Books by Raven McAllan

Diomhair

Secrets Shared
Secrets Uncovered
Secrets Remembered
Secrets Dispatched
Secrets Learned
Secrets Dispelled

Single Titles

Hong Kong Heat
Fairground Attraction
The Earl and the Courtesan

The Earl and the Courtesan

ISBN # 978-1-78686-171-9

©Copyright Raven McAllan 2017

Cover Art by Posh Gosh ©Copyright 2017

Interior text design by Claire Siemaszkiewicz

Totally Bound Publishing

Published in 2017 by Totally Bound Publishing, Think Tank, Ruston Way, Lincoln, LN6 7FL, United Kingdom.

Daring Ladies

THE EARL
AND
THE COURTESAN

RAVEN MCALLAN

Dedication

To Theresa. For your faith and encouragement. For believing in me and cheering me on. This one is yours. To the incomparable Emmy Ellis for the cover, which made me cry in a good way when I saw it. She has the knack of taking my very vague ideas and creating a masterpiece. I am truly indebted to her.
And to Ann Leveille for her fantastic editing.
Thank you all.

Chapter One

"And to my companion, Miss Theresa Kyle, in recognition of all she has done for me and mine, I leave my house in Berkeley Square with all the furniture she wishes to keep and the sum of ten thousand pounds to be hers outright and..."

Theresa didn't hear anything else, other than the gasp that ran around the austere study where the will of the late Sir Humphrey Goddard was being read. She slumped back in her chair — as best she could on a straight-backed Chippendale with several pairs of condemning eyes on her — and put her palm over her racing heart as if to steady it. A handful of silk and lace grounded her. In her eyes, the furniture alone was priceless and more than she could have ever hoped to receive, let alone the building. As for the money?

Ten thousand pounds. That would give her an annual income of around four hundred pounds. A fortune to her. If it wouldn't have looked so stupid, she would have used the hand over her breast to pat it rapidly, just to check she wasn't dreaming. How silly would that appear?

"Good lord, he *had* lost his mind," Mr. Abercorn, the rector, said. "Poor Lord Humphrey, bless him." He looked to the ceiling and put the tips of his fingers together as if he were praying.

Oh my goodness, what sort of person does that in a situation like this? Talk about pontificating. The rector was one her beloved mama would say was full of words and little action. The ceiling was not at all heavenly, being as it was a dull beige and incredibly boring. Theresa was sure she could see a spider's web in one corner, complete with occupant. It was obvious this room had not been used since Sir Humphrey passed on.

"I'm sorry to disabuse you of that idea, Reverend, but his lordship was of a very sound mind and gave me his instructions with precise clarity," the solicitor said with definite annoyance in his tone. "It does you no credit to say such things. After all, he also left money to the church. Some might say that was a sign of a mind lost."

The cleric flushed with anger. "The Lord's house is grateful," he said in a stiff manner "I meant no offense."

"Good," George, Sir Humphrey's heir, interjected, his tone grim "Remember, it was his money to do with as he wished."

The rector reddened. "I stand corrected," he said. His reluctance to admit his mistake was obvious by his inflexible attitude. "My apologies."

Out of the corner of her eye, Theresa watched both Lord George and the solicitor nod. However, it seemed the rector was not the only person to be resentful.

"Never mind that, what's she done to deserve such largesse, then?" a disgruntled Lady Paulina, Sir Humphrey's daughter, asked with a snap Her customary petulant expression was even more pronounced than usual. "I always thought her too forward and encroaching."

George, the elder by several years, frowned at Paulina. "Enough, sister mine, you sound spiteful and grasping. Put your claws away."

Paulina also reddened. Her sharp features stood out prominently and she looked like a weasel about to pounce on some poor unexpected prey. Theresa hoped that she wasn't the target. She wasn't in the mood to retaliate, and if attacked she'd have to. With most daughters you could be charitable and say grief had unsettled them. Not, she thought, in Paulina's case. Her unpleasantness was habitual so this was no departure from normal.

George, a portly man who would no doubt become stout

before middle age, stared at his sister until she turned away with a toss of her head. He nodded then smiled at Theresa. "Miss Kyle did more than any of us could do — make our father happy and whole again for a start. Miss Kyle, you deserve every penny, and I'll be happy to be your mentor and guide in any way possible."

Theresa smiled back somewhat tremulously as Paulina snorted. The woman would never be content, Theresa decided as she looked at the disconsolate long face. Even if everything had been left to Paulina, Theresa imagined she'd still have something to complain about.

Not like dear Humphrey, whose contentment had shone out of him and encompassed Theresa. And now this gift. Was this what Humphrey had meant when she'd lain in his arms and he'd told her she had made him very happy and he'd make sure she never regretted it?

"Theresa, not only did you bring back my ability to be a man again, you taught me much more than how to enjoy making love," he had said. "You showed me how to pleasure a woman in ways that satisfied and gratified us both. Not an easy task, but you succeeded in such a way that I became more of a man."

Theresa smiled at the memory. *Dear Humphrey, I miss you*. Chance in the form of a snowstorm had brought them together. Loneliness had kept them there. And bedroom antics.

She had to be honest. Sex had held them together. Humphrey had evidently been uninterested in sex for many years, until he'd shown her how much enjoyment there could be in the act of copulation. Of foreplay and stimulation, arousal and sensations. He'd taught her how to enjoy everything, how to pleasure him and how to be pleasured in return.

One day he'd turned to her, patted her cheek and told her with a quiet contentment that she knew more than he. Then he'd dropped his bombshell. Whatever she chose to do he would back her and give her an allowance, and a cottage in the village in her name for her to do with as she liked. However, he was certain her talents were needed elsewhere, and he would be grateful if she considered helping his son, who would benefit from her expertise. "As will his women," Lord Humphrey had added with a wink. "Before you say anything, the cottage and allowance are yours outright and with no strings attached. In case you decide not to continue and use your talents as a career. You need never work at anything if you choose not to."

George, a shy and tongue-tied man around women, had added his entreaties to his father's. As later had his friend. And his cousin.

All under the eagle eye of Humphrey, who, although he'd decided he was no longer hungry for sex, had been her willing protector. It was, he'd said, an honor and a privilege to see how well thought of 'Theresita' was. Many people wouldn't understand why she chose to do what she did, Theresa knew. She'd enjoyed it, and understood that to be a lady's maid or a farmer's wife was not for her.

"Miss Kyle?"

Theresa brought herself back to the present as the solicitor addressed her, and turned to the man with a smile. "My apologies, I was wool-gathering."

The elderly man nodded. "Understandable, in the circumstances. However, I'll need your signature and any instructions you have for me."

"Oh…oh yes."

"You will take advantage of the house, won't you?" George asked. "M'father wished it, and I agree with him." He stuck his hand out and put his palm over his sister's mouth. "Ignore Paulina, she thinks it means less for her. It doesn't."

Theresa gaped at him. Did he mean it came from his portion?

"I… You…"

"Theresa, you've done more for this family than anyone could imagine. Papa discussed this with me and I agreed

8

with him. I and my wife have to thank you," George said in a soft voice. The sincerity in his words was noticeable.

Elizabeth, his wife, nodded with vigor "Much more." She stood and squeezed Theresa's cold fingers. "Good lord, you're freezing. Here" — she thrust her muff over Theresa's hands and patted it — "wear that."

"Thank you." Theresa had no idea why she was cold. Shock perhaps? She hadn't expected anything like this. Or thought to be left anything, other than perhaps a few trinkets. Humphrey had given her so much anyway, and he'd owed her nothing. And now, that lovely building where she knew he had been so happy was hers.

Two homes — what more could anyone ask for?

"Are you sure?" she said in little more than a murmur, so only the solicitor and George could hear. "Really?"

"Really. Therefore go and sign your life away." George winked. "I suspect you could do very well in London.

So did she.

* * * *

London
Fifteen years later

"I think we should start a club," Theresa ruminated. "One for people like us who do not want to be ruled by convention."

Her friend Maria sat back in her chair and contemplated Theresa. "There are plenty of us. What's our name?"

"How about the Daring Ladies Club?"

Maria sniggered. "Oh, I like it. And the members?"

"Well, you and me for a start. We can begin small."

"Excellent. When do we have our first meeting?" Maria reached for a nearby bottle of wine and poured two glasses full.

"I rather think we're having it now," Theresa said with a laugh. She took her glass and held it high. "To the Daring

Ladies Club. Be this the only meeting or not, we can at last acknowledge who and what we are."

"Interesting, unconventional and ready to take on the world?"

"Something like that."

Theresa sat back in the large comfortable chair and smiled at her friend over her glass of wine. Theresa's long black hair was half in a knot on the top of her head and the rest had left its pins and spiraled over her shoulders in a waterfall the color of midnight. She pushed it back impatiently. At times it was the bane of her life.

"So, that apart, who is your next client?"

"Who's next?" she said in reply to Maria, her friend, confidante and seamstress to the ton. "Nobody. I've decided to retire." She sipped her wine and savored the silky-smooth apricot and gooseberry-scented liquid with enjoyment. "This is good."

Maria put her own glass down with such a thump that the fine French contents slopped dangerously near the rim. Her mouth dropped open and she gaped at Theresa as if she were hallucinating.

Theresa grinned and held the glass in the air to look at the light amber-colored liquid. "Where did you find it?"

"Never mind the wine," Maria retorted. "Say that again, slowly."

Theresa opened her eyes as wide as possible and waved her glass from side to side as a toast. It wasn't often possible to shock or surprise Maria, and therefore every time it happened was immensely satisfying. "Theresita is no more. From now on I'm plain Theresa Kyle, spinster of the parish."

"Why?" Maria sounded bewildered, as well she might, Theresa thought. She hadn't mentioned her intentions to Maria until she'd firmed up her decisions and set certain plans in motion. "You'll never be plain anything," Maria continued. "Black hair and blue eyes combined with a stunning figure will ensure that." She tugged a strand of her own soft brown tresses. "Not forgettable like mine."

"Exactly." Theresa chose to misunderstand her. "You are not forgettable, and you know it. Your hair is glossy and your figure…"

"Is voluptuous. Top-heavy. Why do you think I became a seamstress?" Maria asked, then chuckled. "I know what suits me."

"You know what suits others as well," Theresa replied. "That is why you are successful."

"Just as well, because now I can afford to dress in the style I enjoy," Maria said. "Something that pleases me. However, stop changing the subject. Why are you retiring?"

"Why?" Theresa said. "Because I've had enough." She shrugged and raised her eyebrows as she tried to put into words just how she felt. "Of men and my life as it has been. Oh, don't get me wrong, I've enjoyed every minute of it, I'd be a liar if I said otherwise. But think about it, Maria. I've spent the last fifteen years earning my living on my back." She snorted then took a mouthful of wine. "Well, not necessarily on my *back*, but you know what I mean."

Theresa winked and Maria choked. "Water," Maria spluttered. "No, wine will do." She took a large swig and wiped her streaming eyes. "How can you say something so audacious with such a straight face?" she asked when she could speak in a coherent manner once more.

"Practice," Theresa responded without any embellishment to her reply. "Back, front or sideways on, it all has the same end. To instruct certain gentlemen of the ton that there are two people in each coupling and both have desires and needs that must be addressed."

"So? You're successful, well liked and a definite asset to lots of relationships, even if that is not admitted to. You can't tell me there are no more men who need help, because after listening to the women in my salon whinge I won't believe it." Maria rolled her eyes. "Some of the things I hear would make the most confident of men blanch. I hear about sizes of appendages, how long a man can last, the best position to ensure you do not get with child... You name it and I probably can give you five different opinions. I'm sure you are needed."

"More than likely, but no more help from me." Theresa sat forward and began to count on her fingers. "First, I'm one and thirty, and would have what, three, four more years before all the bits that are now firm and attractive to gentlemen begin to wobble more than is seemly. Second, I'm not as agile as I was."

She hiccupped as Maria began to laugh uncontrollably. "Not... Oh my, the picture that conjures up," Maria tilted her head to one side. "Just how agile *do* you need to be?"

"As a...and oh, do stop it..." Theresa shook her head and sniggered. "You'd be surprised. Well, no, on reflection, maybe you wouldn't, but believe me it isn't as easy to twist and turn as it was five years ago." She stood and began to pace Maria's snug sitting room. One long stride and her swirling skirts set a side table rocking. She stooped to steady it. If the dainty china figures on it smashed, Maria would not be best pleased. "It's not just that. I think I need to remove from town for a while, and get out of a certain honorable's orbit." She turned in a flurry of elegant skirts and faced Maria. "One who doesn't understand the words 'it is over'."

"Ah, now I begin to see. The Honorable Percival Prendergast?" Maria asked. "Does he think to make you his mistress?"

"Sadly, no. He says he intends to make me his wife."

This time Maria's wine did slop over the rim of the glass. She blotted it with her finger absent-mindedly. "Ah."

"Ah indeed," Theresa replied. "He seems to think I jested when I told him never."

Maria grimaced. "Then you do have a problem."

Theresa returned to her previous position and curled her feet up under her. When the two friends got together for a cozy evening, neither stood on ceremony. The order of the night was that shoes were kicked off, stays were loosened or not even worn, food chosen that could be eaten off a plate with their fingers and fine wine drunk as if it were water.

"It troubles me. There is something not quite right there, but I cannot put my finger on it." She sighed. "He is so damned insistent and does not listen to a word I say. Mind you, I'm not sure he ever did."

"How long has he been bothering you, Tess?" Maria got up, refilled their glasses and sat down in the same position as her friend. "Is it at the harassment stage?"

"No, not yet. But he *does* really worry me, and there are not many people I can say that about. He's" — she paused to formulate her words — "fixated. Our liaison, teaching, call it what you will, ran its course around two months ago, but he seems to think we just move on together. That marriage is the next step. No, no and no. It was over."

"When you dragged me to the cottage for a few days? Respite from our busy lives, you said."

"Just before then. He wouldn't agree. Said we could stay together and be a couple." Theresa rolled her eyes. "It didn't matter how much I told him no, he kept appearing like a jack-in-the-box wherever I went. Then he came up with the idiotic idea that a marriage between us was what he wanted, and I, would you believe, according to him, should benefit. For goodness' sake, apart from anything else, I can give him ten years. And to be honest, I might have taught him, but I have little hope he'll remember anything, and if he does he won't choose to use it. His prick is like a pencil, with a very tiny and soft lead, and not of the highest quality."

Maria sniggered. "The pictures that conjures up."

"Yes, well, 'tis true, I am afraid." Theresa shrugged then grimaced as she remembered the problems she'd encountered in that area. "He neither grows nor shows. Sawdust packs for the pantaloons are his friend. Plus, I am worried he is one of those men who think a woman should be grateful for any attention and he insists he knows what they want. He slurped or bit and it did not matter how many times I told him that although a woman's body could be something to feast on, it was neither soup nor steak, he still carried on. I got that out of him by sheer continual nagging and on one occasion a thump to the head."

Maria laughed out loud and tears rolled down her cheeks. "Only to his head?"

Theresa scowled then giggled. "I did contemplate a thump to his prick — if I could find it — but that would no doubt have given him encouragement. He was and is too arrogant for his own good. I pity his poor wife, if he ever does get someone to accept his proposal. Unless she is prepared to do as I did and stand up to him. Even if it takes a big stick and a locked door to bring him to his senses." She sobered suddenly. "I'm not sure he really put his heart into it. I often got the impression he wished himself elsewhere, and then his attitude changed and I was the person for him. Or so he tried to insist. I almost took another client just to act as a deterrent but decided it would not be fair to the unknown other, or indeed to me. The next man in my hole will be there for love or something similar — so to speak — not money." Crude, but then if she couldn't speak openly and honestly to Maria, to whom could she do so?

"Ah. So do you have anyone in mind?" Maria asked with interest as she wiped her eyes on a lace-edged handkerchief. "Is that why you've retired?"

Theresa shook her head and her black curls danced around her like a dark halo. "No one and not really." She paused and mulled over what she wanted to say. Was there anyone? Not one who would even consider her as a partner, or, sadly, anyone she would want to. "No. Everything I've said so far adds up to the fact that I've had enough of this life. I have sufficient money not to work at any occupation. Two homes, and a nice collection of jewelry. I play the stocks and seem to have a knack for it. I rely on no one and no one relies on me. Staff excepted. I had thought my life would be sweet and simple. I intend to write my memoirs." She giggled like a young girl at the thought of some of those memories. "Suitably discreet and no names mentioned, of course."

"Now those I would definitely give a pretty penny to read," Maria said with a hint of amusement in her voice. "With the Earl of D. M. B. or Lord of the Tiny Penis, and Mole on his Arse sort of names? Have you started yet?"

Theresa laughed. "Definitely the latter sort of names. After all, how many Earls of D. M. B. are there? I'm not that cruel. A Penis, Prick or Uneven Bollocks is so much better. If nothing else, it will prove I do know the men I write about." She sighed. It sounded deep and loud in the quiet room. "Sadly I haven't started yet, and if things go on the way they are I might never do. Unless it is the account of a murder or unmanning. Bloody Lord Percy is proving to be very difficult. His last words to me, as he waylaid me outside my house on my way here, were that if I wouldn't come by my own free will and see reason, he'd use other means." She was silent for a moment as she watched the reflection of the flames in the grate as they danced over her half-full glass. "I am wondering what they are and how I should proceed. Apart from the murder or unmanning solutions." She rolled her eyes. "I fear I would never be able to lie when asked if it was me, and I'm not sure a plea of self-defense would work."

"Are you scared?" Maria asked. "I worry about you. Reassure me. Do you carry your gun?"

"What?" Theresa asked in surprise. "I have a muff pistol in" — she laughed — "in my muff, or course." She nodded toward the swansdown frippery, which Maria had designed a few months earlier. "That muff, not the one on my body. As for scared? Well," she temporized, "not really, but I feel I can't move on until he moves away."

"Shall I arrange for someone I know to press him? There's a ship due to set sail for the Indies within days," Maria said. "I'm sure my friend would take him on without a second thought. The press gangs are very useful for securing extra crew."

Theresa stared at the nearest person to a sister she had. By the look on her face Maria was serious. "I think that's going a bit too far, but I'll keep it in mind." Theresa surveyed the plate of pastries on the table between them and picked up a sausage roll, only to ignore it. "I do think I need to do something, though, but perhaps not quite so drastic." She began to tear tiny bits of pastry off the roll and drop them onto the plate it came from. "Maybe a word in his godfather's ear? The trouble is I like Lord Luscott, and I don't want to upset him if there is no need. He's not in the best of health." She didn't say how she knew his lordship and accepted that Maria knew better than to ask.

As Theresa had once said, "I learn things on my back, with my legs in the air and my cunt full of cock. You learn things on your feet, with your hands full of material and your mouth full of pins," and Maria had nodded. They both were well aware of the need to be discreet.

"Hmm, then we have a problem," Maria said, deep in thought.

"We?"

"Oh yes, we. You don't think I'd let you cope with this alone, do you?" Maria leaned forward and took the mangled sausage roll out of Theresa's hands and put it back on the plate. "What a mess. Let me ponder for a while. I might have an idea how to solve the persistent Percy problem. It may mean pretending you haven't retired, or perhaps that you've gone off in a slightly different direction, but... Look, can you be available tomorrow night if I bring someone to see you?"

"Of course, but who and why?" It wasn't like Maria to be so secretive over something that could involve Theresa. Unless it was a client, of course.

Maria bit her lip. "I think I'd best not say in case the person in question doesn't agree. Not that I think it likely. The person I have in mind also needs help."

"Of what kind?" Theresa asked with suspicion "I told you, no more cocks, unless of the trussed-up-for-the-table kind."

Maria chuckled. "I now have that image firmly entrenched in my mind. But no cocks directly involved." She waggled her finger. "Tut-tut, trust you to think I mean sexual help. I did not. I spoke of the removal of an irritating, interfering mama kind."

Interfering mama? Theresa's stomach suddenly filled with dancing spiders. "Good lord, it's not a woman, is it? I'm not going down that route, pretend or not. It would ruin any credibility I have." She tilted her head to one side. "Not that I reckon I have much anyway, but...*ombttp*." Maria shut her up by putting her hand over Theresa's mouth. Theresa grabbed it and flapped her fingers. Breathing was a necessity and she wasn't achieving it very well.

"No more spouting rubbish?" Maria asked. She sounded quite menacing.

Theresa shook her head and gasped for breath as Maria removed her fingers. Fresh air never seemed so good.

"Good. Stop worrying." Maria picked her glass up and waved it at Theresa. "No, it's not a woman and that's all I'm prepared to say. I'll speak to the person concerned as soon as I can. In fact, I might catch...them...tonight if I send a message. Your house tomorrow?"

Theresa nodded. "For dinner or after?"

"Probably after. Best to learn your fate on a full stomach."

* * * *

"You what?"

Maria looked up at James Howard Edward Weston, Earl of Rushton, and sighed. He narrowed his eyes. That patient 'oh dear, he is but a mere male' expression never boded well for the person on the receiving end. To whit, this time, him.

"Jamie." The familiar tone she used showed how well they knew each other. Ever since, in fact, he had been a toddler tied to leading reins and she a youngster a few years older than him. Maria had seemed to spend a lot of time waiting for her rector father and her mother to leave whoever they had been visiting and retrieve her from whichever willing adult would take her for those thirty minutes or so. It had been, she had said to Jamie many times, one of the trials of being an only child of conscientious parents. If they had happened to be at the castle when her parents had been required elsewhere, she had often told Jamie stories as they had played together under the watchful eye of his nursemaid. His elder brother had ostensibly scorned the stories, but as he had confided years later, he would listen from outside the room. Maria had provided them with entertainment for many a long hour.

"You've got me out of a card game at Radnor's and dragged me here at two a.m. to ask what?" Jamie said. His impatience was obvious "Are you bosky?" He ran his hands through his chestnut hair and swore as he no doubt spoiled his immaculate Brutus cut. Luckily he did his own hair and refused to let his valet fuss. "Lord, Ria, I was winning."

"Good, you usually do, do you not? Let him keep some of his guineas for once. He needs them. Lady Bourne is a greedy mistress, or so I am told." Maria looked at Jamie in speculation.

He laughed and shook his head. "Never been there so I have no idea. The thought of someone wailing, 'oh yes, oh more', in her corncrake voice as I was in the throes of passion shrivels my cock faster than being naked in a snowstorm. You must be tight."

"I am not drunk. I've had precisely three glasses of wine," Maria told him in a testy voice. "Small ones, which, considering my companion, is a miracle. Now, listen to me. Did you or did you not tell me this situation with your mama, Lady Strawbridge and her daughter was getting worrying? That both you and Marion Strawbridge had no thoughts of each other except friendship? Indeed neither of you are emotionally engaged, and Marion actually has her sights set elsewhere?"

Jamie nodded, his mind awhirl as he pondered her words. What was she thinking? "Well, yes, but I fail to see what that has to do with me helping your friend out of a fix. Who is she anyway?" Jamie asked in a rapid manner "And why do you think if I pay attention to her it will dissuade my mama? And what is the fix? You, my dear, are being much too vague." As Maria was usually one of the most transparent people he knew — except with regards to her clients and her crazier ideas — Jamie felt he had every right to be suspicious. "I can't agree to anything without more information." He had a nasty suspicion this suggestion involved both one of her clients *and* a crazy idea.

"Not even if it will help you?" Maria asked him with a quizzical expression. "That's a poor showing."

"Ah but, Ria, there's the rub. How do I know it will without the full facts?" he asked. He had to hope she understood how serious he was It was not a subject to laugh about. "All you have imparted is that someone you know needs to get rid of an admirer and if someone else, name unspecified but of the aristocracy, showed an interest in her it might work."

Maria bit her lip, a sign she secretly agreed with him. Jamie folded his arms and leaned against the window ledge. He knew better than to push her — it was best to let her cogitate over his words.

"I do not want to tell you who this person is if you think it unlikely you'll be interested," she said at last. "It would be betraying a confidence."

Good lord, they could go round the houses forever like this. "Theoretically?" Jamie said He chose his words with care. "I am interested. But, Ria, think about it carefully. If she's an antidote, no one will believe I have any interest in her." His escorting — or bedding — of beauties was well documented.

Maria shook her head and tiny tendrils of conker-colored hair slid over her shoulders. "Nothing like that, I promise you. She isn't of your class and I'm not saying you need to look as if you're about to marry her... Just be besotted. Set her up as your next mistress or something." She blinked in quick succession and looked aghast. "Oh lord, you aren't still involved with Lady Smithers, are you? That would blow it."

"Lady Smithers and I are no longer involved," Jamie said. To his dismay he sounded wooden and stilted; annoyed she'd put her finger on the one thing that irritated him. "It was a momentary aberration." And one he rued. "I, as you so elegantly put it on one occasion, do not have my pudding in anyone's honey pot. Plus, I've never been besotted in my life," Jamie added with perfect truth. "No one will believe it for a second. Nor will they accept I'm chasing a woman not of my class. I've never needed to chase anyone and I have no intention of starting now."

"Goodness, so inflexible." Maria pointed her finger at him. "You, my lord, have been spoiled."

"You think so? With my mama?" he asked in a way most people on the receiving would wince, and stammer apologies. "Hardly."

"Ah, you have a point," Maria said. "However, all the more reason this will work. The lady in question will appear to want you as much as you want her. I hope."

All of a sudden Jamie began to enjoy himself. "Oh there will be no appearing to do so. Come on, Ria, do you want to wager I can't make her want me?" He raised one eyebrow in query. "Really?"

"You will *not* dally with her, Jamie Weston, do you hear me?" Maria snapped as she stood and poked him in the stomach. It was no more than a tickle, but the look on her face showed he'd riled her. "This will be staged to perfection, no more."

"Then you best tell me who you think people would accept I am enamoured both with — and without any dalliance."

"Will you do it?"

He tilted his head to one side and Maria scowled. "Oh all right, but if you say no this goes no further."

It was a fair demand. He nodded. "You have my word."

Maria took a deep breath. "Theresa Kyle."

"Who?" He couldn't fit a face or body to the name.

"Theresita."

The expressions 'the earth stood still' and 'his mind spun' couldn't have been coined for a better occasion. Jamie thought all his breath had been squeezed out of him and he saw stars. How the hell hadn't he remembered her name? It was an open secret in the ton. He laughed inwardly. A curvaceous body, the smile of an *houri* and, if rumor proved to be true, she was proficient if not perfect in the art of lovemaking. Something surely every man dreamed of receiving. And returning the favor. If he hadn't been leaning on the windowsill he'd have fallen over. As it was, he gripped the wooden window surround as if it were the only thing between him and a chasm so deep that once in it he would never get out.

Now a memory of a raven-haired beauty with dark-blue eyes, red lips and an elegant, shapely figure wedged firmly in his mind. To him it was a perfect body. Breasts to fit into his hands and a rear of a perfect shape and size to clutch and fondle. A waist he could almost span with his hands. A woman every man would gladly pay to be with. Except the word was that she was very selective, and only chose certain men who fit her criteria. Jamie had never paid for sex — unless, he thought uneasily, you counted keeping a mistress in style — and needed no tuition, so he had admired and forgotten about her. Almost. To put her completely out of his mind when he saw her around town just hadn't been possible.

So, he knew her, had on more than one occasion wondered what it would be like to be buried bollocks-deep in her sweetness and had known he would never ever fill her criteria or she his.

"Jamie?"

Maria's voice penetrated the haze and he shook his head to clear it. "Theresita? The courtesan." He began to laugh.

Even to his own ears it sounded forced and he stopped abruptly and smiled instead. "Oh that is a good one. Since when does she need a man?"

"Since one of your ilk began to think his gonads meant they could do as they like," Maria snapped. "And he is one man she doesn't need."

Her eyes flashed and Jamie found he'd put his hand over his cock and balls without even noticing. His involuntary gesture seemed to calm her, and she laughed.

"Oh don't worry, yours are safe—for now. Look, Jamie, this is serious. I would not have involved you otherwise. A certain so-called gentleman of the ton is pressing her to marry him, now their arrangement has ended. She has absolutely no interest in his diktat but as she has no client at the moment he thinks she is just being coy. Believe me, she is not."

"Why doesn't she just take another pupil?" Jamie asked, puzzled. "That would solve her problem, would it not?" And why did that solution not please him? Surely he wasn't really contemplating actually taking part in this crazy plot?

Maria sighed. "She's retired. She says enough is enough and…well, anyway, will you do it? Luckily, people don't know of her retirement yet but if she is seen with you they will think she has changed direction. Especially if it gets leaked in the clubs, at tea parties and in my salon that you are both taken with each other, and that she has decided she has a 'new persona', with new ideas. That you both have," she corrected herself. "People will think you've persuaded her you are the one for her, and hopefully it will deter Percy the Persistent Pest Prendergast who we all know can never stand up to any man, especially one higher up the aristocratic ladder than him. Plus, it will sort your mama out. She'd never countenance your parading a mistress in front of the ton, especially in a blatant manner."

"Prendergast? That explains a lot. Hmm." Jamie paced from the window to the fireplace to the tantalus and poured two glasses of port. The dowager had put up with him and his acknowledged lovers many times in the past, although he'd never blatantly flaunted them, probably because each was always someone of their social standing. Any other mistresses had been discreet arrangements and those affairs conducted as such. "I think we need this." He passed one glass to Maria. "Remind me to replenish your cellar. I have a feeling I may be making inroads into it." He suspected he might need to order a few more bottles for himself to get through the next few weeks. Whatever Maria thought, his mama was a force to be reckoned with.

Chapter Two

"Miss Kyle, there's a man asking to see you. He says as it's important." The maid bobbed a curtsy and worried her lips with her teeth. "Miss," she blurted out breathless and full of news. "Oh, miss, I can't say I took to him. He's..." She shuddered. "A real old ruffian. Not a one I'd want to meet on a dark night up an alley."

Theresa's heart missed a beat and she swore under her breath. This jump-at-every-little-thing attitude was ridiculous and it had to stop. "Did he give a name, Kimmie?"

Kimmie shook her head. "No, miss, said you'd know who it was. Right persistent he were. Said that you were to expect him."

Alarm bells rang in Theresa's head. Surely Maria wouldn't have sent someone at this hour? Not when she'd been insistent they would meet that evening. "Where is he, Kimmie?"

The maid's demeanor changed and she grinned. "On the doorstep, miss. Mr. Roberts said he'd inquire and shut the door before the bloke could get his foot inside, seeing as you said no one to come in unless you said yes. He wasn't the sort of man you'd want wandering around, I tell you. Or messing up the study or wherever."

Theresa let her breath out in one long silent *whoosh*.

"That's good. I have no idea who could be calling, and therefore if he won't hand over a card, we need not let him enter. I will come down and speak to Roberts." Her pulse might be erratic and there was a nasty taste in her mouth, but Theresa was determined not to skulk in her sitting room. She checked her appearance in the mirror over the mantelpiece and shoved some of her hair back into her topknot. Her gown was as tidy as ever, but mindful of who might be waiting, Theresa pinned a thin shawl over the low-cut bodice. She might like the comfort of a gown that left the upper swell of her breasts free to expand without too much constriction, but she had no intention of letting just anyone feast their eyes on half of her bosom. Satisfied she looked as well as possible given the circumstances, and that her jumpy pulse would not be noticed, Theresa left the room. If only it were feasible to carry a sword cane like many gentlemen. Instead she would have to make sure the umbrella stand was well stocked and within arm's reach if need be. Her heart thumped as she made her way down the long curving staircase, and stroked the shining burnished oak balustrade with her fingertips. Once again she marveled at her luck in having this gorgeous house as her own.

It was yet another reason why she thought she would never marry. She had too much independence and, if she were honest, too many well-loved goods and chattels to be willing to give them all up to a husband. This house, her cottage, her fortune — were hers and hers alone. It would be no problem to share with someone she loved, but she would not hand it over for someone else to decide what was to be done with it. And as the law was very specific about what a wife did — subjugate herself, in Theresa's opinion — she'd stay single. After all, if there was no man in her life she could always use her darning mushroom to give her body any satisfaction it craved.

Roberts, her general factotum, hovered anxiously by the closed door, his face scrunched with worry and his stance wary. He looked up at her as she descended the last few stairs and smiled with relief. "I hope I did right, miss, but I have no idea who he is. Never seen him before. Not gentry I don't think, not the aristocracy. More..." He hesitated. "Maybe a clerk or some such? One who is perhaps not quite on the right side of the law all the time. Anyway, I minded your words and told him I would inquire if you were at home to callers."

"And shut him out?"

"Well, yes," Roberts said in a worried voice. "I thought it best. Easier to let in than put out. Was that the thing to do?"

"Exactly right," Theresa told him. "Did he not give you his card?"

Roberts shook his head. "Him? I'd be surprised if he's even got one, or would know what to do with it if he did. He just shot his chin out, tried to look brutish and said you were expecting him."

Theresa shook her head. "I'm not. No one is expected except Miss Best—Roberts was one of the few people who knew Maria by her given name and not Madame Meilleur, the name she used for work—and her companion this evening. So, no card, no name, no explanation?"

"No, miss, nothing."

The door knocker rattled on the brass back plate fastened to the oak front door and the noise reverberated around the hall.

"Impatient," Theresa commented. "Now where are two strapping footmen? Ah, Dobson and Frost, good." The two men in question had erupted into the hall as the noise started. "I think it is perhaps time to see who our uninvited visitor is." She waited until all three men nodded, and Frost and Dobson took up their posts, one to each side of her. "Roberts, make sure the umbrellas are easy to reach."

Roberts smiled and nodded. "That they are, miss, and they're the ones with the nice sharp ferrules on them." Roberts was nothing if not precise in his descriptions.

"Excellent." Theresa nodded her approval. "Now, Kimmie, go into the kitchen. If I shout out the word 'now', run to Lord George and tell him what's happening." Theresa had vowed not to tell George anything about her current problems. He was happily married with an heir and another babe on the way, but this was one time she might have to break her self-imposed rule. His wife would understand. They might never be close friends — the class barrier and Theresa's late occupation prevented that — but there was mutual liking and respect between them. They had even shared a few private gossips over the teacups, and Elizabeth had proved to be an interesting and insightful companion.

"Right, gentlemen." Theresa wiped her clammy hands on her skirts and nodded decisively. "Let us see who this person is and what they want. Roberts, open the door."

Roberts inclined his head, took the three steps necessary and swung the heavy door back in one swift movement. The weasel-faced man on the doorstep swayed and almost fell to his knees. He steadied himself and went to take a step forward, only to be halted by the large, meat-plate-sized hand of Dobson, an ex-pugilist who could appear menacing merely by being around.

"Oy, mate, who invited you in?" Dobson asked in his gravelly cockney accent. "No one as far as I can see."

The man swallowed and his Adam's apple bobbed up and down. Sweat appeared on his brow and he cleared his throat several times. "I, er, I'm expected, so show me to your employer."

Theresa sent a warning look toward her staff, who interpreted it as she'd hoped they would. "She never said like." She could recall her childhood intonations with ease. "So I dunno." Would it be over the top to sniff and wipe her nose on her shawl? *Probably.*

The man barely spared her a glance. Theresa bit back a grin. Was her pretty but comfortable day dress so insignificant she wasn't worth more than a passing glance? It must be the shawl that rendered her not worth a second moment of his attention.

"I does, so take me to her quick or it'll be the worse for you." The hopeful interloper peered at Dobson's hand, still flat on his chest. "My master won't stand for this, you know."

Theresa nodded at Dobson and Frost. "Who's your master

then, eh?"

"Why should I tell you?" His eyes slid toward the stairs. "I'll tell the organ grinder, not the monkey."

"Ah, I see." Theresa nodded, took a step forward and dropped her accent to speak in the modulated tones she had cultivated over the years. "Well for your information, I *am* the organ grinder, the woman you insist you need to see."

The man stared and sneered. "Ah so you say, but hows do I know? I was told you'd be awaiting."

"You were misinformed," Theresa told him in an icy voice. "I expected no visitors, welcome, or as you are, unwelcome."

He blanched and no doubt would have taken a step backward if Dobson hadn't gripped his jacket. Instead he swayed like a willow in a breeze and gaped at Theresa in a way that reminded her of a hapless fish out of the water.

"And as you do not know me," Theresa went on inexorably, "I certainly do not know you, and you seem not to want to tell me why you are here or who sent you, we are at an impasse. I think it is time you left. Show him out, please." Theresa turned on her heel just as the man was lifted off his feet and propelled backward out of the room.

Before the door shut firmly on him, he cussed and bellowed at the top of his voice, "He says he is your betrothed."

My what? Theresa waited, but no noise could be heard from outside except the usual sounds of the world going about its everyday business. A flower seller shouted something shrill and a pie seller retorted out loud with several rude words.

Nothing different from normal.

Why? Oh sweet lord, not bloody Percy again? She held back her nigh on murderous thoughts until she reckoned she would be able to speak without stuttering, then eyed her companions, one by one. "Did any of you recognize him?"

They all shook their heads.

"He's no one I've seen before, miss," Roberts offered. "If

he worked for someone around here, we would know it. Servants chat, and The Boar down the road a bit is our place to meet. He's never been in there and no one has said owt about anyone like him nosing around."

Frost nodded. "You know, miss," Frost said after several seconds of deep thought. "He sounds like he's from Bermondsey way. I have some cousins over there. He wasn't one of them, but he could have been, if you get me. Or a neighbor or the like."

Theresa nodded. It was still a marvel to her how some people could pick up on the tiny nuances between all the London dialects. She could just about differentiate between north or south of the river.

"Just keep your ears and eyes open, please. I am definitely not betrothed. Be sure I would tell you if I were." Should she voice her suspicions? Almost she kept her silence but common sense prevailed. After all, if there were any more unwanted intrusions, they would all need to be on their guard. "I suspect it is still the Honorable Percy not accepting my response to his offers." The collective sigh was very welcome. "You all did exactly as you should. Perfect, thank you."

"We protect ours, miss," Roberts said grave and long-faced "You're one of us. And I tell you, miss, if he comes bothering you when I'm about, I'll take Cook's rolling pin to his family jewels, that I will."

Theresa laughed. "I never knew you had such violent tendencies, Roberts."

He grimaced, somewhat shamefaced. "Nor did I, but where this household is concerned it seems I do."

The simple words were balm to her worried self. "Well, I thank you. I hope you can arrange for everyone to get an extra night off in the next couple of weeks. If you come to me, Roberts, I'll furnish you with the silver to get you each a jug of ale." She grinned. "As long as no one forgets to come to work the next morning."

* * * *

It was hard to settle when your maid had brought you the news that she had slipped out and followed the weasel-faced man back to the somewhat shabby office of Wm. Protheroe, Solicitor, in a side lane a few minutes' walk from Lincoln's Inn. Not anyone Theresa had heard of and, judging by the not quite correct address, not a person she would want any dealings with. It was, according to Kimmie, *a bit dodgy looking, like*.

Now, as she left the dining room after picking at her dinner and receiving sorrowful glances from the footman and an anxious message from the kitchens asking if the food was off — she assured the cook it wasn't — Theresa was more than twitchy. She still had no true idea what Wm. Protheroe wanted, or who he worked for — even if she could give it a good guess. It worried her that if his employer *was* Percy, Percy's intentions and actions were escalating. What next? Serenading under her window? Surely not in town. Abduction? The same. He valued his credibility and standing in the ton too much to resort to such things. Or so she hoped. He could be surly and downright nasty when challenged. As his godfather had said sadly, Percy suffered from a syndrome often associated with men who were small in attitude — not necessarily small in stature. Although in Percy's case both were true and he was also mean and mealy mouthed. If his godfather hadn't coughed up her fees gladly, Theresa was damn sure she would not have seen a penny of them.

Percy might pretend to show himself as enamoured with her, but Theresa knew it wasn't so. He was self-centered and couldn't believe anyone dare say no to anything he wanted. Not for the first time, she rued the fact that she'd accepted him as a pupil at the begging behest of his godfather, Lord Luscott, who'd insisted, "The boy needs shaping up and showing how to use his cock properly." She still wasn't sure she had succeeded in drumming all the information into

Percy. As she had told Maria, he was so full of himself he couldn't believe he wasn't perfect in every way. Therefore it was more than likely Protheroe had turned up on Percy's behalf. However, if that were the case, why not say so? Theresa racked her brain and came up blank.

A missive from Maria merely stating '9 p.m. both of us' hadn't helped her to calm down. It was no wonder she was off her food.

Theresa walked into her sitting room, sat then stood again. Moved the decanter of port from one end of the sideboard to the other then returned it to its original position next to the brandy. Ran her finger over the mantelpiece and tut-tutted at herself. Plumped up the cushions and checked her hair in the mirror. As ever, strands were beginning to fall from her topknot and tickle her neck. She sighed and tweaked into place the knee-length string of pearls she had wrapped twice round her throat then made sure it hadn't caught around her breast. Stared at her neckline and wondered if her favorite afternoon gown was suitable for whoever or whatever was about to enter her life, even if just for a short time. At home she saw no reason to dress up, and Maria knew it. They'd spent many evenings together in clothes that would scandalize people if they saw them. As they didn't, neither cared. Therefore to have dressed for dinner, so to speak, would be false. Maria would know she, Theresa, was apprehensive, and that was the last thing she wanted. Instead she'd gone for elegant, smart and as far from a courtesan's see-through voiles and lace as possible. They were for work. She was no longer working and those clothes were packed away in a closet and unneeded.

And hopefully never will be again. Unless of course – She stopped that train of thought. Some of them were so very pretty. Not risqué but teasing. *Do not get any ridiculous idea about anything, just wait until you hear what is suggested.*

She looked at her finger — as clean as it had been before she'd run it over the mantel — and shook her head at her silliness. There would be no dust anywhere, even when the fire was lit. Her staff would have seen to that. The decanters sat on the left-hand corner of the sideboard because it was the most convenient place to use them. Her gown suited her — the shades of blue and green shimmered as if the azure, sapphire, sky-blue and gray-green materials were made of silk, not the finest lawn — and her hair never stayed in place anyway. Even if she put so many pins in it she became a lodestone for a magnet, long curly tendrils escaped and did what they wanted. Theresa had decided at an early age her fine, silky tresses had a mind of their own. Now if she didn't pin it up it fell past her waist in a wave of raven-colored curls. As a child those very curls had caused her no end of tears as her mama had tried to untangle them. Now she accepted such a job as par for the course and suffered while Maisie, her personal maid, tended to them.

Idly Theresa wondered if it was now time to cut her hair and sever one more link with her past. Perhaps not until she understood what Maria had in mind, Theresa thought wryly. It involved a man, of that she was in no doubt, but she was equally sure Maria didn't expect her to reprise her role as sexual tutor to the youth of the ton. However, lots of hair on the lady's head, not elsewhere, seemed to be a prerequisite for a man to look, like and linger.

The longcase clock in the study chimed the three-quarter hour and Theresa jumped, startled by the sudden noise. Fifteen minutes to wait. If it wasn't likely to give the wrong impression, she would have been tempted to have a shot of brandy to steady her nerves.

Brandy-fumed breath is not a good introduction. Instead she picked up her tambour frame and set a stitch…in the wrong place. She threw the embroidery into the corner in disgust and *harrumphed*. It wasn't the half-worked cushion cover's fault she was so on edge. With a groan at her stupid attitude, Theresa picked the mangled material up, smoothed out the creases as best she could and put it in the cupboard where it belonged.

Enough. Take a deep breath and calm down. I can always say no to whatever scheme Maria has cooked up. But could she afford to? Why on earth had she thought life would be simpler once she retired?

Theresa sat, folded her arms and waited. If a voice had spoken in sepulchral tones and told her to prepare to meet her doom, it would not have come as a surprise.

* * * *

"Are you sure this is a good idea?" Jamie asked his companion in a slow, drawn out, heir—much to his disgust—to-a-dukedom drawl as he stretched his long legs out across the floor of the unremarkable, plain black carriage that tooled along Bruton Street. If only his brother would hurry up and produce a male offspring, life would be so much simpler. Or so he assumed. Then he'd be one step removed and in theory less likely to be good husband fodder. However, at that moment in time, Martin's marriage—or remarriage now his period of mourning was well past—seemed as probable as the moon falling into the Thames, or Prinny stopping his profligate, spendthrift ways.

What was it about himself that made women look at him as if they were his next meal, and his mother rub her hands together with glee and plot his life for him, Jamie wondered. Although, he thought philosophically, she did that with all her children, he unfortunately seemed to be the one in her line of fire at that time.

"Why me, Ria?" he asked lazily as he let his body roll in time to their uneven journey over the cobbles. "Why not any other number of my peers?"

"Look at yourself," Maria said. "That is why."

Jamie inspected his semi-prone form in a critical fashion— as best he could within the confines of the carriage. His hessians shone as bright, as his valet could make them, his pantaloons fitted to perfectionas ever, he'd be looking for another tailor if they didn't—and his cravat gleamed pale and ghost-like in the late evening moonlight that showed through the side windows. The perfect aristocrat. At least, he decided, he was well turned out, even if it was for a hum. "It all seems a bit far-fetched to me. There are many with a better physique and both smarter and richer than I."

Maria slewed round in her seat and glared at him. Her eyes sparked with what he presumed was anger, either simulated or real, and she tapped one foot, clad in an encrusted evening shoe, on the floor in a staccato rhythm. She had, she told him as they had climbed into the carriage, a man to meet later. Maybe. "Do not be such an idiot," she advised him acerbically. "Do you think I would waste my time, Theresa's time or, I best add before you spit and snarl, your time, if it was not necessary? For some unfathomable reason women think you should be their one, and your mama is determined Marion must be your one. You agreed last night you would come and hear me...us...out... You will not, my lord, renege."

"Last night I was halfway to being bosky," Jamie said sardonic and, somewhat amused at Maria's fierce attitude. It was so unlike her. "You caught me at an opportune moment." He pondered his words and gave a half laugh. "For you and Miss Kyle anyway. For myself I'm not so sure."

"Ha." Maria sat back and folded her hands over her reticule. "Then why was a certain Lady Strawbridge in my salon this afternoon inquiring how long it would take me to make gowns suitable for a wedding?" she finished. A butter-wouldn't-melt-in-her-mouth expression played over her face.

All Jamie's indolence dropped away as he sat up and turned Maria to face him. "Pardon?"

Maria nodded. "I thought that would wake you up," she said with satisfaction. "Lady S. intimated it would be soon, and a large order would be forthcoming."

"Is that true?" Jamie asked with a snarl. "Or are you trying to make me more compliant?"

"I wouldn't," Maria said in an affronted tone. "I might nag and tease but I would not lie and you know it."

Jamie nodded his apology. She was as honest as the day was long. Sometimes to her detriment. "Yes, that was out of order, I apologize. Put it down to extreme frustration. Of the annoying parent kind," he added as Maria looked him up and down and raised an eyebrow. "So?"

"*So*, she was most chatty, 'in confidence, though'." Maria raised her eyebrows in a theatrical manner. "Stupid woman, I would not last a week if every word said in my salon was not in confidence. I said it would depend on exactly what was needed. The number of garments required and for how many people. I explained I would need to be told how decorative and embellished she would like them—would I have enough seed pearls, for instance—and when they would need to be completed by. Sadly, or perhaps fortuitously, she could not—or would not—give definite dates, people or places. She just smirked in that supercilious way of hers, said it was aristocracy and welcomed."

Jamie sat up straight, all pretense of indolence gone. "Good lord, so that's why Marion was all atwitter when I ran into her at Lady Rancing's. She told me to go away in no uncertain terms and huddled in a corner with Lucy Whatsherface, the chit who almost vomits if I as much as look at her."

"Lucy Chitteringham. You scare her. Even if anyone mentions your name in the salon she goes ashen and shakes. Lord knows why."

Jamie winked. "Chit by name and nature then. Poor girl, has no one told her mama green matches her complexion if I glance her way?" He had no intention imparting the information about how Miss Chitteringham had been an innocent bystander in one forward young lady's ploys. "Nor I."

"Hmm. That apart, now you know about Lady S., and I have broken a confidence. In a good cause I think," Maria said with satisfaction. "Have they tried anything recently?"

He shook his head. "Not since Marion and I were locked in a bedchamber together at the Lauriestons' house party. We scuppered our parents' intentions on that occasion, because I picked the lock, left the room and secured the door behind me. Marion stayed there to give them a perplexing question to try and answer, and I headed to the billiards room to trounce Alfred Holton. It was so ridiculous, I should have suspected a trap when I was summonsed to meet my mama there, but sadly I didn't. Marion answered a similar decree, and thus we were inveigled into the room separately, but within a few seconds of each other. We escaped the marriage trap that time, and forewarned is forearmed, as they say."

He shrugged and rolled his shoulders to de-kink them. "I intend not to give Lady Strawbridge or my mama the chance to do such a thing again. Luckily Mama is still in Bath trying to get some poor unsuspecting laird to offer for Lizzie." Poor Lizzie. He had no hope his younger sister could stand up to their mama and neither he nor Martin nor Freddie, his two brothers, were around. Apart from anything else, Martin had sworn after his wife died he had no intention of remarrying in the near future, if ever. Freddie continued to plow his own furrow and damned the rest of them.

The carriage turned the corner into Berkeley Square and Jamie stretched. "Lord, I ache." The seats might be comfortable but he was taller than the norm and the edge caught his long legs in just the wrong place.

"Too much exercise?" In the pale light he saw Maria's cheeky grin as she winked at him.

He laughed. "Sadly no, not enough. I boxed for the first time in months today. Jackson was most disgruntled with me. Told me all his hard work in the past had been for naught. I found muscles I'd forgotten I had."

"Ah, but I didn't mean that sort of sporting exercise," Maria said. "And you know it."

He tapped her cheek with his forefinger. Lord, she was persistent. "None of your business, but I will satisfy your curiosity…this time. No."

"Between women?"

Jamie inclined his head. "Not a one who takes my fancy."

"Good grief, is that a first?" She fluttered her eyelashes and giggled just like the young girl he had fallen in platonic love with all those years ago. "I must make a note of the date."

"Cheeky brat." He flicked her nose.

Maria batted his hand away and wrinkled her nose. "Ouch, you still deliver a sting when you do that."

"Of course, there is no point otherwise. To refresh your memory, I never run more than one woman at once and you well know it."

"Perhaps that's all for the good if this goes to plan," she said pensively as the carriage rattled to a halt. "It might not be credible otherwise."

It seemed she had an answer for everything. Personally, Jamie didn't think her strategy had a chance in hell of succeeding. Why would anyone think he would settle for a courtesan, however talented, when a goodly percentage of the married ladies of the ton, and a fair few maidens, were prepared to lie down and spread their legs for him?

"It might not be credible anyway," Jamie warned her. "When have I ever visited a courtesan?"

"Ah, but you see, that is why it will work." Maria stood as the carriage door swung open. Jamie exited and held his hand out to her. "Because it is not of the norm for either of you." She alighted onto the flags at the bottom of the steps, which led to a large and imposing door.

"She visits a courtesan?" Jamie asked humorously. "Or not? Now I *am* both worried and intrigued."

"What?" Maria peered at him, bewildered, then rolled her eyes and looked heavenward. "Oh, for goodness' sake, you know what I meant. Now behave or I'll wish I'd never thought of you."

Jamie wasn't certain he didn't wish that either, but chose to remember discretion was always better than foolhardy speech. "Yes, ma'am." He straightened his waistcoat and jacket, checked his fob watch was in place and the chain not crooked, and held out his arm to Maria. "What does Miss Kyle say to all this? About me becoming her devoted companion?"

Maria bit her lip as they ascended the shallow stone steps.

"Maria?" Jamie stopped on the third step from the top and turned toward her. He had a nasty itch between his shoulder blades. The one that had helped him out of trouble in the nick of time on more than one occasion. "What are you not telling me? What *did* Miss Kyle say?"

"Why, not a lot yet," Maria said rapidly. "Mainly because she doesn't yet know you are you or what I intend you both should do."

Chapter Three

Of course, Theresa thought with exasperation, she *had* to be so deep in thought she missed the knock on the sitting room door. It was only when Roberts' head appeared around the doorjamb and he gave a polite 'ahem' that she realized her guests had arrived.

Heart racing, she collected herself and stood. She plucked at the skirts of her gown nervously, flicked away a minute piece of loose cotton and bit back a *harrumph* of annoyance at herself. Anyone would think she was definitely about to do something alien to her nature. She didn't know what Maria was going to suggest and she always had the option to say no.

Or did she? Percy was still a menace. She could have sworn she'd seen him standing in the bushes on the edge of the square's pretty gardens opposite the house earlier in the day, just as dusk had been falling. By the time one of the men had gone to see, the only evidence of anyone loitering had been a few crushed blooms on the ground and an indentation of a boot in the soft earth. Which of course could have been there for days and made by anyone.

Maria entered the room first and handed her pelisse to Roberts, who then exited with a dignified murmur to Theresa to ring if she wanted anything. She nodded and turned to her guests. Maria was her usual cheerful self, her companion watchful and wary.

"Welcome," she murmured, her smile wry. "It's good to know who my visitors are for a change." But surely this man was not to be her savior? That was beyond the realms of possibility.

Maria waited until Roberts had left and indicated the gentleman who now entered. "What do you mean for a change?" she demanded. "Oh, tell me later, Tess. He's theoretically interested. It's up to you to persuade him he should turn theory into practice."

Theresa stared at the tall, elegantly dressed gentleman with something akin to horror as she saw the demonic glint in his eyes while he bowed over her hand.

"At your service, my dear."

She promptly sat with a thud. Surely not? Her ears must be failing her.

"I must say I didn't expect you to swoon at the sight of me," Jamie said in a dry tone. "I anticipate it from impressionable debs, not more mature and, ah, experienced ladies. Am I that formidable?"

"Don't be so mutton-headed and sanctimonious, Jamie, it does not become you," Maria snapped before Theresa had time to reply. "You knew who you were coming to see and why. Theresa did not."

"I stand corrected." He smiled, humor in his expression, and bowed to Theresa. Now she saw why he was considered to be the most eligible of eligibles. "My apologies, Miss Kyle. I was out of order. Forgiveness?"

Oh my. It was plain what Maria meant when she said young ladies talked about eyes to drown in, and a body that made you itch to touch when the earl paid them attention. And added with a sigh it was as if there were no one else around except them. She now saw he had a way of concentrating his gaze on one, as if you were the sun, moon and stars to him.

Probably shortsighted. Theresa blinked and sanity returned. She took a deep breath and waved to the chairs and chaise.

"Nothing to forgive, my lord," she said brisk and all business. *Damn my husky voice.* "I was somewhat taken aback. All Maria said to me was that she might have an answer to my problem. Not how or with whom." She sat on the chaise and stared pointedly at Maria until she followed suit. "Nor indeed was she forthcoming with any other details."

Theresa rubbed her fingers together and looked up at Jamie, who leaned indolently against the elbow cabinet, his eyes on her less-than-smooth movements. She gathered her scattered wits together once more. "Oh, my apologies, my lord. I forgot to offer you a drink. Port or brandy?" She left the words as a question. Some hostess she was to forget even the basic niceties. She began to rise and Jamie waved her down.

"Shall I pour?" He headed to the decanter and held it aloft. "Port?"

"Please."

"Not for me," Maria said in a hurry as she took a step toward the door. "I'll just…"

"Sit down and explain perhaps," Jamie said. He spoke in such a firm way, Theresa thought Maria would be wise to do as he asked. "Whether you drink water, wine or choose not to slake your thirst, you started this. Therefore, as it is your suggestion, you need to be here to answer any questions."

Theresa bit back a grin as her friend's mouth dropped open and she sat as directed with a thump. It was not often she saw her Maria worsted and lost for words.

"Wine then, please," Maria said. "Lud, I have a feeling I might need it."

Jamie nodded, handed over full two goblets to the ladies, poured himself one and sat in an overstuffed armchair to one side of the chaise.

Theresa watched him over the rim of her goblet as he sipped his own drink slowly and returned her gaze.

"Well," Maria said as the silence became uncomfortable. She did her best to use a bright and breezy voice, just as Theresa was about to say something — anything — to break the silence. "Do I start or do we all sit here like corpses?"

"I suggest you explain, then we can ask questions and then, my dear, I'll escort you home and if necessary return to talk to Miss Kyle." He looked over to Theresa, who nodded.

"That sounds fair."

"But—" Maria began to protest.

Jamie held his hand up. "No buts. Some things are best left between Miss Kyle and myself—if we progress to a satisfactory conclusion. It will be better if no one else, including you, knows every little thing. Not that I don't trust you, Ria. I do, or I wouldn't be here."

Theresa nodded, her reluctance obvious, and Jamie half smiled before he continued. "Your surprise, Ria, or whatever is needed in a specific situation, will be so much more effective that way."

"Ria, he's right, you know." Theresa added her entreaty. It might not suit Maria, who after all had engineered the meeting thus far, but it would have a much more dramatic effect on any questioners if she could show she was as much in the dark as they. "I will keep you as up to date as I possibly can, as long as you promise to tell me what the responses are."

Maria scowled then nodded. "Oh, all right," she replied in an aggrieved voice. "You both are cruel and heartless, but reluctantly I agree it would be for the best."

"Then." Jamie sat back and put one ankle on the pantaloon-clad knee of the other leg. "We are *all* in agreement."

The stance stretched the material and highlighted all the areas of Jamie's body that made Theresa's mouth go dry and her body clench with need. She noticed he and Maria were dressed as casually as she. Apart from, she saw with amusement, Maria's jewel-encrusted shoes. Accident or design?

Whichever, Jamie's dove-gray knit trousers outlined his staff in loving detail. She averted her eyes. Good lord, she was no better than the simpering debs he spoke so disparagingly about.

Maria coughed delicately. "Theresa?"

"Oh yes, sorry, wool-gathering," she said and brought her thoughts back to her problem and not Jamie's body. She must take care, she found her mind wandering much too often these days. "Tell us what your plotting has come up with, Ria."

Tiny pinpricks of something she'd never experienced before attacked her skin as Jamie watched her in the manner of an animal about to pounce. Arousal? Excitement? She wasn't sure. It was not comfortable but neither was it painful. It was, she decided, different.

"Right, now, then if I have this right," Maria said in the manner of a governess about to impart something important. "Each of you need help and are happy for me to disclose to both of you all I know about your situations? Correct me if I am wrong and add your ideas and thoughts if needed?" She glanced, bright-eyed, from Jamie to Theresa.

Theresa checked how Jamie appeared. As sardonic as Maria said he could be? She wasn't sure but thought it could be so.

"Yes, get on with it, Maria, clearly, succinctly and without your usual overcomplicated explanations, or I'll be coming back to speak to Miss Kyle at a time of the night that *would* cause a scandal," Jamie said.

Theresa reckoned he was close to losing his patience, and cast about for something to say to help him keep his temper. She didn't have a chance before he spoke again.

"Let's keep the improprieties to a minimum until they are needed, eh?"

What on earth does he mean? Men have always called on me at any time, and the scandals were nothing at all. Not after the first few visitors anyway. Unless, Theresa decided, it was because Jamie Weston was not the sort of man to call on her ever. In that case, then surely a scandal would scotch whatever was occurring in his life?

"Let me recap. As I read it," Maria said without heat, "your mama, Jamie, and her compeer Lady Strawbridge have hatched up a plot that means you will have to marry Marion Strawbridge, and to that end have on several occasions tried to engineer a situation to force your hand.

Something neither of you want?"

Jamie inclined his head. "That is the essence, yes."

Now Theresa understood. Lady Strawbridge and his mama? Surely together they must be a formidable and unstoppable force?

"If you think we can stop their machinations, you have more faith in us than I do," she said.

Jamie raised one eyebrow. "Shall we wager on it? One hundred guineas say we do. By the turn of the year."

Maria gasped. "Count me out."

Theresa grinned. "Done." She held out her hand. "I can always find a use for one hundred guineas."

"So can I," Jamie drawled as they shook hands. "I might even buy you something with it."

"Enough now, the wager is made and noted by me. Time to move on," Maria said. "I know you both well enough to understand you want the best possible outcome, money notwithstanding."

Theresa was amused to see how her friend had taken charge and showed no deference to a man of a higher class than her. Although hadn't she once said she'd known all of the earl's family since childhood? Even Martin, the present duke, the earl's elder brother. Theresa would be the first person to admit she was somewhat hazy about titles and such. Knowing who took precedence over whom had never really bothered her. However, she had an idea that the earl's title was a courtesy one, as the second son of the late duke.

Perhaps she should have taken note. After all, her mama was the granddaughter of an earl. Sadly when she had married well beneath her, her family had disowned her, but the connection still remained.

Now she wished she had listened to her papa's discourse on the subject. Was his role now as the heir of the present duke instead? Some such thing anyway. Really, the hierarchy was much too complicated. She knew which title belonged to the head of each house and that was about it. In her work — her previous work she amended, amused — as long as the man fit her criteria — was an aristocrat and had money — that was enough. She'd never used a title when educating someone anyway. In those sexually charged times she had tried to persuade them it was endearments that were needed. 'My love', 'dearest', or 'my darling'. Not 'my lord' or 'your grace'.

"And now we come to Theresa," Maria said and leaned over to pinch Theresa. "Who is either bored, tired or both."

Theresa strangled the urge to poke her tongue out. "No such thing," she said as her temper flared. "If you must know, I was thinking about something I heard not so long ago," she improvised in a hurry, then remembered something of importance. "My lord, do you plan to attend Lady Derby's house party next month?"

Jamie blinked. "It depends. I was, perhaps I am not now. Why do you ask?" He took another sip of port and sat long-legged and loose-limbed, seemingly at ease. As long as you didn't look at his fingers, which gripped the stem of the glass so tightly his knuckles showed white.

That tiny sign of vulnerability heartened Theresa and gave her strength to go on. "So if you had intended to go, does your mother know?"

Jamie shrugged and his powerful shoulders rippled under his form-fitting dark-gray jacket. It really was enough to make every nerve in her body stand up and demand to be noticed. Theresa's skin once more developed those tiny stings and tingles and that little pulse between her legs throbbed.

"I expect so," Jamie said. "Once again why… Oh, another ambush?" He didn't sound very concerned. "I fail to see how. It's not that sort of party."

"So I believe — normally. However, I did hear that instead of the usual crowd she gathers around her, this party was going to be more young ladies and, ah, men who need to marry. Like Mortimer." She didn't elaborate on who had told her — it was George, when they had gone over some accounts — and Jamie didn't ask.

"Mortimer, her idiot of a son?" Jamie raised one aristocratic eyebrow in a manner Theresa much admired. "Perhaps," he continued in a voice that made her want to hit him. "I agree he needs all the help he can get. But I fail to see why she would do such a thing and ask those of us who would not be impressed by that sort of party."

Supercilious snob. Perhaps this was not a good idea after all.

"I th—"

Maria gave her a sly warning glance and Theresa shut her mouth hastily.

Jamie grinned. Evidently the glance had not gone unnoticed. "It is not like her to put herself out for other people. You must be mistaken."

Was he so sure of his ability to escape all traps he couldn't see the problems ahead? "Do not treat me as an idiot, my lord," Theresa said in a tone that could cut ice. "If you want to step into the lion's den so be it. I can only relate what I heard."

"Pillow talk?" He spoke in a manner designed to wound.

However, Theresa was inured to such things. She smiled and dipped her head in acknowledgment. "If you like."

"Jamie, enough." Maria hit her hand on the chair arm so hard Theresa was relieved no dust flew out. "This attitude is not helpful."

Jamie was silent for several seconds then he drew a deep breath. "I'm not showing myself in a good light, am I?"

"Not in the slightest," Theresa replied. As ever she was composed. "Nevertheless, I will reiterate, it is your funeral — or wedding. I can always resort to violence."

He grunted. "You are correct. My apologies once more. I think perhaps we best let Maria continue with your problems."

"Thank you." Maria spoke too fast as if she was worried she would yet again be interrupted. "You know what Theresa's occupation was." Theresa was amused to see Maria didn't couch it as a question.

Jamie inclined his head.

"Her last client decided that their liaison, relationship, call it what you will, should continue past further than Theresa decreed," Maria said. "He is now on the point of being a serious problem, and insisting she marry him."

"I insist I won't," Theresa interjected. "But he doesn't listen. And today I have had more." She ran through the weasel-faced man's visit and where he had been traced to.

Jamie sat forward, his eyes alight. "Protheroe? That fly-by-night? Then you could have a serious problem." He frowned. "He's on the unpleasant side of shady. You say he never mentioned who sent him?"

"Nothing more than I've told you," Theresa said with a hint of temper. *Why do men never listen?* "I have an inclination it could be the Honorable Percival Prendergast."

Jamie kept his face impassive. William Protheroe had the sort of reputation no self-respecting person would want, especially one in the profession the man claimed to be part of, and he could well believe he had been retained by Prendergast. Jamie wasn't sure either told even half the truth about what they got up to. If Protheroe were sniffing around Theresa, Jamie would bet his month's wine merchant bill—a considerable sum—it was for nothing good. Plus the Honorable Percy was a louse and could be taken down a peg or two. His reputation to dip deeply when gambling and never know when to stop was legendary.

Was he possibly at *point non plus*? But then how would marrying Theresa help him there? Something to think about and set someone on to discovering exactly what the truth was, perhaps?

All of a sudden he made his mind up. "I'll do it."

Both women looked at him in surprise. Theresa jumped. Had she forgotten that, although they had talked about the problems and had even made a wager, neither of them had actually confirmed this mad idea would go ahead and they would be fully engaged in it?

"Then so will I," she said. "Both of us are needed to commit."

"Just like that?" Maria said. "No quibbling?"

"Not with you," Jamie assured her with a grin. "I think it's up to Miss Kyle and myself to iron out all the nuances." Maria glared and he chuckled. How she resisted sticking her tongue out he would never know but he would wager it was uppermost in her mind. "Maria, my dear, you've done all you can for now. Miss Kyle and I are perfectly able to decide the best way to progress."

"By calling her Theresa, I would say," Maria said drily. "I'd wager you're never so formal with your..."

"My?" he asked in his best 'I am an earl' voice. The one that Maria always ignored. No doubt she had told Theresa to do the same.

"Ladies," Maria said, and sniggered.

"Perhaps." Jamie inclined his head. "Now as I mentioned earlier, and I reiterate again now, I am certain it is better not to let you know everything. An element of mystery and surprise from you could help." He held his hand up as Maria opened her mouth to speak once more. "Now don't fly into a temper again, Ria, it is so wearing, and we all know you couldn't keep it up for long. Save your energy."

She *harrumphed*. "It's all well and good for you to say so," Maria grumbled, albeit with a wicked twinkle in her eyes, "but I need some excitement occasionally, as well you know."

Jamie glanced at Maria's shoes and coughed. She blushed. "Yes, well..."

Theresa spluttered and her eyes sparkled with mirth as Jamie raised both eyebrows. Evidently she'd also noticed the shoes.

"Exactly." He nodded, as decisive as he could be "Don't fret, Maria. I'm sure you'll hear a general how and when as soon as we decide." He glanced at Theresa once more, who inclined her head in agreement.

"You know and I know, Ria," he used the affectionate

abbreviation on purpose, "that you can be as close as the grave when need be, but sometimes not to know something is much easier to show than to pretend you don't. If you are goaded, which in this case I have a suspicion may well occur, you will speak first and think later, and that could be disastrous After all, it's an open secret that unfiltered talk happens in the modistes'."

Out of the corner of his eyes, Jamie watched Theresa nod and cough to hide her chuckle. "We will all help each other when we can." Her words were very slow and deliberate and she laughed when Maria stuck her tongue out. He thought he'd better intervene before it dissolved into childish name-calling and hair pulling. Or did young ladies not do that?

"Right, so let's move on," he said before the ladies reverted to even more youthful gestures. "Miss Kyle?"

"Call her Theresa, for goodness' sake," Maria interjected. "Or we might as well stop now."

"Ria, enough. I have to agree with his lordship here," Theresa said as Maria opened her mouth to speak. "It's going to be hard enough to sort out what we want to say and how to act without you adding your two penn'orth," Theresa continued in a strangled voice. Maria puffed out her cheeks and exhaled. It sounded loud in the otherwise quiet room. "We have to do what feels natural and comes to us without having to stop and think how we are behaving or what we are saying." Theresa leaned over and kissed her friend's cheek. "But you thought this up and if whatever we finally decide on works I, and I suspect his lordship, will be forever in your debt."

"Oh good," said the irrepressible Maria. She might have a temper, but both Jamie and, he presumed Theresa, knew it was short-lived. "Order lots of clothes."

"As you always give them to me at a discount, that won't do very much to say thank you," Theresa said dry and droll.

Maria giggled. "It will if you purchase several and have them made up in expensive cloth. Very expensive. I have an idea for a dress for you. It will make Jamie's eyes stand out on stalks and he will worship at your feet."

"Ladies, can we ignore my eyes, Theresa's feet, payments, repayments and rebates for a moment?" Jamie asked not altogether patiently. Two women together was a basket of pitfalls. "The reason I suggest I take you home, Maria, and return, is after Protheroe's visit I would like to make it seem that Theresa and I are…" He hesitated, unsure of what he meant. "Close," he continued. "If I come back, we can talk about what to do next. Anyone around will merely see me return at midnight and not leave until the early hours." He sipped some port and stood. "We can play piquet."

Maria rose and straightened her skirts. "Don't dare," she advised Theresa, to Jamie's amusement. "He is a shark at piquet. Never loses."

"That's a slight exaggeration," Jamie replied in a mild voice. "Let's just say I rarely lose unless I choose to."

Theresa opened her eyes wide and joined the other two. "How about whist?" she suggested. "You see, there…" She ran her tongue around her pink lips and Jamie's mouth went dry. It did things to his libido no one else had ever accomplished.

"…at that game," she went on in a slow drawl, never taking her gaze off Jamie's face, "…I have to admit…" Her eyes were an enticing dark blue, he noted. The color of a pond at midnight, and deep enough to drown in. His cock strained the material of his pantaloons to the limit and he had to be thankful Maria wasn't facing his direction and Theresa wasn't looking down.

"…I rarely lose," she finished, bit her lip and let the skin go with a gentle, sensual movement.

Does she know what that does to me? Of course she does, she is a courtesan, ex or not.

* * * *

Three o'clock in the morning was a strange time to be

50

involved in what was in essence a business meeting, with no sex involved, Theresa thought as she sat opposite Jamie a couple of hours later. She'd stoked the fire, replenished the wine, brandy and port decanters and made sure there was food aplenty. Theresa sniggered to herself. All her other 'business' meetings at this hour had involved naked bodies, and the food suited to copulation, not chat.

Tonight the table of snacks and drinks positioned between them had considerably less victuals on it than there had been before they'd sat down. With the shutters and the long dark red velvet curtains closed, the lamps on low and the fire blazing in the grate, one could almost think it was a setting for seduction.

Except it wasn't.

With her permission, Jamie had loosened his cravat, removed his jacket and unbuttoned his elegant striped waistcoat. "Setting the scene," he said with a laugh. "Or at least acting more like friends than strangers. You can't help but feel somewhat comfortable with someone you have seen slightly rumpled and less than immaculate."

She'd smiled and wished she could discard her stays. As that was probably more than a little too forward, Theresa had unlaced her sandals and wriggled her feet in the pile of the carpet instead. A poor substitute, but better than nothing.

Jamie watched her. A sardonic smile played over his lips. "Do women wear those laces criss-crossed up their legs just to tantalize us males?" he inquired. "For if you do, let me tell you it works. Every time. All I can think of is what is above that tiny knot that holds them in place."

His expression was sinful.

"My knees," she replied. It was a relief that she didn't sound half as flustered as she felt.

Jamie laughed and bowed his appreciation of her reply. "Well said. Mind you, I'm partial to knees..." He paused and sipped some wine. "And what is even higher."

Damn him, did he have any idea what those words,

said in such a deep and sinfully sex-filled voice, did to a woman? One look at the not-so-innocent expression on his face answered her question for her. Of course he did.

"Naturally," Theresa replied composed once more. "You are a man. However, I dress"—she ran her tongue around her lips and was pleased to note how his body tightened and his eyes narrowed—"or not…to please myself."

He raised one eyebrow. Was it a prerequisite of an aristocrat, Theresa wondered, to learn how to make that gesture so effectively? If so, he must be at the top of the class. It was something Theresa had seen done many times, by many people, although never quite so successfully.

"How intriguing. You like stays?" He looked toward her waist for several seconds then let his gaze drift upward to her breasts. "You must be the only woman who does," Jamie continued with a grin. "Probably the only person on earth actually. Although, the untying can be said to be quite titillating, as I am sure you know."

Theresa damned the ready heat that flooded her. It was not all embarrassment. "That is none of your business," she said and hoped her flat, no-nonsense tone would repress his teasing.

"It will be, and, just for the record? I hate the bloody things," Jamie said in an off-hand manner. "They do nothing for me. Don't wear them on my behalf. The laces get knotted, and they can be a devil to remove or push aside when needed. Or," he added almost as an aside, she thought, "put back into place in a hurry."

She gaped and the idiocy of the conversation hit her. Here they were discussing stays when there were so much more important things to talk about. She peered at Jamie from under her lashes and itched to wipe the wicked grin off his face.

"Oh good," she purred. "So do I." His jaw dropped. Perfect. "Hate them," Theresa added. "I was, however, for once trying to be ladylike."

"Not on my behalf, love," he said audaciously, obviously

recovered from his momentary surprise. "I opt for unladylike, every time." He stroked his chin, where a dark shadow of bristly hair showed. "Hmm. I need a shave. Whisker-burn is not to be thought of on delicate skin."

Theresa gasped and he grinned. "Do you not agree?"

Theresa began to realize he would not be a complacent companion, or one she could dictate to. That in itself would be a novelty after so many years. Her core heated and she clenched her thighs together to alleviate the itch of arousal that had begun.

She shook her head. "A step too far," she said, much too breathless for her liking.

"Not at all, I much prefer a little less decorum, especially as we are going to be seen to be close. Very close," he finished and picked up another piece of lardy cake. "This is tasty."

"I'll tell cook," Theresa replied, somewhat confounded at his quick change of subject. She would need to be on her toes to keep up, and not let him see if he flustered her. He'd enjoy that, she was certain. "I suppose I should say I aim to please, but that then poses the question, 'please who'?" She rolled her shoulders and the gesture made her breasts move under the soft material of her gown. His gaze focused on them like a beacon and she licked her lips. "And how."

"You now, and me in the near future, I hope." Jamie dusted his fingers together and steepled them on his chin for a moment. "As we both desire. Thank you." He gestured to the remains of the food on the table. "I hadn't realized I was hungry until I saw this repast. We best plot, I think, Theresa." He paused, and to her amazement colored a little. "Under the circumstances I think we are on first-name terms? Maria might kill us if we are not, apart from the fact that we need to be comfortable using them. I'm damned sure neither of us use titles in the middle of f— Well, you know."

She nodded, and his rigidity softened. "You don't need to spell it out, Jamie. I agree to both of your statements."

"Thank you. Please tell me honestly, you weren't coerced into this by Maria, were you?" Jamie asked. "I know just how persuasive she can be."

His worry and thoughtfulness was unexpected and it curled around her in the way a mama would snuggle her child in a warm blanket. No one had shown so much unspoken sympathy and consideration since she had been a child and had broken her arm falling out of an apple tree. Even then, once it was healed her papa had taken a belt to her for disobeying him. It had not been their tree.

It took a lot of determination not to rub her arse. The scars were still there. Faint, but criss-crossed over her rear, and in the cold weather a reminder of how her childhood had been. An only child, whose mother had disappeared when she was five, she'd bewildered her sire. He had treated her as he would have a son, and although he had been firm, but, she supposed, fair, Theresa had felt lost. When she'd discovered her mama had died, she'd realized she had no woman to turn to for advice. Lord Humphrey's wife had stood in place of her mama until her death, and when her father had passed away just before her sixteenth birthday, Humphrey had then taken over. Although never as a father figure.

"Theresa?"

"Oh lord, sorry. No coercion." She made haste to reassure Jamie, and shook her head. "The only thing she said was she might know someone who could help me out. Not who or how or even when and where. Before this week I would probably have told her there was no need for a third party to become involved. That I was sure bloody pathetic pest Percy—excuse my language but I can no longer think of him without that epithet—would finally get the hint and cease his stupidity."

"He's escalated instead?" Jamie asked, and frowned. "Insolent young pup. What's he done?"

"Threatened to make me give in to his demands, although how he didn't specify," Theresa said in an undertone. "He cannot accept I was doing a job. One I had qualms about from the very first. Between us?"

Jamie nodded his assent.

"I faced an uphill struggle. I could almost own he was my first and only failure. He is one who thinks only his opinion matters, and as he assumes he is perfect in every way, why should a mere courtesan tell him what to do? But even so" — she wrinkled her nose as she concentrated on how best to share her complicated thoughts — "something didn't ring true and I cannot fathom out what seemed wrong. Not that he only went through the motions as if bowing to my whim, but..." She shrugged and tutted. "Something was not right. Then of course, there was Protheroe today. One good thing, I hope, is that bloody Percy has not yet informed the world in general what he intends."

"No notice to the Times?" Jamie questioned. "No special license, or the banns read anywhere?"

Theresa went hot then cold. "He couldn't, could he?"

"He could, or he could have," Jamie amended. "I'll see to it that he no longer can achieve the announcement in the paper at least. The editor owes me a favor. No, don't ask, I won't say. The rest? Not so easy, but as you both need to be in church for the wedding, plus the banns need to be read, that I think we can ignore for the moment. He could go for a common license, I dare say, but we'll just be vigilant." He paused to stand and refill their glasses. Theresa inclined her head to thank him. "I'll put the word to certain people that you are not compliant with his wishes. Hopefully that will help."

"I suppose so, but goodness me, how much happier I would be if I'd never set eyes on him. A most unsatisfactory three months." She shook her head. "I should have listened to my thoughts."

"Why did you take him on if you had misgivings?" Jamie asked. "I'm curious because I am sure you're not so complacent that you thought one word from you and he'd change." He handed a glass to Theresa and resumed his seat. This time he sat with one pantaloon-clad leg crossed over the other.

Lord, how I wish he wouldn't sit like that. It gives me ideas. Ideas she needed not to have.

"Thank you for that," she said as soon as she was sure she was composed enough not to reply in a silly, breathless voice. "Complacency had never suited me. I took him on because I felt sorry for his godfather, who seemed to be forever pulling bloody Percy out of the mire and listening to his godson bewailing how no lady appreciated him."

"Lord Luscott?"

Theresa nodded. "He is an old friend and one who isn't in the best of health. Which is why I haven't approached him about Percy."

To her relief, Jamie didn't ask for any more information. It was just as well, she had no intention of explaining in greater detail. Lord Luscott had never been involved with her intimately. He was, she supposed, almost grandfather-like in his attitude to her. A friend of Sir Humphrey, the elderly peer had championed her ever since Humphrey's death, and been a constant comfort. It was no wonder she'd taken on Percy as a client. Theresa made a mental note never to give in to misguided sympathy again.

"Then we'll have to do the best we can not to involve Luscott." Jamie twirled his wineglass in his hands as he studied the ruby red liquid. "He doesn't deserve it. Do you have any ideas?"

Theresa spread her hands out in a helpless gesture. "None that are legal," she confessed and laughed. "Maria suggested having him pressed. Lots of ships' captains would be glad to have another person working for them. That idea is looking more and more interesting by the hour."

"I'll keep it in mind," Jamie said. "However, for a start, we'll try something less drastic. Marry me."

Chapter Four

He caught her wineglass as it slipped through her suddenly lifeless fingers and placed it on the tabletop. Then he intertwined her fingers with his and held her hand close to his chest.

"Well, that popped out, didn't it." He shook his head. "Mouth before mind."

"Say that again," Theresa said, faint but clear "I must have defective hearing, for I could swear you asked me to marry you."

"Don't get overcome with emotion," he said dry as dust. "As I said, I spoke before I meant to."

"Oh I won't." She tried to tug her hand free and he shook his head and held on as tight as anyone ever had. "You jest."

"Do I?" he mused. "Or is it my inner intentions showing their hand? I wonder." His thumb caressed her palm in slow sweeps. "I really do wonder."

"Well, don't." If she didn't want an unseemly tussle she couldn't do anything about his closeness. Which was a pity as she could see the green flecks in his brown eyes and the golden tips to his dark hair. Scent his own peculiar scent—citrus and woodsy. And feel herself drawn to him. "Of course I'm not going to marry you," she said somewhat more huskily than she wanted. "Why on earth should I?" A pang of 'what if' swept through her and she quashed it with ruthless efficiency. What ifs were not helpful.

"Expediency?" he suggested. "No, don't go up in the boughs. Hear me out." He grinned and again she saw why Maria said so many women sighed with pleasure when the earl smiled at them, or paid them particular attention.

"I accept that is perhaps an overly drastic measure, but nevertheless something to keep in mind," he said as he played with her fingers. "Do you not think we would suit?"

Damn him. That was much too intriguing for her peace of mind. She shrugged. "Well, do you?"

"Who knows? However," Jamie continued, seeming oblivious to the way her pulse raced and tiny goosebumps rose on her arms. *Thank goodness.* "If we were to seem to be interested in each other, and both were breaking the habits of our lifetimes, it could perhaps send a warning to Percy, Lady S. and my mama."

"I would have thought it more likely to make your mama even more determined to get her own way," Theresa observed. "To see you are consorting with a courtesan will surely be like a red rag to a bull. She'll never believe you are besotted with me."

He shrugged. "I've never been besotted with anyone, ever. Unless you count my first pony. Nor do I wear my heart on my sleeve, or parade my current interest in front of my peers. She'll believe it. Not like it, do her best to be obstreperous, but believe it. I'd make sure she understood and accepted it, however grudgingly. As I hold her future comforts in my grasp, she will be careful."

On reflection, Theresa realized that although Jamie was said to be a rake and a ladies' man, no one really had any concrete evidence to produce with regards to his activities. It was all hearsay. "So how will this work?" she asked with interest. "If no one can confirm our...oh, whatever you want to call it."

His mouth quirked. "Our liaison? Your sexual conquest?"

"Mine," Theresa said, astonished at his words and surprised at how they affected her body. Her quim contracted and her thighs were suspiciously damp. "Not yours?"

"Either or. However, I suspect I will be seen as the one who has altered the habits of a lifetime." He grinned and it took ten years off him. "It will be a novel experience."

"But so will I be seen to have changed my ways," Theresa pointed out. "It is well known I only ever have clients. Men who, should we say, need improving. And for a fixed period of time. No one would ever believe you are such a man."

"True but…" He stopped speaking and to her amazement a ruddy hue flooded his face. "Oh Hades, how arrogant do I sound?"

Theresa patted his arm. It was refreshing to see this more humble side of such a supremely confident man. "Somewhat, but it's understandable. Therefore how on earth are we going to achieve our aim?"

"I won't flaunt us. That would be so out of character no one would believe it, especially my mama," Jamie said. "I can't change my basic makeup. But I intend to devote all my time to us, to show I *have* changed my tune and persuaded you to do the same. We will become inseparable whenever possible. As it will be an alien scenario for both of us, that's what will make it believable. If I'm with you, she won't have a chance to do anything."

"Except arrange for my demise?" Theresa said. "I'll warn you now, if she succeeds I will haunt you."

He laughed. "I'd let you. On a serious note, however, I think the best way for us to achieve our desired goal is to show everyone and anyone we are a couple. A word in Percy's ear will show him I mean business. For some reason the family Weston strikes fear into him. It could have something to do with Freddie and a grass snake at Eton."

"A what?" Theresa asked in astonishment. "Do tell."

Jamie chuckled. "Freddie was a year or so older than Percy, but Percy was a pest. To everyone. Always crying foul and never owning up to anything. Plus, when he could be he was an out-and-out bully to the younger boys. Freddie caught him tormenting one of them with a thistle to his sensitive areas. As Freddie knew Percy was somewhat, ah, apprehensive, shall we say, around reptiles, he found a grass snake and put it in Percy's bed. With a note saying 'A grass snake for a snake in the grass'. And a warning... 'We are all watching you. Beware adders.'"

"My goodness." She put her hand over her mouth and bit back a giggle. "Did it work?"

Jamie nodded. "Oh yes. Freddie was not one to be trifled with and Percy knew it. Fred still isn't, to be honest."

"That gives me immense satisfaction. Although, I do wonder whether his mother played his father false. You know," Theresa mused as she ignored Jamie's shout of laughter. "According to Lord Luscott, Percy has nothing of the Prendergasts in him."

"He's wrong, although I bet he wishes he wasn't," Jamie said. "Because then he could wash his hands of the idiot. Percy sports a weak chin like his paternal grandfather, and a penchant for gaming. Even though he has no other Prendergast characteristics, I feel that is enough. Sadly he is not a gamester at heart. No eye and no head for counting. No backbone either and definitely thinks the world owes him. However, I don't think Almeria Prendergast would have found the energy to take a lover, even if it was just the once. She was, as far as I remember, and from a child's point of view, always a wilting violet whose imaginary ills took precedence over all else. Even Percy, which wouldn't have helped his pathetic attitude. I'm as sure as I can be that he's merely and sadly an anomaly." He tapped his fingers on the side of his glass. "Anyway, to get back to *our* problem. There are plenty of harpies who will make it *their* business to tell every lady of the ton, especially my mama, what I'm up to. Therefore, my dear, do we dally?"

Jamie watched a play of emotions cross Theresa's face as she nibbled her lip, and hoped fiercely she would agree to his ideas. He wanted her—his tight body, nerves on edge and hard staff told him that. Every time she took a deep breath he willed his erection to subside, his hands not to move to ease those delicious globes out from under her gown and his breathing to slow down. His immediate reaction wasn't all he experienced, though. He was irate. He couldn't tolerate a man riding roughshod over a defenseless woman.

That gave him pause for thought. Was he not guilty of that very thing?

It's different. Or so he hoped. Apart from which, Jamie was damn sure Theresa would give as good as she got.

"Well?" he asked as the silence stretched. "Is it such a hard decision to make? I'm no ogre. I won't beat you."

Theresa grinned. "That is for certain. I wouldn't let you. I'm a good shot and I wouldn't hesitate to shoot if necessary. In the bollocks." His spare hand automatically went to cover himself. She followed his movement and chuckled. "I've never found the necessity yet."

"Ah, good." He glanced around the room. Then at her face. To say her expression was mischievous was an understatement. "I swear, both you and Maria have a vicious streak. Do you always have a pistol handy then?"

She nodded and withdrew one from behind the cushion. "Always."

Thank goodness she didn't point it at him. She might say she was a good shot, but to Jamie's knowledge saying so and being one were two completely different things. Especially, he pondered, when the shooter was a woman. *Perhaps that was a thought not to be shared.*

"Does Percy know of this?" he asked. "Your propensity to hide firearms everywhere?"

Theresa shook her head. "No, I tend to keep that information to myself. I prefer the element of surprise."

"I'm doubly grateful to you for telling me," Jamie said with honesty. "I'll make sure I make no sudden or unwanted moves. Do you think you could put it away now?" He gestured to the pistol, so at odds with her pretty dress and ladylike figure. "It's probably not the best thing to admit whilst you hold the thing, but in general women and guns worry me."

"And me," Theresa said. She sounded cheerful and

unconcerned. "Which is why I made sure I could shoot well. It gives an element of surprise when someone sees I can hold it steady and point it where I intend the bullet to go."

"Have you had to use it often?" Just who was this woman? All his preconceived ideas had flown out of the window. No common courtesan without a thought between her ears except how to get it over and done with, that was certain. Jamie wondered if he would ever get to know every facet of her. Stories he had heard and dismissed as fallacy now began to make more sense. Intrigued beyond measure, he intended to try to understand what and who she was. All of it. That was another thought that astounded him. He liked most women, and had loved some in a carnal sense, but never before had he experienced the need to know anyone to a greater depth than the minimum required to achieve a comfortable relationship.

"Well I've never shot anyone, if that's what you mean," Theresa said with a smirk. "I've been tempted a time or two, I admit, but as yet I've never pulled the trigger in anger. My shooting has been of the human vermin kind. Oh, and food for the pot."

Jamie wondered where and when that had occurred. He knew next to nothing about her. That would have to be remedied.

"We'll have to arrange a contest at some point," he said and let out his breath in one long *whoosh* as Theresa checked her pistol and put it back under the cushion.

"I'd love to go to Manton's," she said as she cocked her head to one side and contemplated him with speculation. "I am certain I would hold my own."

"I am sure you would as well, but think about it. That would be the day. A woman in the hallowed halls?" Jamie replied. "Can you imagine it? The world of the ton would end. Not to be thought of. Well, not by some. For me, I couldn't care less.

"I could wear breeches."

"Breasts would give you away. Especially such sumptuous ones as yours. Sadly, my love, Manton's is never going to happen. I thought perhaps in the country at Elmwood." He held his breath. To show her that, as well as other things at Elmwood, would be an adventure he would relish.

"Elmwood?" she inquired. "What is that?"

"My house in Rutlandshire. We might find it useful to retire there for a while. To add to the credulity of our arrangement."

"Now I am curious, because I thought you lived in town?" Theresa said. "Or with your brother at Ansterby Grange."

Jamie shook his head. "At my age? Not likely. I've had my own home both here and in the country for years. Although Martin and I are close and do visit each other, we would never live comfortably under the same roof. Mama removed to the dower house, her intention I think to nudge Martin to take another wife. It's backfired. He seems to be uninterested since his beloved wife died. Nevertheless, he can fight his own battles and make sure she doesn't meddle too much. To let her think I dance to her tune whilst I do exactly what I want is an art I have perfected. Wearing but worth it." He tipped Theresa's chin up with his pinkie and watched as the sapphire in his signet ring reflected onto her soft skin, to add to the glow given by her long string of pearls. Just how far would they go if she hadn't looped them twice around her neck? His well-intended, but now, he accepted, foolish thought that of course he was not interested in her in a sexual way was no longer anywhere in evidence. Ever since he'd seen her that evening his body had told him firmly he *was* interested. Very much so. "Now," he said *sotto voce*. "I intend to lavish attendance on you."

She colored, laughed and let her nerves show as she toyed with her necklace. As the soft luster of the moving pearls added their sheen to her skin, Jamie decided he'd love to see her with her hair down, wearing sapphires and pearls and nothing else. He had the exact set in mind.

One day.

"Theresa, what say you?" Jamie appealed to Theresa. "Are we in agreement? I will champion you, stick by you and hopefully do it in such a manner that we will have a good time."

Or so he intended.

"How good?" she asked suspiciously. "In what way?"

"In whichever way you choose," Jamie assured her, quashing his own intentions with a ruthlessness he didn't know he had where they were concerned. "I wish for us both to be happy and comfortable with this arrangement. To be able to say what we think without fear of ridicule or lack of support. Share our wants and needs and work to relieve ourselves of these damned irritants trying to upset our lives." He looked down at his body. "Evidently, it is no secret I want you and before you say want must be my master, I accept that. For now. I will not act on my desires unless you wish it. But who knows what might happen in the future?"

"I do not trade sex for favors, I never did." Theresa blushed. "I do not work in my previous profession anymore. I retired."

"I know that," he said patient and intrigued at how she had colored as she spoke. "Would you have done so if not for Percy?"

She nodded. "Oh yes. I'm too old for all that now."

Jamie could have argued the point, that her age did not affect her desirability. However, he guessed it must be difficult talking about such things with a relative stranger, and didn't carry on in that vein. "Dare I say I'm glad? And that perhaps one day you'll come to me because you want me. For that and no other reason."

"Hmm." She appeared somewhat dubious.

He thought rapidly. "I'll make you a promise."

"Which is?" Theresa asked with skepticism laced through her voice.

Lord she *was* suspicious. Although, he acknowledged,

perhaps with good reason. "Unless you ask me otherwise I will not touch you," he said. "My word on it. You no doubt will make me beg."

Her eyes widened. "Beg on your knees?" That glint of mischief was in them again. "That sounds as if it would be unusual."

"If that is your want. And I will be ready and waiting to do as you desire," Jamie replied.

"No strings?"

"No strings," he assured her. "No coercion. I reserve the right to seduce you, though." He touched the outline of his staff over his pantaloons. "But I promise you if you say no or no more, I will do as you wish. It might be hard, my cock and my decision, but so be it."

Theresa followed the movement of his hand. "I can see that," she said as her eyes danced with devilment. "And at this moment in time, hard they will stay."

Jamie was glad he was not drinking because her audacious statement, spoken in such a deadpan voice, would have made him choke.

"Or not, I'm not sure how much willpower you can use," she continued before he had a chance to come up with a witty reply. Or a reply of any description. "But I'm not around to help," Theresa said. "And I accept your proposition. Plus, you *will* go down on your knees and beg me to take you." She bit her lip and ran her tongue over her lips in that suggestive way she had. "Three times."

Three?

"You drive a hard bargain," Jamie said. "No matter, we have more important things to discuss." He was amazed at the amount of regret that filled him. Until she so very politely turned his offer down, Jamie had fully thought he was teasing. Now he wasn't so sure. "Therefore yes, if I want to touch you, I will beg. On my knees. Thrice. But, my dear, it works both ways. You also have to beg three times, not once. On your knees."

She grinned. "As you say."

"That sorted, here is my plan. I propose we begin to be seen together. A walk in the park and a visit to the theater. Let me accompany you to Maria's salon for a gown fitting. I'll do the 'yes, no, perfect' comments a lover provides, which even if the salon is empty will somehow get back to those we want to know."

"Via the air?" she asked. "Carrier pigeon? Somehow, I'm rather dubious."

"Lord knows, but gossip spreads faster than the plague, you know that," Jamie said. "Tittle-tattle fulfills the empty voids of the ton. So we start the ripples and let them spread. Then let it be known I approve of your new night-rails."

"What new night-rails?" Theresa asked in a startled voice. "I do not need any more night-rails."

"You don't have to need them to buy them. We'll order some from Maria tomorrow. I wager once we are seen entering and leaving, the news will be all over the town."

"From Maria?" Theresa said, bewildered by his intentions. "I thought that was for a gown? One of such a difference people will stop and stare. Which I also have no need of."

"Ah, but did I say a day, evening or night gown?" He laughed as her mouth fell open. "Ah, Theresa, you are so easy to tease, I promise to stop."

"Oh tease away, my lord," she said. "I can ignore you."

"But you won't," he said. "Even though I am confident you will wish to have the last word."

Theresa shook her head in amusement. "We'll see." She stopped speaking and snorted. "Good lord, listen to us. We're like an old established couple griping and snipping."

"Not griping and snipping, love. Teasing and sexual innuendo is something totally different."

She was silent for a while then waggled her finger at him. "As you say." Theresa grinned. "Such fun. Especially as you know if I say no, I mean no." Without warning she yawned and put her hand over her mouth. "Lord, I'm sorry. It's been an eventful few days, and I think they have caught up with me."

Jamie stood and drew her to her feet.

"And the next few days I fear will be even more so. So, a kiss to seal our deal, or do I need to beg for that as well?" He framed her face with his hands.

"Would you?" she asked curious to hear his reply.

"Oh yes," he assured her as he bent his knees. "I foresee fun."

Theresa put her finger over his lips. "No need." She moved her hands to his shoulders and went up on tiptoe. Then she set her lips to his.

Totally unexpected arousal flared. Theresa leaned into him, her mouth parted and she groaned as her tongue meshed with his. He tangled his fingers in her hair, tugged more strands from her bun and spread the tresses over her shoulders. Against his chest, even through his shirt, Jamie fancied her nipples tightened and pushed closer to him.

The grandfather clock wheezed and chimed four times. Theresa jumped back as if she was stung and smoothed her hair behind her ears with unsteady hands. Jamie noticed just how many tendrils he'd loosened from the simple knot at the nape of her neck with his restless fingers.

He stared at her, his breath erratic, and watched as she took in large gulps of air.

"I... You..." She stopped and swallowed. "We..." Her voice trailed off.

"We," Jamie replied, his voice uneven, "mesh. I don't think we'll have any trouble persuading people we have succumbed to lust, do you?"

* * * *

"Do you know what people are saying?" the dowager demanded four days later as she faced him in his dining room. As it was barely ten a.m. and she was rarely up before noon, someone had upset his parent.

Jamie couldn't care less except it meant he was out of bed as well. He surveyed the food on the table in front of him and sighed as he plotted her words in his mind. There was no point in asking her to sit down, or offering her food and drink. She would not only refuse but no doubt also complain about his lack of civility. According to her, a gentleman's inclination should be to phrase it as a request, *not* a demand. He was certain she would deem his words as demands, not requests, however he said them.

"No, nor do I care. Anything else, or have you rushed over here at this hour to inform me that people are talking? Good lord, people always talk. How else would they communicate?" She would seethe at his indifferent and mocking tone, but that, he thought, was her problem, not his.

"Pshaw."

He hated that ridiculous noise. "As you say." Next she would say she was a laughingstock. Jamie poured himself some ale. More to annoy his parent and occupy his hands than for the need of alcohol. What he would prefer was to use his hands to bodily lift her up, carry her to the doorstep and remove her from his presence. Then pour coffee, go for a ride and ignore the pettiness of her and her cronies. As that wasn't to be, he settled with staring at her over the top of his tankard.

She frowned. "Ale at this time of the day. Is that what she is encouraging you to be? A sot?"

Damnation. Why have I never told her to wash her mouth out? She is a first-class harpy. Worse than he had realized. Even though he didn't want it, Jamie took a mouthful of ale and pondered how best to reply.

"I am a laughingstock amongst my friends," his mother said and let her petulance show before he'd formulated an answer.

Thought so. Next will be I do not value her and want her in an early grave.

"They then are no friends of yours." He didn't ask what else irked her. She'd tell him anyway.

"You do not care, do you?" she said in a passionate

68

manner. "You do not value me, your mother. You want me in an early grave."

I knew it.

"People are asking me if you have taken leave of your senses. If you are mad and a candidate for bedlam." She stared at him mutinously. "I assume you must be."

Jamie counted to ten. It was that or scream. "Not at all," he said with no hint of the temper he held on to by sheer determination. "I've come to my senses. My life is mine to do as I choose. I choose my lady."

"She is no lady," his parent said with scorn. She is a nobody, a harl…" Her voice trailed off and she took a step backward as Jamie surged to his feet. His chair toppled onto the floor with a crash that sent a decanter on a nearby table rocking. A footman opened the door, took one look at the two of them as they faced each other and removed himself hastily.

The dowager was red-faced. Jamie was in no doubt that his features were set in stone. Ice-cold anger held him in its grip, the likes of which he had never experienced before.

"Enough, Mama." Was that harsh tone really him? "Do you think that she is different from any one of us? That I have never had sex?"

"Jamie." Her mouth dropped open. "Remember who I am." His mama put her hands over her ears. To his secret amusement, he noticed she didn't blush now.

"I have remembered, or I assure you I would not use such polite language," he said. "Good lord, do you imagine Papa bedded no one else but you and you only to begat his heirs? Rubbish. And, while we are on the subject, what about you, for instance?"

The dowager went white and swayed. Jamie nodded, grim and determined she would understand what he intimated. "Exactly so. You may have been faithful to Papa…" Although he rather thought she hadn't. "However, now?" He shook his head. "Whatever anyone thinks, there are no secrets in the ton. The only difference is my lady does not sugarcoat what she has been. Nor should she."

"Your papa was—"

"Not a saint," Jamie interrupted her with a brusque ruthlessness that no doubt surprised her. "So do not try to tell me he was."

"It is the way of our world," his mother said.

"As you say. To some people, anyhow, changing beds and bedfellows, creeping around and pretending it doesn't happen is the norm. I choose differently."

"But she is not one of us," the dowager said in despair. "How can you be so…so…unfeeling? I will never acknowledge her if you continue on this track."

He shrugged. "Your choice." His voice was icily cold and his mama blanched. Due to his words or his tone? He had no idea, and if he were honest the time to wonder or worry was long gone. She had never considered his feelings in the past, and as much as he ought to have filial affection for her, he accepted he did not.

"Jamie, my son, I beg of you, think."

"I have. Long and hard, believe me. Now if there is nothing else, may I suggest you mind your own business and ignore mine?" Would she never depart? Jamie wanted to leave the capital and breathe fresh air.

"What about the dukedom?" The dowager pointed an accusing finger at him. "Do you not think of that?"

"It is up to Martin. Hound him if you must but leave me and mine alone. I will brook no interference."

"Well, yes, but what about Marion?" his mother said. "Jamie, I beseech you to think again. She expects you to offer. It was decided when she was in her crib. You know that, you both do. She is waiting."

Thank goodness he and Marion had conversed and the last thing either of them wanted was to be wed to each other. "Not by her or me. Face it, Mama, you are just peeved because life has not conformed to what you decree. As for Marion? That is the last thing she expects and you know it. Just because you and Lady Strawbridge have bees in your bonnets doesn't mean Marion and I are going to do anything about it. Let them sting you, I care not. It is your own fault."

Chapter Five

For once, the weather was in their favor. For several days it was bright, sunny with a nip in the air.

Jamie tooled his matching chestnuts through the park and glanced at his silent passenger. It was their third drive in five days, and after the activities of the previous three weeks, his interest in her and hers in him had been noticed. So far no one had openly accosted him about what was going on, but there had been a lot of veiled hints and comments disguised as questions. Their outing two nights earlier, at the theater—in his box, not hers—had caused several quizzing glasses to be raised, and afternoon tea and an ice at Gunter's a few days before had a grand dame and her daughter, both of a lower birth than he, cut him dead.

He'd returned their deliberate non-greetings with a quizzical look that had made the mother blush and the daughter have a coughing fit. Then he had bowed very slowly and shaken his head. "I swear the manners of the ton are sinking to new lows these days."

Theresa had upbraided him but he was unrepentant.

"They could have just ignored us and not been so blatant about cutting me. That way I would have ignored them back. Grief, when Susanna Cousins asked me if I knew what I was about and I said yes, she patted my arm and said good luck. Mind you," he added as he thought over what had happened, "Susie has never wanted to get into my breeches, and that Swanson woman and her daughter do."

"What, both of them?" Theresa asked. She sounded incredulous.

He shrugged. "I'm not one to tell tales."

"Hussies," Theresa said. "I swear, the ton is worse than any other part of society."

"I suspect that is true." Jamie was aware, with every last inch of him, that Theresa looked stunning as she sat next to him in his curricle. There was no other word for it. It was difficult to focus on the road ahead and not keep taking sideways glances at her. Her cherry-red pelisse was the perfect foil for her dark hair, wispy curls of which showed from under her matching bonnet. The shimmering peacock feather attached to the brim was a jaunty and cheeky addition, as was the discreet sapphire-and-pearl clasp that held it in place. A gift from him to her that Jamie was pleased to see Theresa wear. She'd thanked him prettily and offered the opinion that if he had nothing better to do with his money, who was she to persuade him otherwise. Then she had giggled and rolled her eyes. "Really, you didn't have to do this," Theresa had assured him earnestly. "But it is so pretty I cannot refuse it, and thank you." Seeing it now, he was glad she hadn't.

Her hands were sensibly thrust inside a muff, along with, she had told him quietly, her muff pistol, and her feet — resting on a hot brick — were clad in half-boots the same red as her coat. Under the hem he got a glimpse of a warm twill gown in a lighter shade of reddish-pink.

If only she didn't look so worried.

"Having second thoughts?" he asked as he bowed to the occupants of a nearby carriage, drawn up at the side of the track. He kept his voice low. "So far all is working well. Mama is expected back in town within a week, I believe. As I said, she swept out of my house after our oh so interesting conversation. I discovered from Freddie that she went down to Pasterham, the dower house she resides in when she is not making my or my siblings' lives a misery. Probably to plot and plan, but at least it has given us these few days' respite from her. Percy is at present paying attendance on his godfather in Bath. Called away unexpectedly from

Ronnie Roscoff's shooting party."

"Really? Is Lord Luscott ill?" Theresa asked with worry in her voice. "He's a love."

Jamie smirked. "Did I say that? Or that the message was from Luscott?"

He felt her shift on her seat to look at him, and she put one hand on the sleeve of his greatcoat. "Jamie, you didn't?"

He shook his head and laughed. "Didn't what? I merely thought it would do him good to hear stories and not be around to discover how much truth there was in them. He won't be back until tomorrow at the earliest."

"And that will make things better?" Theresa asked. "Somehow I doubt it."

"Of course it will," he said. "Trust me, we are setting the scene most satisfactorily. Now take heed. Lady Jersey is to your left, make your nod to her."

"Second thoughts? Oh my, no. Not just second ones — third, fourth and twentieth," Theresa muttered, as she did as he directed. The lady in question appeared somewhat startled but, after a swift stare in Jamie's direction, gave a stiff nod back.

"Are you trying to give her ladyship a heart attack?" Theresa asked Jamie. "She's just acknowledged me, a common whore in her eyes, and looked as if she might choke. After successfully avoiding me every time she sees me in the square. I swear if she could have blocked my occupancy she would have."

"Let her choke," Jamie replied. "If I sound indifferent it is because I am. For if she thinks that of you, her eyesight is faulty. You were never a whore and common is as common does. Not something I think anyone could ever say of you. And besides, I am aware of your antecedents."

Theresa snorted and her eyes brimmed with amusement. "Thank you. Unacknowledged and so be it. I felt for Mama, not for me. I admit I try not to think of every moment of my upbringing."

"Ah yes, your upbringing." He nigh on purred the words

74

and wondered if it made her wary. "You never have said much about it."

"Not a lot to say, my...Jamie, my dear," Theresa added with a saucy grin. Anything to steer him away from those days. "And definitely not here in the park."

Jamie nodded. "Point taken. Later." It was not a question.

Theresa sighed. "I suppose so. If we are to bare our souls we may as well strip them to the bones."

"Exactly." Jamie flicked the whip off the offside horse's ear and angled around a phaeton drawn up so the male occupant could converse with the two ladies in an open carriage next to it. "Lambton never could park to save himself," he observed as he eyed the skewed vehicle. "Never knows where things should go."

She dipped her head. "That's true, neither his horse and equine equipment nor his hands or his pri...ah..." She lapsed into silence.

Jamie glanced at her reddened face. "Love." It seemed the endearment slipped out as naturally as her name. "If we never acknowledge the fact you know a considerable amount more than most about many of the young bucks and rakes, we will spend the best part of our time together casting around for things to say. What we both are, were and have done is a fact of life. If anyone says anything I will stare down my aristocratic nose and tell them you have saved the best for last."

"Ah...why thank you." Theresa sounded startled. "Even so, that doesn't answer my original question. Why *are* we here? This is prime time for the ton to show off."

"That's why," Jamie said in a cheerful manner. "I think we should begin as we mean to go on, don't you?" He checked the horses and slowed as they approached the end of the park and joined the queue of carriages waiting to turn around and retrace their steps. "Twice earlier to get into the swing of things, as practice runs, so to speak. Now for the real thing. This is the perfect time and place to let our supposed intentions be known."

"I imagine so." Theresa appeared doubtful, which he guessed was understandable. "If we are snubbed, and you are blackballed from Almack's or wherever, do not blame me."

Jamie waited until they were once more trotting down the row before he spoke again. "If I'm blackballed from Almack's we'll do it over and over again until they are forever thankful I'm not longer a member. Nasty place. Weak orgeat and stale cakes. Simpering debs and overbearing mamas. If I never go again it will be soon enough. However, whilst you're with me no one will say a word out of place, I promise you that. There will be no snubbing. Having caught Lady Jersey unaware, she has acknowledged you, so the rest of the flock will follow." He *baaed* like a sheep and Theresa giggled.

"And as I'll be with you the first time you might have occasion to meet some of these old-fashioned stuffed shirts, all will be well," he added with confidence "I won't make any promises about other times, but then…"

"Why should you?" Theresa asked, prosaic, as she often was. "It's not as if I frequent the same places as the ton." She sniggered. "Well, not at the same time, anyway. I visit my modiste at other hours of the day, usually when those people are abed, whichever bed it happens to be. What they probably do not know is that until very recently I knew exactly which beds they were."

Jamie spluttered. "Do tell."

"Pillow talk is never shared," Theresa retorted. There was a twinkle in her eye. "Tempting as it could be. Anyway, 'tis immaterial because now I'm retired my sources are curbed."

"Now that is a pity. I'll tell you what," Jamie said with a grin. "I'll share what I find out. And it will not be pillow talk. Any pillow talk you would be a party to." He glanced at her and saw the moment she understood his words.

"You think so?" Theresa rolled her eyes. "Very confident?"

"I hope so. And sorry, what were you saying before I took

over the conversation?"

"That the park is big enough for them to ignore me if they happen to cast their gaze in my direction. Even my box at the theater is set suitably apart. I know, or knew, my place. Now with all this going on I am clueless."

"Your place is with me and damn them all," Jamie replied. "In bed or otherwise."

"If you say so." She didn't sound too convinced. "Although I reserve my reply with regards to the bed bit. Nevertheless, you *will* get the repercussions in your daily life."

"Why?" He glanced down at Theresa, who was biting her lip. "Martin and my other siblings, if they were around, would tell me to do as I want, friends will accept it. Non-friends are immaterial and my mama may choose to like it or lump it. Balls and soirees hold no appeal and if you present me with a perfect opportunity to give them a miss I will be forever in your debt."

"And Marion and Lady Strawbridge?"

Jamie shrugged. "Marion I sent a message to. Oh don't worry," he added as she jumped in surprise. "My underfootman is friendly with her tweeny. The tweeny passed on the information I deemed it necessary to tell. That you and I were a partnership now and she could respond how she wished as long as it showed she was happy without me in her life, so to speak. Her odious mother? It has nothing to do with her."

"I hope you are right," Theresa said doubtfully. "Because unless my eyes deceive me she is in that dark green barouche to our left, and if looks could kill someone would be in black and choosing the hymns for our funeral."

Jamie glanced toward the barouche, which he noted was parked somewhat apart from its neighbors. "I wish the Lord's Prayer to be said, and *When I Survey the Wondrous Cross* to be sung."

"Good lord, you *are* organized and ahead of yourself," Theresa said in a startled voice. "I've got no further than making sure I'm not in a pauper's grave."

He chuckled as the pink tip of her tongue showed briefly between her lips. Jamie winked. "I promise you that won't be your end. Shall we have a joint mausoleum?"

Theresa gave a tiny amused *harrumph*. "Now you are off into the realms of fancy, my lord. Ah, I think the lady wants you to stop." She gestured discreetly toward the barouche where a stony-faced woman dressed in a brown ensemble that didn't suit her sat next to a young lady in a blue pelisse and bonnet. "Good luck. Shall I get down or pretend I am Lot's wife?"

"Neither. I'm damned sure she does expect me to stop, but she can expect as much as she desires. Let her fume," Jamie said as they drew closer and the woman leaned forward. "I'm in no mood for allegedly polite but actually sarcastic and downright rude platitudes."

"She'll say it's my fault," Theresa warned him without any heat. "That I corrupted you."

Jamie considered. "Hmm. You could be correct. Not, I hasten to add, about the corrupting part. I need no help in that direction. Follow my lead." He slowed the horses so they walked very sedately past the barouche. Then he doffed his hat.

"Hello, Marion, you look very fetching." He deliberately stared at her mother, who firmed her lips and crossed her arms over her somewhat unimpressive bosom. "Lady Strawbridge."

Marion's eyes widened and her glance flickered toward her parent and back at Jamie and Theresa. She swallowed, gave a faint smile and cleared her throat. "Why thank you, my lord. May I say you seem a lot happier than you have in an age."

He nodded. "I am. It's amazing how many cares and irritants drop away once you feel settled."

Lady Strawbridge *harrumphed*. "You are a disgrace. How dare you speak to me, with your present company around." Her voice rose to an unpleasant screech. "Appear here with that…that…"

"Careful," Jamie said so coldly she shrank back into her seat. "I hope the next word was not going to be something you will in the future wish you'd never uttered. I have a long memory, especially for anyone who impugns me or mine."

Impugns? Good grief, I've swallowed a dictionary.

His obvious ire seemed to work. Lady Strawbridge blanched. "I'm sure I do not mean to offend you or your" — she hesitated, glanced at his stony face and swallowed deeply — "your companion. However, I cannot fail to worry about the effect of seeing you here like this, with a who… woman who will be upsetting to my dear Marion. Let alone your poor mother."

"Mama, enough, please," Marion said in an agonized undertone. "I'm glad to see his lordship so content. If only you and his mama would believe that." She turned to Theresa. "We're lucky with the weather today, are we not?"

Before Theresa had time to reply, Lady Strawbridge responded. "I fear you are overwrought and saying what he wishes to hear, not what you feel, my love. As for his mama…" She put her hand to her forehead and let her sentence trail away into silence.

"Enough." Jamie barked the words out. The horses shifted uneasily and he cursed under his breath as he soothed and steadied them. "As my mama well knows, she is my parent, not my owner. I do as I choose. Neither she nor you has to like it, just accept it. Now if you'll excuse us…" He smiled at Marion. "Marion, you will, as ever, be welcome to visit me and my lady any time you choose."

Lady Strawbridge's mouth dropped open.

Jamie refrained from advising her to shut it or she would catch a fly. Instead, he flicked the reins to urge the horses on.

"We'll take our leave."

"Thank you for stopping, my lord," Marion said. "Believe me when I say how good it was to see you both here together."

"Our pleasure," Jamie replied as they moved away. "Very instructive."

"Marion winked," Theresa said in a shaken voice as they left the other carriage behind and re-entered the busy thoroughfare around the park. "She smiled and winked. At me. Goodness."

He weaved the carriage and horses between pie sellers, tinkers and other immaculately turned-out vehicles heading to or from the park and the daily promenade. "Winked and grinned," she said again. "Will she be all right? Her mama looked ready to have a fit of the vapors. My goodness, what a harpy. Maria had intimated that, but until now, I thought she exaggerated."

"Understated it, more like." For several minutes Jamie was silent as he controlled the highly strung pair past a chimney sweep they took objection to and several urchins begging in the gutter. Finally he turned the curricle into Berkeley Square and the animals settled in the tranquil atmosphere. Here, at this time of day, the noise from the main roads was muted and an almost sleepy air took over. Within the gardens a few happy cries could be heard from toddlers and their nannies, but other than that it was a haven of peace.

"She's not so much a harpy as overenthusiastic for her daughter to make a good match," Jamie said as he drew the vehicle to a halt outside Theresa's front door. Jed, his tiger, whom he'd left chatting to Theresa's coachman while they went out, ran up the area steps and took hold of the horses. "Her parents let her refuse a duke, and although Strawbridge is a good fellow, he doesn't have much get-up-and-do-things about him. A bit of a lazy man who lets others do what he ought. So when my mama hatched up this stupid scheme, Lady Strawbridge embraced it with all the vigor of someone who has seen the possibility of her every dream about to come true. The story of them betrothing us when Marion was in her cradle is a total fabrication." He turned to one side as he prepared to alight. "At that point Martin was spoken for, or I suspect he would have been number one on their lists. Since he is back, no one would dare suggest anything woman-wise to him anymore."

"Why not? I thought he was part of the ton again now?"

Jamie hesitated. "He is in body. I'm not so sure in spirit. I think he's had the worst of everything. An arranged marriage because he thought he needed to be wed to be a good duke. Balderdash, but Martin is...no, was, very conventional. Then for Florence to be killed in such silly circumstances, well, it's no wonder he is different now."

Theresa nodded. "It was talked about for weeks. To catch one's shawl in the wheels of one's carriage is unthinkable. Your poor brother."

"Sad indeed, but Florence was never well, and spent a lot of time in bed. I believe they had a fondness for each other at the end, but Martin blames himself because Florence had insisted she was well enough for an outing. She was with child and wanted fresh air. She tried to jump down from his phaeton, overbalanced and hit one of the horses, who bolted. Evidently, the doctor was of the opinion she'd have been hard pressed to bear a child.

"Mama sees Florence's death as one more indication Martin never really cast off his reckless rogue of yesteryear persona to become the oh so proper duke." He sighed. "Poor Martin. Whatever he is now, he is no longer that."

Theresa took a deep breath as she edged toward him. She'd heard stories about the duke's wife running away with her lover then dying along with the lover when their horses had bolted in a vicious thunderstorm. Whichever was correct, it was no wonder the poor man had changed. "It must be hard for him—for all of you," she said and squeezed his hand. "Very hard." She scooted back across the bench seat and folded her hands in her lap as properly as any grand dame or debutante.

"Thank you." Jamie bowed, very formal and aristocratic,

before his somber expression changed to one of undiluted wickedness. The sort of look that made her skin clammy — in the nicest possible way. "Oh it's hard. But hard for other reasons," Jamie whispered as they stood for a second on the pavement before they climbed the wide shallow steps to her front door. "All much more agreeable." He pressed against her to show he didn't lie. His cock rubbed her arse, and even through all her layers of clothes it teased, aroused and gave her thoughts of what next.

Every inch of her body tensed at the idea of his hands on her once more. She wanted it... She didn't want it. She craved it... Worried how she would react. It had been bad enough when he'd helped her up onto the seat earlier. His touch had seared her, made her giddy with longing and speculating how, if only she felt able to let him go further, he would affect her. If such a simple thing went so deep and gave her such exquisite sensations, what would anything more do?

Theresa stiffened her resolve. No more. Not yet. Maybe never?

Lud, that is a depressing thought.

She couldn't describe why she was so determined to resist him. Perhaps because no true emotions other than lust would be involved? Even though that was an honest emotion, with no false pretense to be anything else, it would not be enough. Now she needed more. Not erroneous protestations or promises but something more precious — and something she wasn't sure existed for her.

Love? Surely not. Desire? Yes, but on its own it felt shallow somehow. Admiration and respect were already between them, that was certain, for they wouldn't have survived this far if it had not been. But did it run deep enough? That she wasn't clear about, and she knew she should be for things to appear as they should.

Goodness, what a mess my mind is in.

"Hard and ready," Jamie whispered as he pressed forward once more then took a step back.

Contrarily, she missed the closeness.

"So I can feel," she hissed. "Stop it, anyone might see." She fought not to sway toward him and concentrated instead on placing her feet firmly on the ground before she brushed her skirts into place and allowed him to tuck her arm into his. "We're in the square, and Lady Jersey is getting out of her carriage."

"I know," he said.

How he could appear so indifferent to their surroundings puzzled her. She could never be so cavalier.

"She's on the other side of the gardens and busy making sure she doesn't dusty her skirts." However, he took a step sideways and put several inches between them, and they climbed the steps slowly. Her pelisse swung with each stride. Jamie fell into place beside her and his many caped greatcoat brushed each step. Thank goodness she employed someone to remove any dust or dirt twice daily. How embarrassing if his immaculate clothing ended up soiled.

The door swung open and Theresa turned to him. "My lord, would you like to come in?"

He hesitated. Theresa raised one eyebrow. Not so effective as when he did it, she was sure, but her best effort. However, he grinned, kissed her cheek, drew back and nodded. "I needed that."

He did? "Why?" She was genuinely perplexed. It was the briefest touch, over almost before it began, and in full view of any passerby.

Jamie shrugged. "Do I need a reason?"

It was her turn to nod. "I rather think you do."

"I crave your touch," he said.

His diffidence was hitherto unknown to her, and it appealed more than perhaps it should.

"Which," he continued, "is not easy to admit." He lifted his hand toward her and let it drop by his side again. "It is, at the risk of sounding big-headed, usually the other way around."

Out of the corner of her eye Theresa saw Roberts, her major-domo, beam and look benevolent before he tactfully turned his head. However discreet Jamie tried to be, someone would always notice. They were in luck that this time it was Roberts, who was in agreement with the rest of her staff in hoping more would come of this alleged liaison.

"Crave, thirst for, covet…" Jamie sighed. "Lust after. However, I'm sure one touch would not be enough. You're in my blood."

Craving wasn't good enough but it was a start. Even so, she dipped her head and spoke in a whisper. "And you mine."

He jumped, blinked, and a slow erotic smile grew until he put his lips to her ear. "Say it again."

She shook her head. "Oh no, you do not need any more adulation. You heard and I will reiterate once more, I might wish for something. However, it does not mean I'll give in to that desire."

"Pity…" He winked and Theresa waggled her finger at him in mock—or was it?—remonstrance. She wasn't convinced.

"Not at all. Self-control is important." Even though she was not certain hers would be strong enough to resist him. It would be all too easy to give in and hang the consequences. "*Are* you coming in or do we say goodbye here?"

"I should go and see my godmother, Lady Crane." He pulled out his fob and studied it.

Is that real or an excuse? Her heart fell. The sudden jolt to her senses surprised her.

"However, I see it is early and she is not expecting me just yet," Jamie said with evident relief. "Therefore I would be delighted to accompany you indoors. And thank the lord for that admission, even if it cost you dear."

A day of surprises, I am pleased and excited now.

"About self-control?" Theresa tried, not very successfully, to calm her racing pulse, and chose to misunderstand him. "You're welcome."

"Do not play the simpleton, my dear," Jamie said as he squeezed her arm. "It does not become you. You know what I meant."

She did, and little did he know, Theresa thought, just how much it cost her to refuse to admit how she really felt. She'd need to be on guard. Jamie might want her, crave her, but it was not enough.

A few moments later, Jamie followed her into the small room she preferred to use whenever possible, and Theresa took the opportunity to change the subject—a skill she had perfected as a courtesan.

"Have you heard any more about our situation?" she inquired. "Over and above what we discussed earlier."

They had mutually agreed that the park was not the place to go into anything in any great detail. "For," Jamie had said, sardonic and trenchant, "if we look serious we will be accused of arguing, and that is not the impression we need to give." They had, therefore, become adept at smiling and laughing while talking. It had worked when they had driven at a less than fashionable hour. However, that afternoon, with so many people about, had shown it was not always an easy thing to achieve. In the end they had given up and exchanged quips about some of the fashions they had observed on their outing, and the merits of the various horses going through their paces around them.

Jamie leaned against the mantel and put one foot on the hearth. It was as well the fire was embers. "A little gossip about our situation has been forthcoming. Not a lot, alas." He lifted the poker, bent, and stirred the fire into a blaze then added some coals. "Some sideways glances, a few knowing, a few puzzled, but not a lot of actual to-my-face comments, except… Hold on."

Damn him. The movements outlined his rather perfect arse to perfection. Something Theresa could have done without. She shut her eyes and counted to ten. Luckily it seemed he hadn't—or chose not to—notice.

"Firstly, have you had any more problems?" he asked

as he replaced the poker and turned to her once more. "Protheroe or Percy?"

Theresa shook her head and hoped she once more looked calm and composed. "It has been oh so quiet, except one of the tweenies reported a young man struck up a conversation as she went to her parents' on her afternoon off, twice in succession. He pestered her and when she, I quote, told him to 'shove off, you booger', tried to tell her he was in love with her and asked if there were there any vacancies in this household, 'so they could be together'. Roberts traced him back to a crony of Percy's. I almost took him on just to keep an eye on him but decided I could not be doing with looking over my shoulder all the time. Plus Ellen would have given notice. He was, and I quote again, 'a right old scab'." She stripped off her muff and allowed him to take her pelisse from her shoulders. The sleeves of the garment slid down her arms and she shivered. It was almost as if he undressed her completely, as if in fact his fingers caressed her skin, with nothing to impede his touch.

"And I think...oh I..." Whatever it was she thought, she could no longer remember. Good lord, if she felt like this with material in the way, she would dissolve in a heap if ever they stood skin to skin, be it lust, indifference or whatever they experienced between them.

"I feel it as well," Jamie said with a wry grin. "That connection, need, call it by which name you choose. But as I said, what happens is up to you."

"I remember," Theresa said in an even tone that gave away none of her inner turmoil. "Don't worry, I won't forget. Ale or tea?"

Her abrupt change of subject brought forth a guffaw from him. "Ale and lardy cake?"

"Gracious, you are insatiable." The moment she uttered the words she wished she could call them back. He, the wretch, saw the unintended double entendre immediately and winked.

"Oh yes."

Theresa groaned and punched his arm in mock annoyance. "I meant appetite-wise."

He grinned, wickedness personified. "So did I."

Oh good grief, is anything straightforward? She would need to think twice before she spoke.

"For refreshments," she said in a way she prayed sounded severe. "Food and drink, my lord, nothing else."

He shook his head in what she hoped was mock sorrow. "Oh you are so wrong, my dear, also in everything else. Think about it, what is refreshment if not food for everything that needs feeding?"

"Grr." Theresa stamped her foot then laughed, reluctant to show how he amused her, as she tugged on the bell-pull. "I will never better you at innuendo so I will stop trying."

"Pity. No, no." Jamie held his hands up in surrender. "I promise, no more. Well, not until I forget myself."

"Ha, and how long do you suppose that will be?" Theresa asked. She would give no guarantees except moment by moment.

He shrugged. "Honestly? I have no idea."

At least he is *honest.*

Jamie waited until the housekeeper bustled in and Theresa gave the request for food and drink — ale for him and tea for her — and left, before he spoke again. "Apart from the young Lothario and your tweenie, *have* there been any more annoyances?"

"Not from Protheroe, as I said, although Bill the bootboy is convinced there's a shifty character hanging around in the square. Mind you, as he also thought he saw a unicorn in the bushes which surround the gardens and a cat on a broomstick, we're not sure how concerned to be."

"Well, if he has seen either of the latter, and it can be substantiated, your fortunes will be made," Jamie said. He chuckled. "You can donate them to the suffering of broomstick-flying cats and lost unicorn societies. As for the rest, I'll get Jarvey, my man of business, to employ someone to look into it," Jamie said. "No point in not checking, eh?"

There was a tap at the door and a maidservant entered with their victuals and departed with a bobbed curtsy. Theresa sat and waved Jamie to a nearby chair. "Thank you."

It was all well and good thinking you were strong enough to cope with everything life threw at you, but these last few weeks had shown her the opposite. Jamie's intervention was more than welcome. "I try not to worry, but no news is almost as bad as a surfeit in this case."

"True, but as I was going to mention earlier and never got round to it, last night I was asked, in a most convoluted and roundabout way by no less than three cronies of my mama and four rakes, if we were actively together. Something will come to a head soon, I'm certain." Jamie divested himself of his greatcoat—why on earth hadn't he handed it over to Roberts?—sat, undid the buttons on his gray jacket and pushed the sides apart.

Theresa wished he hadn't. The dove-gray and silver-striped waistcoat he wore underneath showed off the contours of his chest much too well for her comfort. It was hard to move her gaze upward, not downward to peek at just how snugly his pantaloons fit. She dragged her wayward thoughts away from his body and to his words instead.

"As I said, Prendergast is out of town, but I'd bet my chestnuts that someone will have hotfooted it to Bath to tell him all the on-dits about us. I am in no doubt whatsoever he will return to the capital post haste to discover what is true and what is fabrication. We will be ready for him when he arrives back. Then we'll see what happens next."

"What did you tell people?" Theresa asked with interest. She'd wondered how he was going to explain things, but previously Jamie hadn't gone into great detail, merely said he'd sort it.

"That my life is my own, and if I choose to share any of it they will discover what in due course. Then I copied the way Martin stares down his nose and gave an aristocratic inquiring glance, to show I was not best amused at their impertinence. It worked. A few mumbled apologies and excuses, and several red-faced busybodies were dispatched."

Theresa laughed. "You've done better than me. I've had a quiet couple of days catching up with my household affairs and not been out and about." She didn't mention the instructions to her solicitor, which had earned her a nice sum by selling and buying shares.

"I added to a couple of people I thought could be entrusted, if that is the correct word, to spread the information without too much embellishment, that we are very much involved and money isn't," Jamie said. "I thought it best to be crass and say that outright, rather than invite vulgar speculation." He slid a large piece of cake into his mouth and began to chew.

"Then if I am asked do I say the same?"

He nodded, as his mouth was full of lardy cake. "Please," he added once he'd swallowed. "I also mentioned we were very enamoured with each other and looking forward to our—a word I emphasized—future together. As I told these people in—allegedly—confidence, they will be careful what they spread."

"Did anyone faint?"

"No, but a couple of the grand dames swayed." He rolled his eyes and Theresa laughed.

"I bet."

"Lady Ferris came up to me at one point and said she hoped I'd take you to one of her at-homes. Evidently she's never had a chance to thank you." He raised one eyebrow in query and she waggled her finger at him.

"I do not kiss and tell or even not kiss and tell," she said. "Well, except for bloody Percy."

"Oh, him," Jamie said with indifference to Percy's fate "He deserves it. Now, about Lady Ferris. That is different. Oh yes."

Theresa groaned. "What about her?" she asked wary of

his teasing.

"Whatever you say, she intimated she really wanted to meet you in the flesh, so to speak. I was instructed to tell you she will not take no for an answer."

"Good lord, what did you reply?" Theresa asked, alarmed. Several years earlier, St. John Ferris had been the perfect pupil, and evidently his wife was grateful. Even so, how on earth did you act when confronted with the wife of one of your ex-pupils? Surely it could prove to be somewhat embarrassing? So many pitfalls and subjects to be avoided.

Jamie smiled. "Why, that we'd be delighted, of course. She added that she owed you so much she'd be happy to repay the favor in whatever way she could."

"Jamie, you do know that whatever people like Leonora Ferris say or do I will always be persona non grata in the ton, don't you?" Theresa said. "If you intend to spend time with me, your usual haunts will be off limits. Although, as this is a hum, once it is over you can move on and it will be forgiven if not forgotten, as one of the excesses of youth. The question is, can you cope until then? It strikes me you have a lot to lose."

"You think so? You don't know how perfect that sounds. I won't miss the idiocy of the ton or its members," Jamie replied with a quirk to his lips. "Not to have to listen to the wittering, the pettiness and the boasting is almost enough to make me ask you to marry me all over again." He grinned. "But as I know fine well you will say no, I am going to bide my time and catch you off guard at the perfect moment."

Theresa put down the half-drunk cup of tea she was holding. "Thank goodness it's only almost." She ignored the rest of his statement. Even with her noble descendants it would not do. "Had we wanted to, it would never be permissible and you know it. Now drink your ale, eat that last slice of lardy cake and tell me what is next—or may I offer an idea?" Anything to change his train of thought.

Chapter Six

Jamie picked up his mug, took a deep draught of the contents and regarded her over the rim. "Well, we need to go to Maria for you to try on the gowns you ordered the other day, before we do anything else, but that apart? Offer away."

Damn, now I need something to suggest. All her previous thoughts on what might be acceptable had gone out of her mind. The words 'take me to bed and show me what I'm missing' hovered on her lips and she shivered. They could not be uttered. For he would, she was certain of that. Theresa was equally as sure that, if he did, she would rue the day forever. To know him and lose him would not be bearable.

She might not know him in the biblical sense, but she understood herself. In all her thirty-odd years no one had ever affected her in the way Jamie did. He was like a disease inside her, an illness that only one thing could cure. As she couldn't apply the remedy, she was stuck with it.

He put the mug down and ran his fingers over the top of the last piece of cake. "Should I?" His eyes twinkled. "After all, I need to make sure I don't become portly and suffer from gout and irascibility, but I do need to keep my strength up. Just in case."

"Somehow I don't think there's much chance of gout or bad temper." Jamie wasn't rake thin, but as far as Theresa could ascertain there wasn't an ounce of fat on him. Nor had she seen any signs of excess drinking. She picked the plate up and handed it to him. "Here, just eat and listen to my proposition, if you will." She waited until he took the plate from her and began to eat. Then she leaned toward him, eager to discover if the suggestion she was about to put to him would be acceptable and he would agree to it. "Do you know what I would like more than anything?"

He shook his head. With a mouthful of cake it would be difficult to do anything else without spraying her with crumbs.

"To get out of the city for an hour or two. To walk in fresh air and forget about all the troubles and woes that seem to be besetting us. Not to worry about people and places, what is correct and what impossible. To sing and shout if I want to. Paddle in a stream, pick daisies and wear them as a crown." She shrugged, embarrassed at her impassioned statement. "Although I rather think most of that is not possible at this time of the year."

"Perhaps not all, but the walk and the fresh air can be arranged." Jamie brushed her cheeks. She looked up at him in query and managed—just—not to turn her head so his fingers were over her mouth and she could kiss them.

"Crumbs," he said as his let his hands drift to the nape of her neck and linger for a second before he sat back. "I best brush them off or they will make you itch."

The sense of loss was so silly, if she'd been alone, Theresa decided, she would have screamed her frustration. Instead she focused on what he had just said.

"I haven't eaten anything," Theresa told him, bewildered both by his statement and her state of mind. This giddiness had to stop. Sadly it was easier to say than achieve. "Not since breakfast, and I know that I was crumbless then, so to speak."

"No?" He raised one eyebrow and assumed an oh so innocent expression. "Then I'll hold my hand up and say actually I just wanted an excuse to touch you." His smile was tinged with something she couldn't decipher. Perhaps, Theresa thought, it was just as well. This deception was taking on a life of its own, and she hated not knowing what direction her life was heading.

"Richmond perhaps?" Jamie asked.

He can read my mind? She went hot and cold at that thought before common sense reasserted itself. This was not a scene in one of the romances she read for relaxation. For a moment she had no idea what he meant then it dawned on her. Their outing. "That sounds perfect," Theresa said honest as ever. "I can hardly wait." It was true. Until she had made her plea, she'd had no idea how much she missed the countryside. Perhaps it was time to visit her cottage on the Devon coast. At least there she'd be well away from bloody Percy. Thank goodness the only people who knew about it were Humphrey's family and Maria. Should she mention it to Jamie? There seemed to be no reason why she should, but hadn't they decided to be honest and open?

"I'll pick you up at eleven." Jamie spoke and the opportunity passed. "We'll have lunch out."

Theresa nodded as Jamie stood and redid up his waistcoat.
"Until then."

"Until then." She watched as he kissed her hand, then took a deep breath, hesitated and shook his head.

"No. Ah...lord." He ran his hands through his hair and rearranged his Brutus cut into an unruly mess. Theresa itched to smooth it down again. Instead she curled her fingers into her palm.

"Sort your hair out," she advised him in a voice that wasn't as steady as she would have liked. "Or the gossip will escalate faster than the Montgolfier balloon rose." Even though it might show someone—for instance, Theresa—had run their hands through it, it would also look somewhat suspiciously like a frost. A noted gentleman such as Jamie would never be seen less than perfectly turned out, unless sparring in Jackson's, and even then he would restore himself before he ventured forth.

Jamie blinked. "Eh?"

She pointed to the bronze fluted-edged mirror that hung over the mantle. "Hair."

"Ah." Jamie stared at his reflection. "A mess indeed." He

ran his fingers through it once more, this time to return his locks into a reasonable facsimile of his intended look. "My thanks, and it is no good, I have to do this, and bugger the consequences."

He moved nearer and put his arms around her. Theresa stiffened and Jamie groaned into her neck. "Please, love, just once."

It was his anguished tone that melted her resolve and she relaxed. *Why not?* She ached for his touch. Once more wouldn't hurt, surely? Even though she doubted her sanity, her lips softened.

"Just this once," she agreed. Why not let her dreams become reality? She turned her head to his.

This time his lips lingered on hers long enough for her nipples to tighten and her pulse accelerate as her whole body quivered with the need for more.

To hell with decorum. It's just this once. Theresa returned his kiss, deepened it, felt his body tighten against hers and his tongue slip between her lips. She welcomed the intrusion gladly, allowing herself to draw him hard into her body. That he was aroused was in no doubt. His cock pressed against her, urging her to go further and let herself enjoy every second. His scent surrounded her, and his harsh breath showed he was as affected by their closeness as she was. By the time Jamie gentled the embrace and drew back she was as involved as he.

"I won't apologize and say I didn't mean it," Jamie said in a rapid undertone. "I hadn't meant to kiss you so thoroughly, that is true." He half laughed and retucked his shirt into his trousers. *How on earth did that happen?* "It was supposed to be a tiny salute, no more. However, that idea soon left my head, and from then on my instincts took over and I meant every second of it. And now I best go before I follow my other inclinations and take you here and now and thus break every promise I made. Until tomorrow."

He bowed, spun round then turned back with sudden abruptness. "I meant to ask if you will wear these. They were my mama's and she gave them to me." He held up a long and impressively matched string of pearls, finer by far than the ones she already owned and fastened together with a series of diamond and sapphire clasps.

"Your mama's." Theresa stroked the fine pearls to find them warm to her skin. The diamonds and sapphires sparkled and shone as the light caught them. "Why lend them to me?" She used the word lend on purpose and his eyes glittered as he acknowledged it.

"Mama made the mistake of making me promise I would give them to the one who means the most to me. She assumed it would be Marion, but as I promised faithfully to adhere to her wish, I will do just that. You are that person, so not only would it make me happy, it would show her we are serious."

Theresa considered him. Her heart thumped as she thought over the ways she could take his words. "As a loan," she said. "I mean it. And I will relinquish them at any time. Just say the word."

Jamie studied her until she shifted uneasily from one foot to the other. Then he nodded and carefully put them over her head, wrapped them around her neck once and fastened the row of evenly spaced clasps. "Strange to say, she never wore them, saying she was more suited to rubies, but nevertheless we all knew the importance of the necklace. It was, I have been given to believe, bestowed on my mama by an old admirer who sadly disappeared before he could make an offer, and has, in her words, great meaning and is considered an heirloom. She might have very odd ideas at times, but she is very strong on what should be revered. He took her by the shoulders and turned her so she could see her reflection in the mirror. "Now how's that?"

Theresa blinked as the iridescent pearls and exquisite gems glittered and glistened as Jamie swung the string gently to and fro. Wrapped twice around her neck, the string fastened in two places. One so a strand was tight— but not too tight—around her neck, the other so the rest of the lustrous drops hung down past her waist to end, tantalizing and teasing, just over her mound. "Stunning," she said. There was no reason not to be honest "But how do I undo it?"

He smiled, wickedness and all-out devilry in his expression. "You don't. I have the key. It is on for however long it takes." He kissed her cheek, tucked the end of the pearls with one overlarge sapphire at the end of the necklace between her breasts, shook her gown so the stones slipped downward then walked out briskly.

But not before Theresa saw exactly how aroused he was. The large stone caressed her nub and she bit back a grin. The tease, he'd known it would end up there.

I wonder how much give there is in the material of a pair of pantaloons? For his sake, she hoped it was generous.

Theresa waited until she heard the front door close then slowly made her way upstairs to peruse the clothes in her wardrobe. It seemed her life was about to head in the direction of Richmond.

* * * *

Jamie had dispensed with his greatcoat, choosing to stow it instead of wearing it, and was attired in a formfitting jacket of navy superfine and, as ever, shining and polished-to-the-highest-degree hessians. His pantaloons were a mastery of knit and his cravat tied in the simple but perfect way only someone confident could achieve. That it took him a quarter of the time it would take most people to achieve that look was a credit to him not his valet, who frequently complained he was underused.

Was it a sign of good things to come that the weather gods seemed to have had heard Theresa's plea for fresh air and sunshine? After a night of relentless rain that freshened the air and the streets, Jamie drove his curricle into Berkeley Square the following morning, in a mood of happy anticipation. A drive around the park then luncheon was just the ticket.

He halted the horses just as a bird flew up from the bushes opposite Theresa's house with an indignant squawk. Jamie glanced idly in that direction and stiffened.

"Here, walk them." He threw the reins at Jed, his tiger, slung his hat and gloves in the general direction of the seat and jumped down in such a bouncing way it set the horses moving and the vehicle swaying before he stalked across the road toward the garden. A flash of red in the bushes made him run, just as a body burst through a gap in the hedge, vaulted the railings and darted down the square away from him.

"Hey, you! I want to talk to you," Jamie shouted as he began to give chase.

If anything the youth ran even faster and turned the corner into Bruton Street. Even though Jamie knew he was fit, by the time he reached the place he'd last seen the fleeing figure, the street was empty of anyone with a red muffler on, and he himself was out of breath. He put his hands on his knees and heaved as he did his best to get air back into his lungs. The reverberation of pounding feet behind him made him swing around and rest one hand on the wall of a nearby house to steady himself, and fumble for the knife concealed up his sleeve with the other. He'd thought it overkill when he'd placed it there, now he wasn't so sure.

Two of Theresa's servants reached him and scanned the area suspiciously.

"Who was it?" the first asked.

"Where is the bastard?" the second demanded aggressively. "I bet it's that skulking bugger young Bill the bootboy says he saw."

"Along with the unicorn?" Jamie asked drily as he remembered the names of the men who now observed him with sympathy as his words were forced out of him. He coughed and swore. They, of course, weren't even breathing heavily.

Frost and Dobson. One an ex-pugilist and one who

appeared as if he could also account well for himself.

"Ah well, we pick and choose what to believe, but this we did think had the ring of truth," Frost said in his slow and ponderous way. "Because young Bleddows, him that's Lord Marton's doorman, reckoned he saw someone yesterday as well. He was asking us last night in the Boar if we'ud noticed anything."

"So we kept us eyes open," Dobson added. "And when Mr. Roberts heard the commotion, he sent us to see what's what."

Jamie straightened up, replaced his knife in its concealed holder and tugged his jacket and waistcoat into place. He pretended not to notice the expression of satisfaction the other two men exchanged. "Did either of you catch a proper glance at him?" he asked.

Both men shook their heads. "We only got to follow after he was well away," Dobson offered apologetically. He hit one huge fist into the palm of the other hand and spat in the gutter. "Young Bill says he looks well like a right mumper."

"A tramp?" Jamie said in surprise. "Really?"

Dobson shrugged. "So he says. Strange really. Round here, I thought it'd be more likely a body from the stews, but who knows. He got the lurker bang on, so he could have it."

Jamie nodded as by common, unspoken accord they turned and stalked back up the square. As they reached Theresa's house Jed stopped walking the horses for a moment and squinted at Jamie before he let his breath out in a long *whoosh*. "You didn't get him, my lord?"

Jamie shook his head. "He was too fast for me."

"Ah, he had too much of a head start on you," Jed said loyal to the end. "You'd 've got him otherwise, no problem, my lord."

Jamie smiled at the way everyone was quick to assure him that the man's escape wasn't down to him. "I'm unfit," he said. "Too much town living and not enough exercise. An occasional sparring session in Jackson's salon is not enough.

A salutary lesson, I'm afraid. Ah well, can't be helped now. Though perhaps the bootboy could be put on guard?"

Frost and Dobson exchanged wary glances. "Ah." Jamie understood why. "I will of course ask your mistress. If she can't spare him I'll send one of my men, don't worry."

"Ah, that be better, my lord," Frost said in a relieved voice. "We've all worked out how to keep an eye on Miss Theresa, you see. She still doesn't take this as serious as we thinks she should."

Even in the short time he'd known Theresa, that didn't ring true. It was more likely she was doing her best to reassure her staff that everything was under control. He chose not to upset their ideas.

"She's lucky to have you," he said as they mounted the steps to where a worried-looking Roberts stood next to the open door. He smiled reassuringly at Roberts. "We missed him, but the lads here think it's the same man that Bill says he saw." An expression of horror crossed Roberts' face. Jamie made haste to allay his fears. "We're taking care of all that can be done, don't worry." He glanced swiftly at all three men, noted their anxious expressions and decided to take them into his confidence. "I've arranged for one of my men to keep an eye on the man who keeps an eye on you," he said before anyone could object. "Unfortunately, he had to do something else first." He chose not to say that Hewson had been checking out Protheroe and pretending to avail himself of the solicitor's services. "Hewson is capable and I doubt you'll know he's around." He grinned. "Unless you need him, then send a two-note whistle like this," he whistled softly, "and it will bring him to your side. He'll be around during the day. Merchison, another of my staff, will take over at night." The sense of relief was palpable, and their demeanours reflected that.

"Same whistle, my lord?" Roberts asked.

"Or, oi, help," Jamie said with humor in his tone. "They are well primed."

A maid poked her head out. "Mr. Roberts? Miss Theresa's

on her way."

All four men straightened. Jamie checked his appearance as best he could. Roberts took his position by the side of the door. Frost and Dobson disappeared down the area steps and the noise of a door closing drifted up to Jamie as Roberts cleared his throat and bowed, very ostentatiously. "My lord, Miss Theresa is about to join you."

Saved by the maid.

* * * *

Strangely, after such an enjoyable day, Theresa hadn't slept well. The drive, their lunch and the chat they had afterward had been so pleasant she could almost have forgotten it was all a sham. It wasn't until Jamie had departed and Roberts had informed her all was well she'd remembered none of it was real. She'd gone to bed in contemplative mood. Her cottage in Devon was looking more and more like her home once this was over.

As she didn't like the shutters closed, in the early hours, the moon had managed to find the thinnest of cracks between the curtains and light the room enough for her to wake. Then of course she'd tossed and turned until, as the clock in the hall chimed three a.m. she had given up, slipped her robe on and made her way to the kitchen.

Luckily her staff were used to her nocturnal wanderings and no one woke from their slumbers. This time it was for warm milk for herself. Often in the past it had been for other drinks and not necessarily for herself. Luckily, she thought, those days were long gone, and she didn't have to worry about men and their foibles.

Unless of course one day Jamie…

No, no and most definitely no, do not go there. That was as likely as she be given a peerage for services to the aristocracy. She stared out of the window into the still garden as she sipped her milk. An animal sneaked across the lawn and disappeared as silently as it had arrived. The old house creaked as all old houses did, and she sighed. Why was she so unsettled?

Bloody Percy. Up until he'd decided to rewrite the rules, her life had gone as she'd planned, right down to how and when she'd retired.

Now she was on edge and had no idea which way her future would go. Theresa drained her cup, washed it and returned it to its allotted place. She'd choose a book and take it upstairs to read with the aid of a lamp. Then perhaps she'd be tired enough to rest.

Theresa took one last perusal from the window and froze.

Someone was skulking around near the wall to the mews. She backed away slowly, determined not to make any sudden movements that might alert the intruder to her presence, and peered around her carefully. The meat cleaver? That might be a bit too much. Likewise the bread knife. The flour crock could work, but what a waste of flour. If only she had her pistol handy. It, however, was upstairs in her bedside drawer. Relieved, she remembered with glee that her muff pistol was tucked inside her swansdown muff on the seat of the overlarge chair situated in the hall. She'd forgotten to remove it after she'd visited Maria earlier that day. Theresa watched the figure approach stealthily across the shadowed lawn as she continued to move backward, her hand behind her to find the door latch.

She found something soft instead and bit back a scream.

"Miss Theresa," Mrs. Penicuik, the aptly named cook, hissed in a loud undertone. "What on earth are you doing?"

"Look outside without moving," Theresa whispered back. "What can you see?"

Theresa watched as Mrs. Penicuik tensed, screwed up her eyes, relaxed and stared toward the glass. Then she stiffened. "On the lawn?"

"Yes, outside coming closer. Keep your eyes on whoever it is whilst I go and get my small pistol. It might not kill but it will blow a hole in his — if it is a he — bollocks."

"Mighty me." Mrs. Penicuik put one hand on her throat

and gripped Theresa's arm so tightly Theresa was certain she'd have a four-fingered bruise there. "You can't shoot him, miss. That's young Archie Frost, that is. It's his turn on guard duty. I dare say he's about to be relieved by Teddy Dobson."

Theresa turned around. Had she heard aright? "Say that again, Mrs. Penicuik. Slowly."

"Well, you didn't think we'd not protect you, now, did you, miss?" the cook said, defensive and brusque. "You're special you are, and no uppity aristocrat is going to do you any harm whilst we're all here to make sure no one harms a hair on your head." She let go of Theresa, who forced herself not to rub her maltreated arm. "I've got a pistol in the pantry and one in the pot cupboard. Roberts has one hidden in the hallway, and we set up a rota, sort of, and his lo…"

"Go on," Theresa said mildly. "His lordship agreed?"

Mrs. Penicuik nodded. "He worries for you, miss. As well he should. Sometimes a man comes in handy. Not often, mind, but on occasion. His lordship, he said he was a lot happier now we were on our guard and his men were in the square."

His men? In the square? What else has been going on without my knowledge? The words stuck in her throat. She couldn't put the onus to explain on Mrs. Penicuik. The poor woman was only doing what she thought best.

"Excellent, then I'll leave you to it." It was no good, she had to ask. "Er, why are you up, Mrs. Penicuik?"

The woman became embarrassed. "I woke up and had to spend a penny."

Damn. Now she'd said it, so did Theresa.

* * * *

"So I went back to bed and seethed." Theresa prowled around Maria's sitting room. "How dare he?" she asked rhetorically. "Now he's had to go to Elmwood for something about the river flooding and saving a barn, so I cannot ask him what on earth he is thinking. I hate that. My dander is up and he is the cause, I need to let it down by taking my grievances and temper out on him, and I've been foiled."

"Perhaps as well," Maria said. "Or I could lose two friends in one fell swoop. Calm down and think, Tess. They care."

Theresa ignored her friend's well-intentioned advice. She was in no mood to do what was in essence common sense. It had been a long time since she had allowed herself a temper tantrum, and no doubt it would be as long again before she had another one. She might as well milk it to the full. "And of course I can't say anything to my staff, who are all treating me like a piece of precious glass or a flower that will blow away as soon as looked at. Good heavens, I accidentally banged my wardrobe door by mistake before I left to come here and three maids, two footmen and Mrs. Penicuik—plus rolling pin—appeared within thirty seconds. Roberts was half a minute later, because he had, as he explained, puffing, whistled for the earl's man to be aware of what was going on. The earl's man, for goodness' sake. As if we can't take care of ourselves. Oh all right, he might have been correct if, and I stress if, someone had invaded us. But good lord, Ria, he had made sure Frost and Dobson were on guard at the doors to prevent any intruder from escaping, and the gate to the mews is now guarded night and day." She rolled her eyes and wrinkled her nose in disgust. "I tell you, Ria, I'll be scared to use the commode soon in case I drop the lid and someone bursts in on me."

Maria's mouth dropped open and she burst out laughing. "Oh my…"

"Hmm." Trust Maria to see the funny side of it. "You aren't the one cabined, cribbed and confined, damn it." With a thump, Theresa dropped into the armchair she'd left a few moments earlier to pace. "Gah, I need wine."

"Ohh dear me, you poor thing, having people who love you and want to keep you safe." Maria stood and pointed her finger at Theresa. "They are there for you. Be thankful.

Don't push them away." She tucked her finger under the jewel and pearl rope that Theresa had perforce to wear. "Most people would commit murder for something like this."

"Yes, well," Theresa said as her temper abated by the second. She was more than a little ashamed of her outburst. "It is to set the scene, that is all. No murder or even grievous bodily harm committed."

"You had no need to be so upset. Take the care when it is freely given and embrace it."

The expression on her face made Theresa draw breath. Maria looked bereft. Sad, lonely and lost. Theresa stood rapidly and put her arms around Maria, who, she noticed, stood rigid and hardly breathing. Maria's pulse was rapid and shallow and her skin was clammy. "What's up, Ria?"

"Eh?" Maria visibly collected herself. "Oh." She sighed heavily and managed a half smile. Theresa could see the effort it took and her heart ached for her friend. Whatever was wrong hurt Maria deeply. "Once I had someone who thought I was his sun, moon and stars. Who cared for me. I miss…it." She shook her head, wriggled out of Theresa's embrace and poured red wine into two heavy goblets. "Don't carp over concern, especially in the manner it is given to you. Such loyalty is above most all things." She passed one glass to Theresa, who grasped it automatically.

"Thank you. Oh, lord, Ria, whatever it is, for your sake I hope it is soon sorted. I won't pry, but I'm here if you need me." Theresa understood all too well how lonely it could be when you felt part of your life was missing. "At any time. You come first."

"I know, and I appreciate that." Maria sighed and shook her head. "Sorted? Unlikely, so I have stopped thinking about it." She twisted her lips, mocking her statement. "Mostly." Her carefully neutral expression, so at odds with shadow in her eyes, forbade Theresa to pry.

"Therefore," Maria continued. "Be thankful for your supporters. So many people have no one to stand up for them."

Theresa nodded, sick at heart as she watched her friend struggle to put whatever ailed her to one side. "I am, really," she said. "I know I am being crotchety, but believe me, it is a comfort knowing I'm watched over and looked after. However, it was a cupboard door, for heaven's sake. Not even the door into the bathing chamber, or the outdoors. A plain, small cupboard door."

Maria scowled and pointed her finger at Theresa. "And they knew that how? It could have been an intruder through the window or…"

"A mouse via the wainscoting carrying poison?"

"Yes, well." Maria grinned. "The scullery cat with doctored paws to scratch you?"

"Lady Milfried's dog and its bad temper to bite me?" Theresa shuddered in an exaggerated fashion. "God, I swear, its eyes are evil." They both dissolved into giggles. "It fixes them on you and you look for some basil or brass to ward off witches and the devil." The dog had a reputation for biting unwary people's ankles and several ladies had refused to attend anything at the Milfrieds' unless the dog was kennelled.

"That apart," Maria said when each had wiped their eyes and sobered, "think about it calmly for a moment. If Jamie has put everyone on high alert he must think there could be a threat to you. He is thorough but not one for excessive worry, or shows of emotion where none is needed. Or so I would say." She paused. "Tess, you do know we've only ever been platonic friends, don't you?" she asked. "I promise you that. He is like the brother I never had."

As she rarely shortened Theresa's name, and had done it more than once in a short time, Theresa knew how earnest her friend was. "Of course I do," she said and was both reassured and relived when the anxious expression on Maria's face softened. "Stop worrying. Yes, I overreacted, I know. I promise no more. Now, how about showing me that new Brussels lace and the silks you have and decide on how best to make me something very" — she paused and lowered her eyelids slowly — "exotic, erotic and designed to drive a certain earl mad."

Maria's eyes widened and a slow grin spread over her face. "Drive him mad?"

Theresa nodded. "Just to show him what he's missing, for now."

"Oh my," Maria said as she pulled a parcel out of the cupboard and let the contents spill over the table. "Cruel. I love it. He is somewhat sure of his charm." A long bolt of silk in shades from midnight to midday blue shimmered as if they were sapphires tossed in a sun-swept sea rippled as it settled. "I have the most perfect creamy lace to complement it."

"Beautiful." Theresa fingered the silk and smiled at the thought of what Maria could create with it. "It makes my mouth water."

"Thank you. I must admit I thought of you the moment I saw it. So how enticing must this garment be?" Maria lifted the silk to let it drift through her fingers and back on to the table like a glorious waterfall of material.

"Very," Theresa said. "Oh yes, incredibly so. I've had enough of cutting my nose off to spite my face. I want him as much as I think he wants me. But…well, sufficient to say we have a bet I will need to lose, a bargain which means I have to concede quite a lot before we can move on. Therefore if I have to suffer and allow him to subjugate my independence, he can suffer and deprive his cock for as long as it takes."

"It sounds so very complicated, but I'll admit, you take devious to new heights," Maria said in obvious admiration. "Oh I like it." She picked up a red length of a material Theresa had never seen before. "Your new dress will be in this, with no back, long sleeves and enough allure to drive a man mad. Ask no more for I will not say. Except it will be my gift to you and Jamie. We will work on deviousness instead. I love it."

"Good," Theresa said with a chuckle. She understood Maria enough not to mention that amazing, unusual material. "So do I. Let's plot."

Maria nodded. "How long is he thought to be away?"

"At Elmwood?" Theresa asked. Maria nodded. "He went the day before yesterday and said he would be four or five days," Theresa continued. "I assume we have until the day after tomorrow at the earliest. Perhaps not long enough for you and truly, I'll understand if it isn't. I know you have many other calls on your time that must take priority."

"Rubbish," Maria said. "Plenty of time to make a negligee and robe to go over it. It will be our number one priority." She picked up a sketchpad and pencil and began to draw.

"But what about your real customers?" Theresa protested as she stood and looked over Maria's shoulder. It seemed wrong that her friend should miss out on money to accommodate Theresa. "They must come... Oh, that is beautiful." She gasped, blinked then snorted as Maria waved the sketchbook at her. "Ria, those feathers are positively indecent. I love it, but surely you will need time to create this? I'm certain you can't put all your other orders to one side, just for me. They are the ones who pay properly. Until you let me do the same you should put me to the bottom of the queue." She grimaced at Maria's 'I beg your pardon, why?' expression. "You know what I mean. Those to whom you charge a realistic price are those you need to attend to first. The proper customer. That way you ensure you are paid enough that you and your staff do not starve."

"Ha." Maria added a few strokes to her sketch and held it at arm's length to study it. "One tie here, I think." She outlined a bow on one shoulder. "There. Perfect. We will start tomorrow. As for proper or not? You may at times have been considered improper, my dear, but never in regard as my customer." She put her pencil down and held the lace across Theresa's bosom. "This color suits you. You were the one whom, when I asked for a chance to show you my amateur sketches of my designs, never hesitated and gave me an order on the strength of them."

"Well, of course. They were outstanding." Theresa remember their excitement as Maria had put the finishing touches to that very first gown, and how well it had been received by those who'd seen it. "You have dressed me superbly ever since. Which could have worked against you, I know that and am grateful. Dressing a courtesan." She rolled her eyes. "Outrageous." The last word was spoken in the perfect tones of one of the starchiest of matrons.

"You must be joking," Maria said. "I, however, am serious. It was all the ladies needed. If they chose to believe it was my clothes, not your..."

"Assets?" Theresa supplied. "Bosom?" She patted said part of her body and wriggled her bottom. "Rear, ankles... and any other parts we will not mention at present."

"Assets, intelligence, call it what you will. You are more than your body. But if they wanted to believe it was a gown that worked wonders, who was I to disabuse them?"

"Put like that, I see what you mean."

Maria pulled Theresa to stand in the middle of the room. "Strip and let me begin to cut and pin. I'm off to get my shears."

"It's as well we are friends," Theresa said as she began to unlace her sandals. "Anyone else hearing you say that might get the wrong idea."

Maria grinned. "Perhaps we should be relieved I am a dab hand with my shears then." She made a snipping motion with her fingers before she left the room at a brisk pace. Used to her whirlwind impression, Theresa had a sip of wine, put her goblet down, kicked off her sandals and started to unbutton her gown.

Chapter Seven

Typically, it was later than she had meant it to be before she left Maria's. Chatting, trying on *toiles* and drinking wine did that. Plus that amazing red dress. Four sketched-out designs later, she refused her friend's offer of transport. After all, a hackney could be picked up by standing on Maria's doorstep and waving. Theresa hadn't arrived in her own carriage. She and Maria had been to Hatchards and the park before making their way to Bruton Street for a late afternoon meal and she *had* intended to have an early night and mull over her situation. Now it was more likely going to be the opposite. Mindful of Jamie's warning to be vigilant, she waited with Paxman, Maria's doorman, until the hackney drew up and Paxman handed her inside. Deep down, she was somewhat ashamed of putting the jarvey to so much trouble for such a short distance, which during daylight she would have walked, but she accepted it was probably the correct thing to do.

Theresa sat back with a sigh of relief as the carriage drew away. She was twitchy, imagined unseen eyes everywhere and sported an almost constant, nasty prickle on the back of her neck. Something unheard of until recently, and it wasn't an experience she relished.

A man stood on the corner of the street and Theresa clutched her muff pistol just to reassure herself it was still there. When she saw it was a policeman she relaxed and laughed. She didn't let go of the gun though.

A few minutes later, the carriage turned into Berkeley Square, and she leaned forward to tap on the roof as they approached her house. Strangely, it seemed Roberts hadn't heard the hackney, because the door stayed firmly closed. Theresa wriggled her shoulders, suddenly uneasy. However, it was a matter of seconds to pay the man, gather up her reticule, straighten her pelisse and begin to walk toward the flight of wide stone steps.

What on earth could happen a few yards from home? But why was the door still closed?

A clatter made her turn and look down the cobbles. Several yards along the square, a carriage began to move in the opposite direction. Amused at the relieved jolt in her pulse as the vehicle went farther away from her, she turned back to the front door. Why was the house so devoid of activity? Theresa experienced a moment of disquiet and moved rapidly to the first step.

Nothing alerted her to someone close by until hands grabbed her from behind. Startled, she scrabbled to pull her gun out of her muff. It was too late. *Idiot.* She berated herself as the strong smell of something noxious made her eyes sting. Her muff was torn from her hands and thrown away, and Theresa heard the clatter as the pistol slipped out and skidded over the cobbles. *Now if only the damn thing would go off.* Typically, it didn't, and someone began to drag her toward the carriage.

She screamed and bit the hand that tried to cover her mouth. Where was anybody? A peeler, a lamp lighter, even a burglar might be of some help.

"Booger." Someone swore in the rough accent of the stews. "Oy, the bleeding bitch bit me." A large hand struck her across the cheek and lights flashed in front of her eyes and caused them to water. That sudden pain inflamed Theresa even more. She might be overwhelmed but she would not go down without a fight. With a surge of energy, she jerked her head up and back, kicked out wildly and evidently caught someone in the bollocks.

"Whore. Enough now, or it'll be the worse for you." The meat plate of a hand lifted off her mouth enough for her to draw breath. "Give over."

"You snot, you are a blister, a scab." Why oh why hadn't she taken her pistol from her muff and secreted it in her pocket? One of the men — she had decided there were two — began to pull her ever closer to the black carriage while the other one hugged himself where she had caught him.

"You ruffians, get your bloody thieving hand off arghh —" The one whom she hoped would no longer be able to perform or sire children took hold of her feet, thereby stopping her frantic kicks.

"Oi, you, what the devil?" someone else shouted as she heard footsteps getting louder. Both men stopped and turned in the direction of the newcomer who sprinted down the side of the square toward them. "What's going on?"

The inattention of her captors gave Theresa the opportunity she needed. As her feet were dropped unceremoniously to the ground she elbowed one man, kicked the other — sadly behind the knee and not in the groin — and struggled free. She ran toward the newcomer, who she saw had drawn his sword from its covering stick as he ran.

Theresa flung herself at him, taking care to stay clear of his sword arm. "Please play along, sir, please," she said in a low voice. "My lord, I know you said wait for you," she said continued as loud as she could in an apologetic tone. "But I thought I'd come to join you instead."

"Indeed." Her rescuer put her firmly behind him and turned to the two men, who seemed mesmerized by his presence. "Why are you attacking my lady? I should run you both through."

The two men stopped dead in their tracks and looked at each other.

"Well? Cat got your tongues?" her rescuer demanded in a much more forceful manner than she thought the question warranted. "Tell me why I *shouldn't* run you both through. And before you think two on one, think again. I can do it easily." He held his saber out so the steel glittered in the moonlight. Even though they *were* two to one, Theresa reckoned his greatcoat made him appear incredibly dangerous and his sword doubly so. A good illusion to create, whether it be true or not. "Sharp, isn't it?" he said, as if it was something he hadn't noticed before. "Goes through skin like it was paper." He held the sword high and pointed it in the ruffians' direction. "Whom shall I test it on?"

"Eh, no need for that." The taller of the two men spoke in a thick London accent. "Mistekken identity, like. She's not who we's thought." The man began to edge away. "We were just passin' like and well…" He trailed off and gaped warily at the stranger. "We wus wrong."

"You think so?" the gentleman asked. His tone was not pleasant and Theresa was glad she wasn't the person on the receiving end of it. "What else do you have to say for yourself before the watch arrives?"

The taller man gazed toward the other, who shrugged and spoke. "Don't need no watch. The besom — "

He coughed as the gentleman took a step toward him, menace in his movement, and his sword waved gently from one to the other.

"Beggin' your pardon, sir. 'Scuse me, the lady, she were all alone and we thought we could prang some of those sparklers."

The gentleman turned to glance at her neck briefly and his eyes widened. "Indeed. Fine, are they not? However, not yours." The second man spat on the ground and immediately the gentleman refocused on the pair. "Now you know she is protected so you can go before I hand you over. But remember this, I have an excellent memory for faces and if she or I set our eyes on one of your ugly phizogs again, you'll wish we hadn't." He lifted his sword high and touched the top of the chin of the nearer one. The man went white and swayed toward that lethal tip.

Idiot. Although Theresa wondered what would happen if he swayed a little too far. No court in the land would find her rescuer guilty of anything except chivalry.

The gentleman shook his head pityingly and adjusted his hold. "You seem not to value any life, including your own. In case you didn't know, this is a saber. It's sharp, and believe me, I have no hesitation in using it." He pointed it to the ground. "Now cut and run and get out of my sight, before I change my mind and give you at least a little scar to remind you of what could be worse."

With one wary glance they ran down the road to where a coach—presumably, she decided, the one she'd seen earlier—had returned and parked, and clambered ungainly into it. As it moved away at a pace that made it rock violently over the uneven cobbles, an arm shot out of the window to make a rude gesture.

"Charming company you keep, my dear." The gentleman held on to her arm as if she were about to make a run for it, and waited until the coach rounded the corner into Bruton Street and out of sight before he turned to her. "I thought the coach yours. It seems I was mistaken."

She shook her head. "I had just stepped out of a hackney and started to mount the steps to my house when they accosted me. I'd seen the coach but thought it was moving away. It did move away, but I swear the one they vanished in was the same vehicle."

"Hmm. Perhaps." He stared at her. "So why did they want you?"

She bit her lip and knew fine she would come across as wary, as heat flooded her. "I have no *idea*. I live a quiet life with my companion." *Lord, I hope he doesn't ask who that is.* Making up stories on the spur of the moment wasn't as easy as she'd hoped. "I'd, ah, been to the theater with friends."

"If you say so."

She bit her lips but kept her mouth shut. Some information was not hers to impart. Thus it was easier to say nothing rather than be embroiled in half-truths she would need to remember.

"Do you feel ready to share your name?" the gentleman asked. "I'm sure you will in a moment. Therefore, let me escort you. Even though those ruffians seem to have left, who knows if they are lurking somewhere nearby to see if we give lie to our account of things. Which house?"

Theresa glanced up at him and saw his face clearly for the first time. She groaned under her breath. Of all the people it could have been. "The one with the blue door, your grace."

"You know me?" he asked. "You have the advantage over me."

"I recognize your features," Theresa said slowly to Martin, the Duke of Anster. "Your brother is very like you. My name is Theresa Kyle." She stared at him with intent and wondered if the name meant something to him.

"Nice to make your acquaintance, Miss Kyle. You say you know my sibling?" Martin asked. Now I am curious. Which one?"

Obviously it didn't. Was that a good or a bad thing? She shrugged and her shoulders moved under the elegant velvet cloak she wore. Her shadow on the ground changed as her gestures caught the light of the flares in the sconces on either side of her front door. "Er, let's just say one of them, just a little, no more than that. I don't generally move in such exalted circles. There the door is here, I am here and you…"

"Are here," he finished. "And you wish to invite me in." The look he gave her dared her to contradict him. "As I admire your pearls and diamonds. Unique, wouldn't you say?"

The necklace. Had Jamie been economical with the truth over why he had them?

"Invite me in," he said again, with a hint of menace in his voice. "Trust me," he said, as she hesitated. "It is in your best interest to do so."

She looked into his eyes and shook her head. "I shouldn't but… I suppose it may as well be now as later. Your grace, would you like to come in for a nightcap? Of the alcoholic kind."

Martin bowed. "My dear, I thought you'd never ask. There is nothing at this moment in time I'd like more."

That was what she was worried about. Theresa rapped

on the door and glared at Roberts, who opened it. His jaw dropped.

"Miss Kyle? Did you change your mind?"

"Change my mind?" What was the man talking about? Another nasty shiver of apprehension skittered down her spine. She was having far too many of those for comfort lately. "About what, Roberts?"

Roberts went white. "We got a message saying you'd not be back tonight. That's why I'd left the door. There was a ruckus in the mews and stones came over the wall. I went to help check the windows and such."

He stared at Martin and took a step back. "Your grace?" He looked at Theresa with puzzlement. No wonder. His grace was not the sort of person who would have needed to use her services in her previous life. Roberts, who insisted it was his duty to recognize all about the nobility, and be cognizant with their needs and foibles, would know that. "His grace encouraged you to change your mind?" He sounded aghast. Theresa made haste to disabuse him of that idea. The last thing she wanted was stories about her and Martin doing the rounds.

"No, his grace saved me from abduction. I owe him a drink." She watched Roberts go even whiter. "I think you'd better have one yourself. We'll talk about it in the morning. Go to bed."

"But, miss," Roberts protested without a lot of conviction. What's going on?"

"It's all right, Roberts. It's his lordship's brother, not a client."

* * * *

As he reached the outskirts of St. Albans, with its impressive cathedral on the skyline and the dusty road getting busier by the yard, Jamie urged his tired horse on. Now eager to get back and see Theresa — since the previous evening he'd had an irritating niggle that something was wrong—he cursed every slow cart and pedestrian that held him up. Annoying and without foundation, he'd found it in his best interest in the past not to ignore that alarming sensation. Hence his return south a full day earlier than he'd intended. First though, he needed to eat, change horses—his had carried him far and well, but enough was enough—and take half an hour to stretch and roll out some of his aches and pains. Not only had he ridden to Rutland and back in under four days, he'd also mucked in and helped with flood barriers and replacing a weir. Hard physical work that he'd enjoyed, but it had demonstrated to him he wasn't as agile as he had been five years earlier. Replenishment of the body and soul accomplished, then he could begin the last few miles.

Rare roast beef, a pigeon pie and a jug of ale worked wonders for his hunger and his weariness and within the hour he passed the boundary of the city once more, this time going south.

The horse was one his brother kept at the inn especially for the family. The landlord had seemed somewhat surprised to see Jamie, and apologized that the horse was not the one he usually favored, '*Seeing as your brother took that one, m'lord*'. As he had no intention of letting the landlord know he had no idea what he was talking about, Jamie had nodded reassuringly. "No matter, the roan will be fine."

It was, and although not up to carrying his weight for long distances, Jamie was happy enough with its performance as he cantered through the late afternoon sunshine and estimated he should reach his London town house—a legacy from his godfather—well before sunset.

He made it, but only just. An accommodation coach with a broken axle held him up near Watford. He'd decided it behoved him to see if he could offer any help. Therefore he'd spent a good thirty minutes, greatcoat, jacket and cravat off, shirtsleeves rolled up, unloading trunks and boxes and re-stowing them on a farmer's cart, which had been found to take the goods and some of the late occupants of the coach to a nearby inn.

By the time he'd finished he'd found somehow his cravat had been cast into the dust and his greatcoat looked as if had been dragged through a hedge backward. Combined with the manual labor, it was no wonder he was dusty, sweaty and weary when at last, he handed the horse over to Cherry, his stableman, and made his way indoors. He'd hardly managed to open his greatcoat before what seemed like half his staff appeared and began to assail his ears from every direction. His valet bore his outerwear away, took one look at his boots with a long fresh scratch in the leather, groaned like a dying man and pointedly stared at Jamie's cravat, which now just hung around his neck.

"My lord," he said in an agonized voice. "Oh, my lord."

"Here, do what you think fit with it and my apologies." Jamie thrust the mangled strip of cloth into the man's hands and proceeded to ignore him — Edderidge was a dramatic person — and instead tried to decipher the cacophony around him. He understood about one word in ten. He heard, "she", "shook", "extreme", "him", "why"…and that damn itch appeared threefold. He couldn't make head nor tail of it all. Not one person seemed capable of being coherent.

In the end he put his hand in the air. "Enough, all of you. Be *quiet*." He roared the words and waited, tapping his foot, until silence reigned once more. "Thank you." He looked around the packed hall and caught the eye of Thaw, his major-domo.

"Thaw?"

Thaw bowed and elbowed his way to his master's side. "My lord?

"Are you well enough informed to be spokesperson?"

Thaw nodded. "I believe so, my lord. You see — "

Jamie stopped him before he had time to get into the explanation. "Not here. In the study." He spied his valet still hovering on the bottom stair and beckoned him over. The poor man had only been trying to do his job, and he,

Jamie, had been incredibly off-hand.

"My apologies once more for the state of my attire, Edderidge. I became involved with an incident concerning an accommodation coach and played the Good Samaritan." A concerted gasp ran around the hall. "Contrary to what it looks like, I was not set upon, or bucked from my horse, I promise you. I ended up half under the coach in the mud, pulling people and luggage to safety and aiding others to right it. Sadly it wasn't able to continue on its journey, but, thankfully, the passengers and cattle were not badly hurt." He smiled. "Only my clothing. Lud I am weary, now. Could you try to resurrect my coat as well as my cravat, please? Although I think the cravat is past redemption." He waited for Edderidge's nod and turned toward his study. "I myself was a mere passerby."

The general sigh of relief that spread around the hall stopped Jamie mid-stride.

"Why?" he demanded. "What did you think?"

"That perhaps you had been set upon," Thaw said with care. "Now you have told us that is not the case, the household is relieved."

There was obviously more to the palpable tension that almost shimmered around the hall like an entity of its own, but Jamie decided he'd prefer to be sitting down when he learned about it. "As you now know that isn't the case, shall we return to normal as best we can? Dinner in an hour."

The chef, a temperamental Frenchman called Jean-Jacques, gasped and swore under his breath in French.

"Not at all, I was born a full five years into my parents' marriage," Jamie said, urbane as ever, and kept his face straight as the chef went red. A reasonably new addition to the household, Jean-Jacques obviously hadn't believed his peers when they had told him Jamie was fluent in the chef's mother tongue. Or thought that fluency didn't relate to the language of the gutters, which he now knew it did. "Plus," Jamie went on in the same unaggressive, level tone, "according to the portraits in Anster's great hall, the perfect double of my grandfather on my father's side. I do not expect a banquet, Jean-Jacques, just a simple meal to your usual high standards. Plus brandy and a report in my study immediately, conveyed via Thaw from whoever is best informed." He didn't wait to see if his diktat was obeyed. He knew it would be. With a nod to encompass everyone, he went into the welcoming room and didn't give in to the temptation to sag against the door and count to twenty. Instead he took several deep breaths and sank into the large buttoned leather armchair set to one side of the glowing embers. It was obvious the fire needed livening but he hadn't the energy to move.

He was still slumped in the same position a few minutes later when Thaw entered with the brandy bottle.

"I need that," Jamie said, heartfelt, as Thaw busied himself in pouring some of the dark-gold liquid into a rummer and passed it to Jamie. He took the heavy glass by the short stem and sniffed the contents appreciatively. "Thank you, where is yours? I have a feeling you might need one. Help yourself and then take a seat."

Thaw's eyes widened and he blinked before he cleared his throat. "Ah, if you are sure, my lord."

Jamie didn't bother to vocalize a reply but merely nodded and waited until the man sat rather nervously on a Chippendale chair to one side of Jamie's more comfortable armchair. He didn't argue over Thaw's choice of seat. The man would, by his very profession, be extremely careful over how he reacted to invitations or demands from his employer.

"Now tell me what's been going on, why are my staff up to high doh and do I have justification for that something-isn't-quite-right itch?"

"The, ah, what, my lord?"

"Why do I have a feeling of disquiet?" Jamie explained as patiently as he was able. "Of something not being quite as it should be?"

Thaw's Adam's apple bobbed vigorously as he drank

some brandy and cleared his throat. "Well, last night young Toolan was walking down Berkeley Square like you suggested, my lord. Casual like and not exactly on watch but well…"

Jamie nodded, impatient to find out more. The sick tension that gripped him increased threefold. "Yes, I know what you mean. And?"

"And he saw the lady have a problem with a couple of unsavory types. Before he had a chance to reach her some toff got there first and ended up going inside with her." He coughed delicately. "Very pally they seemed, he said, no making her go with him like…"

No coercion? Spiders crawled over his spine as well as churned his stomach. His lady with another man? The sense of betrayal made him feel sick. That was replaced by anger. No one but no one was taking Theresa from him. *She is mine. Mine?* Since when had he thought of her quite in that way?

Since the beginning, he realized.

"Go on," he said. "Was she harmed at all?" If she was, heads would roll, he'd make sure of that.

"Well, Toolan thought mebbe he should follow the men but they got into an unmarked carriage and drove off. Toolan hung around for a bit, but the bloke didn't come out." He looked fearful being the harbinger of bad news, and a tic showed erratically by the side of his eye. The poor man gulped then took a mouthful of brandy. "I'm sorry, my lord, but he didn't know what else to do, so he caught Godfrey on the corner and told him. By the time Godfrey got to the house, no one knew if the man were still inside or not. And as Miss Theresa had given strict instructions not to disturb them unless it was a fire…" He shrugged. "Well us didn't. He were unsure of his role but stayed on watch, like you said."

"Best thing, if someone was struggling with the lady that would have been different, however in this case, he was right to do as I asked."

But it is a pity he didn't.

Who was the man? The sharp stab to his gut brought Jamie up short.

Jealousy? Surely not? "Anything else?"

Thaw shook his head. "No, my lord. We've got our rota set up for tonight and tomorrow. Unless, of course, you ask us to do otherwise, we'll carry on watching."

"Thank you, for now anyway. I'm back in the capital for a while, and I'll call on the lady in the morning." He didn't have the energy to move at that moment. Plus, Jamie knew himself well enough to accept he needed to get his temper in check before he approached Theresa, with or without her unknown companion in attendance.

He'd find out what was going on, one way or another.

* * * *

"Your grace, I'm sorry, I can't tell you any more than I already have." Theresa worried her bottom lip, realized she was doing it and that her unwanted visitor noted it *and* her agitation. By the gleam in his eye he intended to capitalize on it, if she wasn't careful. She forced herself to calm down. "A friend gave it to me." She touched her necklace, and the heat from the pearls gave her some comfort. Why she shouldn't tell Jamie's brother how he had put the necklace on her she had no idea. Was Martin in his confidence? She rather thought not, and it wasn't up to her to change that situation, however uncomfortable it might become for her.

"It is not yours." Martin paced the room, swung round suddenly and pointed at her. As he held a glass of robust red wine in the hand he gesticulated with, Theresa worried that her cream and blue Aubusson was about to become cream, blue and red.

"Careful," she warned him. "France's finest wine has no need to become acquainted with its finest floor coverings." The carpet had been a present to herself when she finally felt she was proficient in managing and growing her money, and it represented independence.

He straightened his glass in a hurry. "Sorry," he said apologetically. "My mind was elsewhere, and I was distracted."

She nodded. "However, to the best of my knowledge the necklace is not yours either. So we are at an impasse."

Martin seemed bewildered. "What? I hope not." His glass tilted once more and he put it on a side table. "Look, all I'm asking is how you got hold of that necklace? It's unique and I know to whom it belongs. It is not yours, that I do know."

"And as I said not two minutes ago, it is not yours either," Theresa said with a snap. "That *I* do know."

"If she's pawned or sold it I need to know why," Martin said, almost to himself. "Surely she would not?"

So he hadn't been told it had passed to Jamie. *Oh dear.*

"It was neither pawned, sold nor stolen." Theresa chose her words with care. "It was given to me by someone who is..." She hesitated. If ever there was a time to tread cautiously, but also forward their deception, this was it. "Someone very dear to me," she finished.

"My mother?" He sounded aghast, then swore. "Damn, now you know whose necklace it is."

"Was," she said, nowhere near as calm as she sounded. "No longer. And before you ask or attack me with words or more, I can say nothing else except that I believe it was passed to whoever gave it to me freely and without coercion."

"You make no sense," he said in a menacing voice. "I suggest you try."

"My apologies," Theresa replied. She was amazed her nerves did not show in her voice. "It is the best I can do." She hoped her earlier words, when Roberts had recognized him and she'd confirmed his identity, hadn't registered with him and made him wonder if she had been given the pearls from Jamie. There was no real reason why he should, but then stranger things had happened. She didn't want to inadvertently be the cause of bad blood.

He growled deep in his throat. Instead of scaring her it made her smirk.

"Who?"

She shook her head. "I cannot tell you."

Martin glared. His behavior was akin to that of a ten-year-old denied an extra pudding. She rolled her eyes.

Throwing things and stamping his feet next?

"For god's sake, woman, it is no laughing matter. Here I am worried sick my mama is in some sort of trouble and has had to part with a family heirloom, and all you can do is smirk? Smirk for goodness' sake. I'm *worried sick,* woman, and you are treating it as a laughing matter."

Now she felt bad, but really, he had to be in her shoes to see how sulky he sounded. "I'm not laughing at that, I promise you. Just at your petulant, little-boy-thwarted, it's-not-fair attitude. Believe me, you have no need to be worried, sick or otherwise." She reassured him as best she could. "Really, it is nothing untoward, but it is not up to me to explain the whys and wherefores."

"Then pray tell me, who is it up to?" he demanded. "I am beginning to lose what little patience I have left. The man in the moon? Prinny? Boney?"

"Someone else." Theresa spread her hands in supplication.

"I know that, you infuriating woman." Martin hit the mantelpiece hard with his fist. "Bloody hell that hurts. So who in Hades is this mysterious one? It has to be one of my brothers, which bloody one?"

"Truly, I cannot tell you yet." Theresa thought she sounded like a poor, pathetic, whiny woman, but she really had no other answer. "I would if I could, but I will not break a confidence."

"I suppose not, in your profession," he said

That is nasty.

"Ex-profession," she said, much too calmly for the state of her mind. "But it has helped me learn the art of discretion."

"Then when *can* you share such a snippet?"

"When I can contact the person concerned," she said. "I'm

not being obstreperous, I promise, I just cannot say."

"Infuriating, argh…" Martin stood four-square with his hands on his hips. "Woman, this is serious."

His eyes flashed and for a brief moment Theresa saw what so many other women did. A man who knew what he wanted, went after it and did not take kindly to being thwarted. She could admire that, but her heart didn't quicken, her skin didn't tingle and her juices didn't gather. He did nothing for her at all. One swift thought of Jamie and it was the exact opposite.

"Man, I know."

He blinked and ran his hand through his hair. "I'm worried."

"I truly am sorry," she said. "But not even for a duke will I break a confidence."

"Then believe this, until you send a message to say you *can* tell me, I will have someone watch your every move."

"They can join the queue," she muttered.

Chapter Eight

Jamie ducked as a dictionary, a cushion and a shoe whistled past his ear at a rate of knots. The leather-clad tome that came next caught the edge of his chin, and it hurt. He swore and grasped the Ming vase that followed it, put it firmly on the half-moon table that sat beside the door of the study and studied Theresa warily.

Her eyes sparkled with rage as she glared at him. Her luscious lips were red and full, her cheeks rosy with temper. She clenched and unclenched her hands and her fingers twitched. With her dark-as-midnight hair as ever spiralling down her back and over her shoulders, she looked magnificent.

I could love her. Where had that come from?

"What on earth?" he demanded, his own anger rising at his wayward thoughts. After a long, arduous three days in Rutland sorting out such things as floods, hayricks, a nest in the earl's bedroom chimney and who should supply the game, the next batch of cheese and the kneelers for the church, he was tired. Those times had culminated in riding through a heavy rainstorm, and that infuriating accident as he'd approached the capital. Now he was finally with Theresa, and this was the last thing he'd expected. He had hoped for succouring not stunning.

"Grr, you…you…*argh.*" Theresa flung her hands in the air, looked around wildly and marched, poker backed, across the room. "You turncoat, you, liar, you…"

"Oi, no more, you'll hurt someone." Jamie stepped to one side and a tambour frame clattered harmlessly against the doorjamb. He reached Theresa before she aimed and threw the firedogs, and held her arms tightly against her sides.

"What's this all about?" Jamie demanded. "What brought this on?"

"What?" Theresa demanded. "You dare to ask me what? Underhand, deceitful... *Argh*..." She stomped her foot on his instep. He wriggled his foot gingerly inside his hessians. Even through the leather, she inflicted serious pain.

"Bloody hell, Theresa, that hurts."

"Good, I wish I'd broken something. How *dare* you?" she asked in a voice tight with temper. "To put your men in the square is one thing, even though it would have been nice to know about it, but to have my staff on guard and say nothing? That is beyond the pale."

"It was their idea," Jamie pointed out. "I just agreed it was a good idea and offered any assistance they might need. They persuaded me they could protect their own without any help. Who was I to argue?"

"Pah." Evidently her temper was receding a little, for that word had lost the forcefulness of her prior speech. "Men."

"Theresa, they needed to," he said. "They wanted to be useful, to feel they were keeping you safe. Who was I to dissuade them? Their loyalty is not to be sniffed at. Many people would gladly hand over half their fortunes for such a happening."

He released her arms and watched warily in case he needed to restrain her once more. He hadn't been on the receiving end of this fiery side of her, and it both fascinated him and made him take care.

"And it was not just the men. All your staff love you and want to keep you safe."

She narrowed her eyes and muttered as she sat on a chair with such a thump Jamie wouldn't have been overly surprised to see dust rise around her.

None did, of course—she had excellent servants. He regarded her with amusement as she tried—and evidently failed—to get her rage back. "Damn you, Jamie," she said and sighed. "Damn you to wherever and back. You have just made me lose a perfectly good bad temper."

He dipped his head. "That is a contradiction in terms. No, don't get your dander up again. Just do the damning bit. People frequently do, love." The endearment slipped out as naturally as if it was always used, not just on those occasions when he forgot himself. "It's a national pastime. You know, along the lines of 'Damn those Ansters, they are'... Insert whatever epithet and description that riles you. We are all used to it. Even my esteemed elder brother." He rubbed his chin where the book had clipped it, and groaned. There would be a bruise there, which would be hard to explain without appearing an idiot. Perhaps a dignified silence and a blank expression might be the best answer. "You have good aim."

Theresa began to laugh. "Of course, why else bother?" She stretched her arms above her head and yawned. "An excess of anger always tires me out. That is why I try to exercise discretion as often as possible. This time though? Ah, not possible."

The stretch revealed a perfect bosom pressed tight against the delicate, low-cut lawn of her dress. The yawn, her perfect teeth. Damn he had it bad if he was about to wax lyrical about molars, for goodness' sake.

"I'm sorry," Jamie said. "I mean it. In all honesty I did what I did for the best. I'm not used to having to consider someone else when I make decisions. I vow never to be so arbitrary from now on."

She raised one eyebrow and slowly the second one rose to join it. "Damn and blast." Theresa giggled. "I've been practicing how to do this one brow thing and still it doesn't really work. But even so, you say you are sorry and you vow, but how much do I take from that?"

"All of it. I promise. Or," he temporized, "I promise to try."

He felt like a schoolboy under the eagle eyes of his headmaster after some supposed misdemeanor — or, he guessed, a felon in front of a judge about to pronounce sentence. It was a most unpleasant sensation. As if long-legged spiders were crawling over his skin and choosing where to bite.

Eventually Theresa shook her head and laughed, reluctantly. "If you believe any of that, you need committing. You have 'in charge' stamped all over you. However, be warned, if you do try anything like that again, you will get the same response. Ask me, for the lord's sake, and do not tell me. I am not some shy and retiring, simpering and silly deb. I have a mind and I use it."

Jamie clapped. She half rose, and he put his hands high in the air. "No, don't go up in the boughs again. I meant it as a sincere compliment. I wish more ladies were like you."

Theresa sat again. "Courtesans?" she asked with a chuckle, her humor seeming to have been restored.

He laughed. "Ex-courtesans and no, ladies with a brain and not afraid to use it."

"Ah." She was silent. "Yes, well, they probably didn't have the upbringing I had. Are we going to Richmond?"

She might not think she had the knack of changing a subject down to a fine art, but Jamie disagreed. Nevertheless he intended to return to the subject of her earlier days at a time where he hoped she'd be more amenable to sharing the information. "Of course," Jamie replied smooth as silk. "My horses are being walked as we speak. Do you need long to get ready?"

"Ten minutes should do."

He chose not to answer. It was his conviction that it would take four times that before she reappeared. However, it was little more than fifteen minutes later when they turned out of the square and wended their way through the busy street toward Richmond.

"I didn't see any watchers," Theresa remarked as Berkeley Square was left behind them. "Yours, mine or anyone else's."

"Good." Jamie pulled over to one side to let the Exeter to London stage pass. "The whole idea is not to see them, just know they are there, and act accordingly." He glanced up at the stage. On the last leg of its several-day journey, the outside passengers appeared drawn, bedraggled and weary. "Thank the lord we do not have to suffer thus." He nodded to the coach as the horses plodded by.

"Speak for yourself," Theresa retorted. "Some of us do not have the luxury of a coach and four, and rejoice there *is* even a stagecoach to use."

He set the curricle in motion once more and navigated around a dead dog and a young lad hawking pots and pans. "You use the stage?" Jamie asked, surprised. "I know you have your own coach and horses."

"I do now," she said impatiently. "But once I didn't, and the stage or the mail were the only way to get around. That or—"

She broke off and Jamie waited with as much patience as he could muster for her to continue.

"Or," he prompted.

"Eh? Ah, or Shanks's pony. Luckily I like walking. However, now I walk for pleasure, not from necessity. Oh, my, how pretty is that beech hedge?"

As a change of subject it wasn't up to her usual standard, but it did the trick. Jamie risked a quick glance as he checked the horses, who seemed to think the hedge was about to jump out and bite them, and forgot about her childhood until the supposed dangers had passed and they were once more moving forward properly. He supposed he'd have to quiz Maria. If anyone knew anything, she would. Mind you, he thought ironically, she could be as closed-mouthed as Theresa.

Never one to flog a dead horse, he changed the subject and began to chat about Anster, his brother's castle and his brother. "Martin, of course, is supposed to provide an heir but seems inclined not to do anything in that direction at the moment. I can't say I blame him, not really. He's had a hard time of it, and for all he says he is fine, I am inclined to believe he is still affected by his wife's death."

"Talking about Martin," she said in a voice little above a whisper.

He watched Theresa swivel and look at him.

"Yes?" He returned his attention to his horses. There was too much traffic around to do otherwise. "I am listening, I promise you." What on earth did she want to say about his brother? "But I need to keep an eye on this pair and their tendency to take fright whenever my attention is elsewhere."

"He was the man who thankfully rescued me from those thugs. Although, I have to say he recognized the necklace, and was quite truculent when I refused to tell him why I was wearing it."

"Ah." Now he'd have to sort his brother out as well as his mama.

"Ah indeed. He demanded several times to know where I got it from. I wouldn't be surprised if he thought I'd stolen it, or acquired it by some nefarious means or another. He was insistent I tell him which brother must have handed it over. My fault, because when I let slip I recognized him, I said it was because I knew one of his brothers a little. A strange man," she said. "One who holds himself so stiff he must ache. I mean that metaphorically."

"Grief does that to some people and then it is hard to shake. What did you tell him?"

"That until I had spoken with the person who gave it to me I could pass no information on. He said he'd be watching me. I muttered he could join the queue."

"That wouldn't have pleased him," Jamie said. He understood his brother. "But it delights me, he needs taking down a notch or two at times. Far too pompous for his own good. I'll speak to him. They were Mama's to do with as she liked but as she delights in not confiding her intentions to all of us, I doubt he knew. Plus, he is now back and spending most of his time at the castle. I never thought to inform him. He… I suppose you could say he needs to be there to become himself again."

"It sounds a lovely place," Theresa said wistful at the thought. She had never experienced that sense of truly belonging somewhere. "A place you can identify with, and love. Your heritage. Perfect."

Damn. He hadn't meant to upset her, just the opposite.

"You wouldn't say that when you've ice on your washing water and it was allegedly piping hot when it left the kitchen," he said before he chuckled. "Or when to have only three chilblains is a success. It might be my history, but it isn't my present or my future. I prefer my own home. Martin has all the discomforts to deal with, poor man. Now he's home again it's up to him to sort all the disadvantages and change the negatives into positives. It's a long job, and I do not envy him one jot." He chuckled. "I won't bore you with it all. Suffice it to say, whilst he was a…not around, Mama managed the estates as she wanted, and I fear a lot of her ideas do not mesh with those of Martin. I can't totally blame Mama, she was rather left just to get on with it all, with of course no training. I wasn't around as I was away at Cambridge, and the others too young. Poor thing, my mama was bewildered a lot of the time and at odds with change regarding the rest. It's been a hard few years for us all. She couldn't help rubbing me up the wrong way, and I can't help not doing as she would prefer. It is life— my life—and she has to accept it as it is. Now, though?" He raised his eyebrows. "Now we seem to have turned the corner and I can concentrate on me and my life." He chose not to speak further on the duke or his problems. Martin's life was *his* own and it was all down to him to mold it to his own desires. Just like Jamie intended to.

"I thought if we left the horses at the inn, walked in the park for an hour and had lunch we could still have a brief wander later if you wish?" he said a short time later as they approached their destination. "Enjoy the good weather."

"It sounds perfect," Theresa replied as Jamie directed the horses through the narrow archway entrance that led into the inn's courtyard and handed the reins to a waiting ostler.

"I have a private parlor booked." Jamie helped her down from the curricle and held out his arm. "Do you wish a bedchamber as well?" The look on her face would have been funny in other circumstances. "To freshen up," he added before she berated him for his impudence.

She inclined her head. "When we return."

Damn if it wouldn't have been good if she said yes and for other things as well. His cock hardened at the thought.

Bloody thing really does have a mind of its own.

"Let's walk," he said. Come on, a brisk walk will do us both good." He steered her away from the building. Hopefully the fresh air would cool his ardor *and* his prick.

The sun shone down and the few white, fluffy clouds in the sky stopped on the horizon. Although there was a chill in the air that hadn't been there in the city, or a few weeks previously when she and Maria had stolen a couple of hours to walk on Hampstead Heath, it was invigorating to stride out briskly with no fear of someone looking down on her. Or being scandalized by the brief view of what she had been informed were very appealing limbs, which she was sure was revealed as her skirts swished with each step. Pleased she had worn very attractive, albeit practical sandals that showed off her ankles, Theresa relaxed and enjoyed herself. Arm in arm with her, Jamie matched her pace, adapting his longer stride easily to her shorter one.

"Until I get out of the capital I forget I'm a country boy at heart," he remarked as they slowed their steps to watch a tiding of magpies fly over and land on clumps of bushes ahead of them. Theresa crossed herself and laughed self-consciously at Jamie's sardonic expression.

"Yes well, heathen-like no doubt but..." She shrugged. "I like to hedge my bets."

He laughed. "As do I, but perhaps in a different way." He paused for effect. "I duck as they fly over, do not consider bird muck lucky and know a very good poacher who takes excellent potshots if they become too worrisome."

Theresa missed a step. "My, you do like to live dangerously, don't you? Potshots?"

"Oh I tell him to miss," Jamie said with an audacious wink. "But the noise scares 'em away. Pigeons now, that's a different matter. I like a bit of pigeon pie."

Theresa nodded — she'd been partial to those in her youth. Lately, though… "I haven't had pigeon pie for an age," she said and sighed. "Maybe it was time to spend a week or so in her cottage. Except she had the urge to be near, but not *too* near Jamie, and wasn't sure the cottage would help. The visitation from Protheroe and another unsigned missive that morning had ensured that.

"Damn, I forgot I had this left on the doorstep this morning. Under a stone of all things, slap bang where anyone who left the house would put their feet." She rummaged in her reticule and withdrew an expensive vellum sheet of paper and handed it over. "It was lucky no one tripped over it and fell head over heels down the steps."

Jamie opened it and read out loud the words she knew by heart. "Good lord. 'If you don't come willingly, you'll come by force.' Melodramatic bastard."

"That's as may be but it's not the sort of thing to read over your breakfast kippers," Theresa retorted, "and not get indigestion."

"Hmm, I think something needs to be done about Percy," Jamie replied. "I'll work on it. Perhaps a notice in the *Times* announcing…"

"*No,*" Theresa shouted, and choked as her heartbeat sped up to an alarming pace and she became short of breath. She took several deep gulps of air as Jamie turned to consider her in concern. The last thing she felt able to cope with was more and more people getting involved and adding their two penn'orth to her troubles.

"I didn't finish what I was going to say," he said, so mild she distrusted his reply. "Are you all right or have you swallowed a fly?"

"All right," she gasped, mortified that once more she was

wrong-footed. "But I might suffer a relapse if you send a notice to the *Times*."

"Why?" Jamie asked. "What on earth do you think it would say?"

"I do not know, do I?" She bit back a snappy retort. "But it sounded as if it was going to be a betrothal notice."

He stopped walking again and took her arms to twist her to face him. "One bloody day you'll trust me, love." By his demeanor, her lack of faith had hurt him.

"I do," she protested, uneasy and aware that perhaps that was not the whole truth, even though a lot of the time he gave her no reason *to* believe in him. "Or I wouldn't be here, would I?" she finished. It was hard not to add, *so there* in a triumphant voice.

"Really?" Jamie ran his hands through his hair again, and put one long finger under his cravat to loosen it. "You have a strange way of showing it. I said I would never do anything like that until you begged. Do you not believe my word?"

"Not about a betrothal," Theresa replied. Now was the time to be honest. "Just about two people and s...se... seduction." Her cheeks were warm and she wished she carried a fan. Dare she waft her hand in front of her? "You know, sex," she ended in a hurried mutter.

His anguished expression stopped her. Had she killed anything they may have had? It was so stupid. She could teach any man about how to treat a lady in the most explicit terms ever. Had no problem in not mincing her words regarding what needed to be done for the ultimate satisfaction. But to just say the most innocent of those words to Jamie was so hard. Why? Surely not because he was an earl? In her previous life she had fucked those of a higher rank.

Because he matters. Because I want him to see me in a good light, and how pathetic, I want to be ladylike around him.

One day she would learn to think before she opened her mouth. And begin to trust what she saw and learned. "I'm sorry," she mumbled. "But…"

"Good lord, woman. You *were* put on this world to try me." Jamie swung her around to face him and grabbed hold of her shoulders.

Which would be most effective? To shake her or kiss her senseless? He ground his teeth to stop himself from saying harsh words that would do them no good whatsoever. She was what she was and a few days in his presence was not going to change that.

But how, oh how, had she been a successful courtesan, someone evidently sexually active, when it seemed she was somewhat of a prude over describing the act?

It intrigued him and fascinated him — and he liked it. "Sex, seduction, fuckery, buggery, sodomy — although that is not my area of need — marriage, bed partners with or without a license, call it what you will, they're different sides of the same coin. Nothing like that would be done without your knowledge and you should bloody well know it."

"Well, some of it, unless I was comatose you'd have a hard job to achieve," she said, "but the rest?" Theresa considered him with skepticism. "Hmm."

"Yes all right, I did things without your say-so and I have apologized." Damn she knew how to make him feel a heel and respond accordingly. "I've learned my lesson, believe me. Nothing without telling you from now on."

"And my consent?" she persisted. She noticed he hadn't added 'before it happens' either.

"Don't push your luck," Jamie advised her. "If necessary, of course, but I reserve the right to do what is imperative in an emergency." He would do anything to keep her safe. Even if it meant abducting her and removing her from danger in a way he was damn sure she would never forgive.

Theresa bit her lip. The silence stretched until a crow or raven landed on a nearby tree with a screech and she jumped. "Lord, my nerves must be shot. How ridiculous. So, therefore, yes…"

Jamie took her hands once more, and began to walk again. "If we skirt the pond..." He gestured to where a circle of water fringed with bulrushes glinted in the sunlight. Three ducks swam across it busily and every so often only their feathered rears showed as they hunted for food. "It will bring us back to the inn just in time for lunch." He bit back a grin. "And to freshen up."

"Alone?" she asked suspiciously as one duck reappeared and quacked several times. "To freshen up, I mean, not to dine alone."

He laughed. "As I have probably mentioned on more than one occasion, love, you strike a harsh bargain." He kissed her cheek and for a brief moment let the scents of her tease his senses. "If you must."

"Oh I must." She purred the words. "I really must."

Damn. She just has to have the last word.

* * * *

"My, that was excellent." Theresa slid back in her chair, regarded the remains of their repast and sighed in satisfaction. She was as full as it was possible to be. "This chef could be the toast of the ton if he moved to one of the grand dames' establishments." Thank the lord she hadn't laced her stays up too tight. She would have passed out if that had been the case. The meal had been so excellent and tasty she had eaten far too much to be comfortable if constricted to any great degree. Stays, she was sure, were why so many women only picked at their meals when in company.

"Young Kenny, the chef, is a marvel," Jamie agreed. "But as he said when I tried to poach him, 'Eh, it's me granddad's inn and he'd fair kill me if I went elsewhere.'" Jamie did a creditable copy of the chef's accent. "Therefore here he continues to tempt us."

Theresa giggled. The day had turned out so much better than it had seemed possible when she'd found out about his perfidy. Then to add worse to already bad, she'd received that bloody note. She now felt slightly guilty about hitting Jamie. It was not easy, but she accepted he was only doing his high and mighty aristocratic best to take care of her.

"Did you see the title of the book that touched you?" she asked with a note of humor in her voice. She studied his chin, where a tiny red abrasion stood out, and touched it carefully. "Hopefully the mark will fade." She dropped her hands to her lap and stared at him with concern in her expression and her bottom lip caught between her teeth.

"Touched? You mean clobbered," Jamie retorted without any heat in his reply. He fingered the spot where her missile had made its mark. "No, I was too busy dodging everything else. What is it called?"

She rolled her eyes. "A Touch of Temper."

He laughed. "How apt. You know, I dread to think how lethal you could be when not in a rage."

"I'd hit everything I aimed for," Theresa said matter-of-factly. "Except with a knife. Then I am useless. I'm not even the safest person to cut my meat. If I aimed at the door over there with a knife or stiletto, I'd hit the cat on the window ledge." Unconcerned, the animal continued to clean itself. "Give me a pistol, a saber or a slingshot," she went on, "and I'm on target, ninety-nine times out of one hundred. When I am not in a temper."

"Impressive, love." Jamie saluted her then bussed her cheek before he flicked her nose. "And the one hundredth?"

She grinned and scrunched her face up. "Oh, around half an inch out."

The astonishment on his face was another notch in his favor.

"I'll remember never to rile you," Jamie said. "Silly question, but do you keep a pistol handy at all times?"

"I do, I promise. I have one in my reticule or muff."

Whatever else she was about to say was lost as Jamie spluttered and guffawed as he glanced toward her cloth-covered cunt. "In your muff? "

Theresa rolled her eyes and went hot, cold and hot again. He was a master at innuendo and she would never best him. "Not that muff. My swansdown one I keep my…"

Jamie shook his head and wiped the tears that streamed down his face. "It must be something to behold. How on earth do you retrieve it in a hurry?"

"Stop it, do." She began to giggle. "Oh lud, the vagaries of our language. You know exactly what I mean. I carry a pistol around with me and also have several situated around the house. So does Mrs. Penicuik. The night I was accosted I'd let my guard down and didn't have one ready in my hand. That will never happen again, I promise you. So do not come upon me unawares. As for the rest of my staff? Roberts would rather have a knife and I do not ask the footmen their preferences. I just trust them all."

"Mrs. Penicuik? From Scotland?" Penicuik, pronounced 'Pennycook', was a good Scottish name, not often heard in London. "Who is she?"

Theresa giggled. "The cook, who hails from north of the border."

"Ah." He joined in her laughter. "A perfect name. And you say she can shoot?"

"Her common-law husband was Two Pistols Parlan, a Scottish highwayman who, if she is to be believed, plied his trade between Perth and Pitlochry. Allegedly he could hit a wren on the wing at fifty yards." She grinned. "Or so the story goes. Mrs. P. says he was a thatchgallow regarded by all his peers as the one to aspire to become and deserved all he got."

"Hanged? Transported?" Jamie lowered his voice. "Fed to the hogs?"

Theresa shook her head, enjoying their repartee. "No such luck. I think Mrs. Penicuik would have watched if that had been the case. Leg shackled to Bessie Boulter from Auchterarder. A harpy of the first order with a voice like a shrike. Mrs. P.'s words, you understand. I've never met the woman. For which I am devoutly grateful. But all that apart, we are as protected as best we can be." She paused and licked her lips. His eyes narrowed so she did it again. "And you are here to...take care of me in every way..."

"Cocktease." Jamie ground the word out.

His face was impassive, but true to what he called her, his cock was not. Theresa couldn't help but notice how it struggled to grow under his pantaloons. Perhaps it was unfair to be such a person. Although, there was a way she could redeem herself. If she dared.

"I'm sorry," she apologized and meant it. "But I... No, ignore me. It's not right to act so."

"No it isn't," Jamie agreed. "But you might as well tell me what you were about to say."

Theresa breathed in then let that breath out in a long hiss. I am an adult, I deserve a chance to know. "How long do we have our private bedchamber for?"

Whatever she thought he might do, she never expected him to stand grab her hand and put her over his shoulder. Half her hair fell out of its knot and three jeweled pins spiraled to the floor as her tresses spilled down his back to sway over his jacket round his waist and arse. From her upside-down position, she could tell he really did have a splendid rear. One she itched to clutch and stroke. Even so...

"Jamie, people might see," she protested as he began to walk across the polished wooden floorboards. Not to the door, though, but strangely toward a cupboard next to the blazing fire. "What are you doing?" Surely he wasn't an advocate of sex in a closet?

"Taking you to our private bedchamber," he said huskily. "There is not a chance we will be seen, so do not worry about it. Unless they can see through walls. We have a private stair. Duck your head. You don't want a headache to spoil your enjoyment, now, do you?"

"Well, no, but..." She shut her eyes as he ducked. The headspace was so low it seemed impossible they would be able to get through the tiny aperture. "Ah, lord, this is not possible surely?"

"Perfectly possible, stop worrying. We even have the occasional lamp to light our way. We're all right now, it's head height," Jamie said in a level voice that showed no sign he was carrying her. "Just the stairs to climb. If I go sideways, I reiterate. Do. Not. Worry. I have you safe." They moved upward steadily. His breathing never changed, it was even and it seemed his journey was effortless.

Theresa had to be impressed. She knew she was no lightweight, and the stairs were narrow, steep and twisted in a tight spiral. Her head bumped off Jamie's back as they turned one particularly compact bend. He moved his arm until he was able to put his hand on her skull and hold her close to him.

"Almost there, only one more turn. Yes, hold on. Ah." Her world spun as she heard a thud, a squeak, then her world lightened as they emerged into the bedchamber she had visited briefly before they had eaten. Visited via a difference entrance.

Jamie put her onto her feet and closed the door. Once more the hinges complained as the door met the frame and the aperture disappeared. He leaned back on the wood and observed her thoroughly from head to toe. It was unnerving, as he inspected every inch of her, and it took all of Theresa's self-control not to fidget or shift from foot to foot.

"And now we are here?" he asked. "What then?"

Dare she? It was going against everything she had held dear. She reviewed and revised her parameters about what was acceptable to her and what was not. Could she do it?

Yes she could. A woman had the prerogative to change her mind, surely? And if she were honest she wanted to know what those women who had enjoyed him meant when they had spoken in hushed tones about his prowess and inventiveness. It was all well and good living it third-hand through Maria's repeated reports, but she wanted more.

And, she owned, she had a deep-seated desire to discover

how it felt to have sex for enjoyment with someone she wanted, rather than paying attention to where her partner needed to improve his technique.

Maybe even be the pupil, not the teacher?

"How long do we have the room?" she asked once more. "An hour? Two?" She prayed it was two, or could she dare hope for longer? For once she didn't want to set a strict time limit in her mind about how long she could be involved.

I just want to be. To live for the moment, however long that is, and enjoy whatever transpires.

"Blenkinsop senior would never countenance that," Jamie said serenely. "The scandal, you know." He winked. "He keeps a respectable house, he says. Therefore, I have bespoken it for the night and arranged for a portmanteau to be delivered. Oh he knows we are not wed, probably had no idea we'd use it for more than lunch, but as he tells me on every visit, this is a respectable house, no shenanigans under his roof."

Damn. He comes here often. Her dismay must have shown on her face because Jamie shook his head and flicked her curls.

"Tut, tut, what a suspicious mind you have, my love. I can see your thoughts whirring like the spring of the clock on the mantel. I use this if I go to visit friends in the south. My Aunt Fewson lives far enough away for me to call here for lunch, or if I have a late start, to stop overnight. At times I have stayed when, as Blenkinsopp commented, not all of the guests were of the caliber he prefers. Breaking my journey here means I do not have to fight the traffic to get a head start. Plus the food is superb, the beds comfortable and Blenkinsop's homemade ale a cut above the rest. All a man could wish for." He grinned and unpinned the rest of her hair so it fell in rippling curls down her back. "Except for a willing woman, of course."

Theresa gasped and put her hand to one long strand that stuck to her cheek. "My hair, Jamie, it takes an age to arrange." And a couple of dozen hairpins that now rested in his pocket.

He patted said pocket. "Pinning hair is one of the many accomplishments of a rake, I assure you."

She shook her head in amusement. "Is there anything you can't do?"

"Who knows? With luck we will find out soon." He winked. "There's no such thing as rake school, so perhaps I've bypassed something important. But let's hope not, eh?"

Drat him. His gravelly tones made her channel muscles contract and her body send urgent messages to her brain. Of the 'I need him now' sort. Theresa smiled limpidly and sank into a deep and, she hoped, breast-revealing curtsy. "Then this visit should encompass all those things." She slipped her footwear off and wriggled her toes. "Should it not?"

Jamie took three steps toward her until they were almost touching. Slowly he put one finger to her chin and tilted her head so their eyes met.

"Say that again," he requested. His voice was hoarse and sounded rusty. "Slowly."

"Shall I put it like this instead?" she asked with a smile. A sultry, come hither, take-me-I'm-yours smile, she hoped. "Please, Jamie, take me and show me what it's like to make love to a man."

His jaw dropped. "Please repeat yourself," he entreated in a voice she had never heard before. "Slowly, so I make no mistake."

"I believe," Theresa said in a voice husky with emotion, "I have to beg twice more. Please, my lord, make love to me." She stretched up and traced the outline of his jaw with her fingertip. "Please show me how it should be."

"Why now?"

He took hold of her finger and suckled the tip. Red-hot sensation flooded her and her knees almost buckled. Why did such a tiny thing make her quim damp and her nipples hard?

"I...ah." She did her best to sort her scrambled thoughts

but it was difficult as ever more hitherto unfelt experiences bombarded her. "I need to know. Please, my lord." Surely that was enough?

"What do you need to know, love?" He was inexorable, like a terrier with a rat in its mouth.

"The difference," she panted. "How it…"

He pushed the neckline of her dress to one side and sucked on the soft skin that swelled to his touch. "Ah…I…"

"What difference?" Jamie asked. "Tell me or I stop."

Oh hell, not that. "Between making love and teaching the mechanics." Theresa fought not to sob. "Please show me. Take me and—"

Jamie put his finger over her lips. She looked up into his dark eyes and blinked at what she saw there. Tenderness and more. A need and an ache? For her? Oh please let it be so.

"Oh I won't take you, Theresa," he said, and paused before he continued. "That is not how it works."

"No?" Sick, helpless despair rolled over her, darkness filled her soul and she began to struggle against his touch. Embarrassment made her sway and push at him to get away. "Let me go then."

Jamie held her still with ease. "Stop it, you termagant. I will not take you—because this is a two-way experience. We will take each other."

Chapter Nine

Would she agree? His cock was so hard the slightest scrape of his pantaloons across the engorged head sent a spiral of need into him and more than a few drops of his need down the length. If she *didn't* agree... Jamie now was certain it was all or nothing. He wanted them to take that journey of discovery together.

The silence was overwhelming. Perhaps his wording had been less than perfect but for the first time in his life Jamie felt himself at a disadvantage. As unsure as a virgin on the cusp of the discovery of sex, he stood motionless, hardy daring to breathe as then, very slowly, he moved his arms away from Theresa then took a step back. It was the most peculiar feeling to experience such an acute sense of loss, especially as Theresa seemed to have no inclination to return to the circle of his arms.

Moisture gathered at the backs of his eyes and Jamie blinked rapidly. Men did not cry. Not under any circumstance. He watched the hand of the clock jerk to indicate a full minute had passed. Was it time to bow and say, 'Very well, goodbye'?

No. That would be cowardly. Somehow he would have to try to persuade her it was together or never.

Theresa circled him, and she pressed up against his back. Her breasts caressed him—even through his jacket Jamie felt they imprinted themselves onto his skin. Her breath teased the hairs on the nape of his neck as she brought her arms around him, then rested her cheek on his back and held him close.

"You are, my lord, something special. Usual—" She

stopped speaking abruptly and Jamie understood. He put his hands behind him to tap her rear.

"It is impossible for us to forget who either of us are or were, love. We will just have to put up with it and accept our past can only help our present and hopefully our future." He chuckled and held her hands over his cock, pleased when she curled them to encase him in her palms. "Who knows? You might teach me a thing or two that has up to now escaped me."

Theresa sniggered. "As you were frequently named as the person most people told me they aspired to copy, it is not likely. Although, I must confess to being intrigued. For if some of the things you are purported to have done are correct, you must be first cousin to a particularly limber ape."

"What?" Jamie tried to glance at her over his shoulder and failed. "Let me look at you, woman, for the lord's sake." He lifted Theresa's hands from his torso and tugged her around so they faced each other. "I hadn't realized how tiny you were," he remarked with surprise. The top of her head only reached up to his chin.

"Stockinged feet," Theresa said in a prosaic manner. "Plus, you are so tall."

He rested his jaw on her hair and moved it around. Theresa snorted. "That is irritating."

"Ah, see, I have learned something already," Jamie said in a humorous tone. "What else? I need to stand on my head? Never touch your ears? That could make things interesting, I must say. I'm partial to your shell-like lobes."

"Really?" Theresa said, "Permit me to say I am skeptical with regards to that. On my part, I'm partial to your…" She licked her lips suggestively and tilted her head back so her dark-blue eyes looked directly into his.

"My?"

"Shall we find out?" she purred and tugged on the waistband of his pantaloons. Her thumbs stroked over the tip of his cock and his heart missed a beat.

He couldn't have articulated how it affected him, not even if his life depended on it. Instead he began to open the long row of tiny, fiddly buttons down her spine. Not easy with her hands between them, but oh so necessary.

Theresa's lips parted and she swallowed as she used one digit to stroke his length. "I think you want me."

"I damn well know I do, and I want this as well." He gathered his scattered wits and eased the gown carefully down and over her shoulders, effectively trapping her fingers as they circled his staff. His pantaloons covered his torso *and* her hands. Her luscious breasts slowly showed over the lace and fine lawn that had titillated and shielded them from his eager eyes.

Jamie licked his dry lips and bent his head to take first one hard nub then the other in his mouth. He sucked and nipped. Theresa's fingers tightened on his cock, relaxed and tightened again. It was heaven and hell all rolled into one. Very reluctantly he moved his lips from her nipple with a wet plop that sounded loud in the room.

"That, my love," he said fervently but honestly, "will guarantee I come before I get inside you. I usually pride myself on my control, but this time I think will be the one occasion to go against that." He tugged her dress over her wrists until she moved her hands, then let the material drop even lower until she was able to step out of the garment.

No shift. Just the most erotic pair of stays he had ever feasted his eyes on. And there had been plenty. These were in a shocking deep red lace and matched the rose-speckled garters that hugged her thighs and held gossamer silk stockings in place.

She took his breath away. "Oh my," he said when he found his voice and decided he could speak without stuttering. "Yes." He stroked the silk from the top—just under her breasts—to the bottom, which skimmed her muff. "Exquisite and begging to be removed, I think." Jamie spun Theresa around and admired how the corset drew his eyes to the soft rounded globes of her arse with that tantalizing shadow between. "I have now discovered not all ladies' undergarments are designed to annoy a man."

With shaking, fumbling fingers, he unlaced the criss-cross satin ties on the garment until it fell forward and he was faced with a shapely naked rear. "The stockings and garters stay. I never realized I had a fondness for them until now." He skimmed his fingers around the garters and slowly trailed his digits upward to cup her arse then stroked the soft skin of her waist before moving higher caress her nape. Tiny freckles dotted her shoulders, powdered her spine and invited kisses.

"I wonder where these enticing freckles stop," he said in a throaty voice. "Maybe I should map them over you and see where I end up."

Theresa shivered and tiny goosebumps appeared on her skin. She moaned deep in her throat and pressed back into him. "Please." She breathed the word. "I need—"

"*We* need." Jamie lifted her up and carried her to the bed. He dropped her carefully onto the mattress and grinned as she bounced and shook. "That, my love, is a sight for sore eyes."

"Really?" She sniggered. "As I bounce and jiggle?"

"Oh yes, definitely." He nodded and smiled. "Each jiggle tests my resolve. And it weakens every time. Now, for the love of all that's holy, stay still while I get ready to join you." Jamie pulled off his boots with the convenient jack, stripped off his cravat and jacket and tugged his shirt over his head. That followed the other garments in the direction of a nearby chair. None of them actually reached it.

"Maybe I can help?" Theresa said. She wetted her lips with her tongue. "Two minds or, indeed, four hands, are better than one, or so they say."

"Oh I'm sure you could help, but on this occasion I reckon you'd be best not to or I might spill in your hands, not your cunt," he said, candid as ever. "I am teetering on a rope edge."

"Or in my mouth." Theresa got onto her knees and

crawled across to the edge of the bed. Before his sluggish sex-filled brain reacted, she slipped his pantaloons down and his cock jutted out of its nest of wiry dark curls, slick and engorged.

"Mine, I think." Theresa licked the tip delicately and gave a moan of approval. "Oh yes. You are ready, aren't you? So damned bloody perfect."

Jamie swore his eyes crossed. His balls tightened so much they would bruise her if he put them near her body. On any other occasion he would have tipped himself back and let her eat him to completion. However, not now, not for their first time. This time he wanted to bury himself deep inside her cunt, not her mouth, and watch her face as they both exploded. Ruthlessly, he tugged a handful of spiral curls until, with a final graze of her teeth, Theresa let go of his staff.

"First we'll be conventional." Jamie pulled the covers back on the bed and plumped up the pillows. "Here, on your back and fast."

Theresa grinned and obeyed while Jamie toed his pantaloons off, then joined her. With little finesse, he pushed her knees apart and crawled between her legs. He didn't have to ask before she raised them and rested one slender ankle on each of his shoulders. Her toes tickled his ears and she smirked. "This is nice."

Nice? I can do better than nice.

"This is a view I never thought I would be lucky enough to enjoy," he said with frank admiration as her position opened her to him, and he flicked her quim with one fingernail. "I'm not going to be kind or gentle, I can't."

"Why should you?" Theresa took in a shuddering breath. "I'm as ready for you as you are for me." She lifted her arse from the bed. Jamie needed no further bidding. He put his hands either side of her shoulders and surged into her.

Fast and furious, she met him thrust for thrust, and used her internal muscles to alternate holding him tight and letting him fill her. She exulted in it. In him and her together. Her body was on fire, her vision clouded and her mind full of him—only him. Each nerve end throbbed and she would have sworn every hair on her arms stood up. As their rhythm meshed, their breaths became shorter and harsher and Theresa tensed, shuddered and shouted. Jamie made one last move and pulled out. To spill his hot, plentiful seed over her, not in her.

He slumped onto her and sticky wet seed coated them both and held them together.

Theresa cuddled the man who pressed her into the soft mattress and reveled in both his closeness and his weight.

"I never realized it could be so different," she said in an awed tone. "To make love, not have sex. It is as different as night and day." She pressed a kiss to the top of his head. "Oh my, I never knew."

"'Tis only the start," Jamie said, his voice muffled by the way he slumped. It reverberated over her skin and into her soul. "The beginning."

Into my soul. The words echoed again and again in her mind. She wasn't sure it was possible to put her emotions into words, but hoped he understood as they lay there quietly, relaxed in each other's arms, until somewhere a clock struck the hour. She counted the gongs absently and jolted. "Good god, did you hear those?" Theresa sat up and stared at the mantel clock as if to dare it to not be the hour it said it was. "I cannot believe it."

"What?" Jamie lifted his head and smiled at her. Toe curling and spine tingling, full of the promise of things to come. "I like this. It is never something I have ever had the desire to do before."

"Pardon?" His words distracted her. "Have sex in such a way? Why ever not?" Warmth crossed her skin. "It was amazing."

"And that. But I meant snuggle," he said. "For want of a better word. Enjoy the aftermath. The closeness, the togetherness. I now know what I have been missing." He tried to tug her down onto him again and she resisted.

"It is perfect," she agreed. "But, Jamie, the time isn't." Her voice rose, as did her panic. "That was five o'clock and we are still here. The staff will be at twos and threes and beside themselves with worry. I didn't say we would be back late, and I can see the state they will be in, especially in the light of all the goings-on." She bit her lip. "What do we do?"

Jamie stretched, stood in one lithe movement and dragged Theresa to her feet after him. "We do not panic. Instead we dress and return to the world where others populate our time. I wish it was not necessary, but I respect the care and attention your staff pay to you. It is not to be messed with, or taken lightly." He looked at the water in the ewer. "Lukewarm at best and we both could do with a bath, but I suspect this will have to do. Come on, let me play lady's maid and remove my essence from you. Make you all nice and clean and tidy again."

Theresa nodded and stood still until his cloth-covered hands strayed to the hairs that hid her quim. She wriggled and he grinned ruefully. "Do not encourage me." Jamie moved his hands and completed his ministrations on her somewhat perfunctorily before he helped her into her stays.

"Not too tight," she said with a laugh as he began to retie them. "I am past the stage of holding everything in for vanity – or a man."

"Good. If it wasn't such an arousing thing, I'd say don't bother." Jamie slipped her dress over her head. "In fact, it's the first time I've ever appreciated a corset. Even so, next time I will demand, please don't."

"No stays?"

Jamie inclined his head. "No stays, nothing like them and no shift." He winked. "Hell, if it were possible I'd say no gown. I want to see you, all of you."

She rolled her eyes. "Now that would give the tabbies something to talk about. I can cope with no stays but sadly not the rest."

"Pity." He patted her bottom and began to don his own

clothes. It should have felt uncomfortable with her gaze on him. It didn't. It was, he decided, perfect.

He needed to ponder why.

Theresa watched him with interest. "Impressive," she said as he tied his cravat with scarcely a glance in the mirror. "And no need for a valet?"

"I'm well known as a rake. I should be able to do this with one hand tied behind my back in the pitch black."

"Ah, yes." Theresa nodded in agreement. "Point taken. And do rakes always get out of wherever they are unscathed and unseen?"

"Of course. Well, the competent ones do. And fix their ladies' hair. Come here." He finger-combed her hair, plaited it swiftly, wound it into a coronet and pinned it in place. "There you are, basic but neat."

She stood on tiptoe to peer into the mirror. "Very impressive. I know where to come if my dresser is indisposed."

He kissed her cheek. "If you ever need help dressing, or indeed preferably undressing, just give me a call. However, for the love of God, don't ask me to remove those titillating garters."

* * * *

"What now?" Theresa asked. She tucked a warm rug around her legs and sat as close as possible to Jamie as he urged the horses forward on their return journey. The nip in the air was a perfect excuse to snuggle up to him. Dusk was fast approaching and she could only thank Jamie's forethought, that once he was presentable he had asked for a rider on a fast horse to go and tell her household they would be back later than anticipated, but all was well.

The thoughtful man in her mind looked at her briefly before he returned his attention to the road and maneuvered around a cartful of cabbages. "That's up to you."

The carter pulled over and Jamie nodded his thanks and

once again gathered his reins and the horses surged on.

"May I suggest dinner at my house and a bath?" Theresa said. Even after Jamie's close attention to her, she still felt sticky. "I'm sure both will be very welcome. After all, food is a dim and distant memory and we didn't have the option of the bath."

He chuckled. "That sounds a good plan. Which way round?"

Theresa watched the illusion of trees rushing by as they headed away from Richmond, and considered his question. "Well, I always think if you bathe on a full stomach you feel sluggish," she said with a grin. "But I have a niggling suspicion that if we did bathe first we might never reach the dinner table..." She paused and swiveled sideways on the seat to look at his profile. She could see his amused expression even though he concentrated on the highway, not her. The first houses had appeared and the road was considerably busier. "But of course I will defer to you, my lord."

"Good of you," he said dryly. "Something unusual?"

"Oh yes, most definitely, but I have made a vow to try to be more..." She paused for effect and lowered her voice to what she hoped was an arousing undertone. "More accommodating to the right person."

Jamie started, dropped his hands several inches from where he held them to control the horses, and his perfectly matched chestnuts broke stride. "Hellfire." He spent several seconds bringing the horses back under control before he answered her. "That right person better be me."

"Well, of course. Who else?" Her stomach gurgled and she grimaced, her attempts at eroticism foiled by her tummy. "Oh dear."

Jamie shot her a swift glance. "That solves our dilemma. Eat first and play...ahem, bathe later."

I hope it is bathe then play? Or should that be the other way round?

"Of course," Jamie continued as they turned into a busy

thoroughfare and the horses slowed to a walk. "It might be too late for me to brave the streets of London at that time of night." He slanted her a glance from narrowed eyes. "It is alleged not to be safe if one is out late, alone."

Even though she liked the sound of him stopping—for the night perhaps—a disquieting thought hit Theresa. "What about your horses?"

"When I sent the messenger to say we were on our way, I also sent a message for my groom to meet us at your house."

He sounded so satisfied and complacent, Theresa bit her lip to stop herself laughing. "You think of everything." Amusement aside, she didn't know whether that thought was pleasing or not. Had he taken it for granted he would stay?

"Not really." Jamie shook his head. "No, do not pucker up, your thoughts showed in your expression. I just knew I wanted to see you home and we both need to know what's happened whilst we were away, if anything. Therefore I needed someone to look after the horses. I'll just arrange for them to be taken straight back to the stables instead of walked until I reappear. What happens after we've checked all is well, or not, is up to you." They turned the corner near her home, wove around a milk cart and a chimney sweep, and Jamie reined the horses to a halt. "I hope what you want is the same as I do, but I have never coerced a woman in my life and I do not intend to start with you. Apart from the fact it goes against the grain, you wouldn't let me."

She giggled, all good humor restored, as the front door opened and a footman came running just as Jamie's groom appeared from the area steps to catch the reins. The footman took up a wary and alert stance next to the curricle as Jamie jumped down, held out his arms and swung Theresa to the ground before he turned to his groom to give him instructions. He watched the curricle maneuver out of the square and scanned the passersby. It all seemed somewhat cloak and daggerish, but he was not taking any chances. However, no one watched from the bushes, or the gardens beyond as far as he could tell, and he could spy no loiterers in the shadows. All seemed well, so perhaps he could now relax a little?

Nevertheless, the hairs on his neck still stood on end, and Jamie had learned over the years never to ignore that feeling of disquiet. With a last careful scan of the immediate area, Jamie followed Theresa indoors.

Roberts, her major-domo, held the door open as they and the footman entered.

"That's all for now, Michael." Roberts nodded at the young man, whom, Jamie estimated, wasn't yet out of his teens. "Off and get your supper." He waited until the young man disappeared behind the green baize door, and turned to Theresa. "Is all well, miss?"

"It will be once we've eaten," she said with a laugh. "His grace is stopping."

She didn't say how long for and Roberts didn't ask. "I'll let the appropriate people know, miss. Dinner will be about an hour, if that works for you?"

"Perfect, in the small dining room. I refuse to shout down three or four leaves when we can converse perfectly well if we are informal." She turned to Jamie. "Do you wish to freshen up? I'll have a bath later." She winked swiftly and he bit back a grin. He had very specific plans for her ablutions.

"But for now, as we will be informal, I think to wash my face and hands will do. If you agree?" she added.

"Perfect. For now."

* * * *

"If we splash and soak the floorboards I will be mortified," Theresa told Jamie as she leaned back so she rested on his chest in the bath. She had pinned her hair high and he was amused to see that, as ever, it was already escaping the confines of those pins. He guessed she usually put it over the edge of the bath, but with them sharing the tub, that was not possible this time.

He reveled in the way she was so at ease, with his long legs either side of her and his cock pressed against the top of her bottom. Her nipples almost seemed to bob up and down in the water, and every so often she lifted one foot to swirl the rose petals scattered on the surface.

"It is one thing for the servants to guess what we are doing, another for them to know for sure," she said, languid and at ease, and blew wisps of hair off her face.

"I think asking for plenty of water and towels might be a giveaway," Jamie remarked. He soaped her shoulders and breasts with one hand. "And me smelling like a cottage garden or adding not to bother to fill mine could have been another." Somehow he managed to hold a glass to her mouth. "Sip and savor." She did as he requested.

"What about you?" Theresa asked him once he set the glass down again. "We are to share and share alike, remember?"

"Oh I'm going to sip and savor later," Jamie assured her. "Although in my case it's you I will be enjoying." He rubbed the soap between her legs. "We have a lot to thank Andrew Pears for. The scent of this soap reminds me of you."

"Soapy?"

"If you want." Jamie nuzzled the top of her head. "I was thinking more along the lines of flowery myself. Pretty, pleasant, heady and sweetly perfumed. A teasing, mysterious mixture, just like you." He dropped the soap and used his fingers to trace the outline of her nether lips, delicately slid one digit inside her and cupped her mound with his palm.

Theresa mewled and bucked up into his hand. Water sloshed dangerously near the rim of the bath and Jamie chuckled. "Careful, love. Who was it who was concerned about soaking the floor?"

"Ah, but I didn't know what you were going to do then," she gasped. "And I cannot ignore what you are doing to me."

"Then, as I intend to do a lot more of the like, we had

better get out." He leaned her forward and stood. Water streamed off him. Theresa chose that moment to look up at him and squealed as droplets rained down on her.

"Ugh, that hit my nose. And it is cold." Which was strange as the water she still sat in was the opposite.

"Then you best get out and get warm." Jamie climbed out of the tub and wrapped a towel around his waist before he helped Theresa to her feet. "This will get you warm." He took another towel from the pile and tucked it around her shoulders. "Or pre-warm. The actuality I reserve for myself."

She looked startled then speculative before she licked her lips in one long sensual sweep of her tongue. "*Brrrr*, I am *so* cold." She shivered then spoiled her exaggerated gesture by sniggering. "Soooooo cold. Now you know once more why I chose not to go on the stage. Any of my acting has been reserved for pumping up men's egos... Oh lord. What a crass thing to say. You do know I do not mean you, don't you?"

"Oh yes." Jamie purred the words into her ear as he began to dry her body in long arousing caresses. "Just as I would never speak anything but the truth to you. But, my love, I comprehend what you mean. It is not exclusive to you." He patted the still damp ends of her hair, picked up a dry sheet of linen and wound that around her toga style. As he drew her out of the bathing chamber, he continued his conversation. "I have in the past employed similar tactics to get myself out of a situation that otherwise would perhaps not make my companion feel comfortable about herself. I'm not in the business of making ladies feel they are not up to scratch."

Theresa wrinkled her nose. "Boxing cant, but I understand what you are saying. For myself though, I know if I do not do something as I should I want you will tell me. You will, *won't you?*"

He tapped her bottom. "We both will, but so far, I can think of nothing you could do I would not enjoy. Shall we go and see?"

"Now that, my lord, is one of your better ideas." She stood on tiptoe and wound her arms around his neck, pulled his head down closer to her own and pressed her lips over his.

His towel slipped unheeded down his hips to land in a heap around his feet. All his blood moved downward until his cock made its presence noticed in a most insistent way. By springing up and teasing her belly.

Jamie slid his tongue between Theresa's lips, nipped the soft flesh and leaned back a little to tug her towel away and let it drop to the floor. She swayed and he took advantage to bring her closer to him so their bodies touched at every possible opportunity. Every nerve stretched to its limits as her scent surrounded him.

"Bed," she muttered then she tore her mouth away. "Easier."

"Later," Jamie murmured while he nipped his way down her shoulder, bent her backward and took one hard nipple in his mouth and sucked. "I want you here." He lifted her and walked across the room to put her down in front of the long mirror next to her dresser. "If we were in the country, in my rooms, I'd stand you in front of the window so you could see us reflected in the glass. And take you from behind. Then take you in the summerhouse as you stood and looked over the lake. By the lake, in the woods... But here, we use the mirror. Watch me take you here."

His hopes were realized when Theresa leaned back on him and stared misty eyed at the glass in front of them. "See how well we look together," Jamie said softly once he stood behind her and circled his waist with his arms, one hand lower to almost reach her feminine core. As he often did, he rested his chin on the top of her head. "You reach up to my heart."

Chapter Ten

Such a simple thing to say, but such a magical thing to hear. Theresa stared at their reflections in the mirror. Lit by candles and not lamps, they were mere shadows and outlines with light and dark to show who they were and how they touched. His hair-sprinkled arms, dark from when he'd toiled outdoors with his estate staff, stood out next to her milky skin. The way one long finger stroked the dark shadow of the curls that hid her quim created patterns on the ceiling that shifted and reformed as he worked his magic. For once she was glad she had let those particular hairs grow again after she had given up her profession.

With their heads together there was no indication of where the long, raven tresses that covered her scalp ended and his shorter but no lighter ones began.

Jamie kissed the top of her head as he slid one hand lower. So he could play with every inch of her body?

Oh yes.

"Now watch," he said in a quiet voice, but with a hint of command. "Watch and enjoy us together."

He moved his other hand to tweak one nipple, alternating a stroke and a pinch until that invisible cord that stretched from her breasts to her core sang. He slid two fingers inside her and began to scissor them. Theresa sighed, groaned under her breath and panted before she leaned on him heavily and closed her eyes to savor every tiny nuance.

"Open your eyes, love, and watch." She moaned but did as he asked, thrilled at the sight of his powerful legs and thighs as they showed on either side of her softer, more feminine ones.

Cradling her, embracing her, keeping her safe.

Over her head, his face was partially in shadow but she could see his eyes. Dark sparkling pools, both watchful and tender.

"See the rosy hue...or the shadow that if it were illuminated would be rosy," he said in an undertone. "Watch as you embrace my touch."

Her breath sped up. His words, uttered in a low growl, were as much an aphrodisiac as the finest wine. Theresa sighed once more as her body tingled and she stirred restlessly against him. His staff stroked her rear, and she pushed her arms between them to cup that silky soft hardness. She loved how his body responded instantly to her touch. Already liquid gathered on the tip and she ached to lick it. But this, she reminded herself, was Jamie's directive.

This time.

Jamie used his clever hands to touch, tease and entice her senses as he stroked, nipped and caressed her breasts, her curves and her cunt. His chin made those teasing circles on her scalp that she both loved and hated. Being able to watch him caress her sent sharp stabs of arousal through Theresa. Fiercely she tried to shuffle sideways to face him. She wanted to return the favor but he held her firm.

"You've stopped watching, love."

"I want to watch you as well," she said desperate to see as his nails scraped over her nub in a touch so full of pleasure it was just short of pain. "I want to..."

"You will. Later. Now where were we?" He turned her around to once more face the mirror. "Enjoy this, it is so arousing to see you watch me watching you as I touch you. Caress you and bring you to the edge." His fingers moved inside her and on her breasts and her inner muscles contracted.

"Oh, so wet for me, love," he said, husky with emotion. "Spread your legs, yes, like that."

It seemed, Theresa thought hazily, that she'd obeyed and

159

not even realized.

"Are you watching?" he asked.

She nodded and his chuckles reverberated through her. "Oh God, do not stop. Now let me...ah...yes..."

Enthralled, Theresa kept her eyes on the glass and saw Jamie bend his knees, guide his cock between her thighs and very carefully put the tip inside her. That sight was enough for her to bend forward to give him better access.

"Don't stop watching us."

"I won't, but I want...oh, please—"

"So do I, love, so do I." Jamie entered her another inch. Then another. "Shall we fly, love? Keep your gaze forward, watch us...watch us... Now." He thrust hard and set up a bucking, furious movement that she caught and matched. It was hard to stay upright and be equal.

"Hold on to the wall."

Could he read her mind? Whatever, willingly, Theresa let herself fall forward a little to put her palms flat on the wallpaper to get a better stance. Her hair swayed around her and let her breast play peekaboo. Whenever had her nipples stood out so proudly, or the nerve between her legs throbbed so hard with anticipation? Her body was so on edge, one touch and she would scream.

She bit her lip and concentrated on every emotion, every tiny feeling and waited...waited until she had no idea where she was or where her body ended and Jamie's began.

It was not for many moments.

"Now." Jamie groaned, stiffened and pulled out of her just as she screamed her completion, stuffed one hand in her mouth to muffle her shouts and joined him in that spinning vortex of ecstasy.

Oh my, am I still alive?

Jamie slumped against Theresa, took a deep breath and half carried her, half dragged her to fall onto the bed. It was a long time before any other sounds joined those of their harsh, uneven breathing. Eventually Jamie stirred and lifted himself onto one elbow. Theresa rolled over onto her stomach before she peeped at him over her shoulder then took a deep breath.

"Am I alive?" she said in a voice she wasn't sure belonged to her. "I just wondered." For that matter she wasn't sure of anything anymore. She who had been a teacher had never ever experienced anything before like those last few minutes. Somehow that pleased her. It was special to both of them, and them alone. She refused to think that, although of course it was nothing new to Jamie, or how else would he be so proficient? To *her* it was something new, and anyway, she reasoned, it was something new to him to make love in that manner to *her*.

"Alive? I'm not sure. Hold on." Jamie nipped one plump globe of her rear and she squealed. "Yes," he said with a lilt in his voice. "I can confirm you are indeed alive."

He gathered her into his arms and she went gladly to rest her head on his chest and play with the whorls of dark hair that covered it and arrowed downward.

The candles flickered and their silhouettes showed large and dark on the pale wall across the room. "This is different," she said. "New and amazing."

"And good?"

Did he sound a little concerned? She rushed to put his mind at rest. "More than. I am rejoicing in every new thing I learn, and believe me there are many."

His arm tightened around her. "As am I, and for the first time ever, I'm loth to get up and clean up. At the risk once more of improper comments, I do not usually like to linger. With you it is different. I want to stay here with you and hold you tight to me. It is our protection against the world."

"Then don't. Move, I mean. A little bit of sticky will not kill us and anyway..." Theresa hesitated. To be crude or not? "You pulled out," she finished.

"True," Jamie said. "Even so. Ah well, the floor will be sticky, so remind me to do something tomorrow with it so you won't have to bother your staff."

She forbade to say that in her previous profession the staff had on occasion had to deal with worse than seed on the floorboards. That was then, not now, and to be honest she appreciated his thoughtfulness.

"Later," she said instead. "Snuggle and sleep first."

* * * *

A most annoying and persistent sound reverberated through his skull. Jamie sat up abruptly as he sadly left his erotic dream about Theresa and himself, a deep bath and some cream, and fought off the veils of sleep that held him in their thrall. The noise registered as something unwanted. He heard shouts and swearing, then the sound of running feet. He swore and removed the pillow he cuddled.

The pillow swore and morphed into Theresa as Jamie flung back the covers and cold air hit him. "Bloody hell."

"Wha…"

"Breaking glass," he said in a terse voice. "Somewhere downstairs I think." A door slammed and the running feet got louder. "Light a lamp if you can, love, while I dress and investigate." He got out of bed, winced as his warm feet hit cold floorboards then fumbled his way to the window to open the shutters and let some moonlight in.

Someone thumped on the door that led to the hall. The candle flared and Theresa struggled into a robe. "Shall I?" She gestured to the door.

"Give me a second." Jamie tugged on his pantaloons and gave thanks for their stretchy knit. "I do not want to shock your staff more than necessary."

"They will be shocked anyway. I have never had a man in this room." Theresa knotted her gown and thrust her feet into a pair of embroidered slippers.

"Never?" Jamie found his shirt—what on earth was it doing draped over the tallboy?—and tried to thrust his head and arms through wrong openings. He swore, tried again, and this time succeeded. "What about…oh, no time." The knock came again. "Right, love. Open it and let us see what has happened." He worked his hessians onto his feet and up his legs as he spoke.

"Never anyone else in here except me and now you. My haven. I used elsewhere for tuition, and no one ever stopped overnight," Theresa said before she flung open her door.

Mrs. Penicuik stood there resplendent in a voluminous dressing gown and her hair in rags. She was an awesome sight. The cook took one swift glance at Jamie and sighed with relief. "Thank the lord you are here, my lord." She didn't appear fazed at his appearance. "What a to-do."

"What?" Theresa grabbed her arm. "What has happened? Who is hurt?"

"The dining room window was smashed, miss. Frost gave chase, and Dobson went down the mews and checked all was well there. Mr. Roberts wants to know what he should do, miss."

She glanced at Jamie. He had no intention of giving his opinion until Theresa asked for it. Luckily she did immediately.

"Jamie?"

If Mrs. Penicuik noted the informality she gave no sign. Although considering the circumstances she had found them in, it would probably have caused more conjecture if Theresa had addressed him formally.

"You and Mrs. Penicuik dress and get anything ready we might need," he said in a hurry while he went over every possible scenario in his mind and a few impossible ones as well.

"Brandy and bandages?" Theresa said, ever practical. "Hot water and clean cloths."

Jamie nodded. "Something like that. I'll take whoever gets back first and go for a scout around." He picked up his jacket as Mrs. Penicuik curtsied and departed, closing the door after her. "I wish I had my pistol," he added. "Somehow I didn't expect to need it."

Theresa considered him as she dropped her robe on the floor. Her body gleamed in the candlelight, and he regretfully told his half-erect cock that it was not the time or the place to stretch his pantaloons.

"One moment." She rummaged in the top drawer of a walnut bureau and produced a key. "Cupboard to the right of the fire in the library. Help yourself."

Jamie took the key and nodded with relief. "Thank you. I'll be back as soon as I can be."

He clattered down the stairs just as Dobson shot from the servants' corridor like a bullet out of a rifle. "My lord? What on earth is going on?" he asked. The poor man's breath came out in short, harsh pants, his hair was on end, his shirt tails untucked and his jacket buttons done up wrongly. "There's no one around in the mews. Where are the men?"

"I was going to ask you that. Something is gravely wrong. Follow me." Jamie walked without undue haste, but with an economy of effort to the library and unlocked the cupboard Theresa had mentioned. He glanced at Dobson and trusted he would do as he was asked. "Can you shoot a pistol?"

"Eh?" Dobson blinked and a slow grin lit up his face. "Oh yes, I learned as a lad in the country. I can hit a pheasant on the wing."

"Good." Jamie handed him a weapon and found one for himself before he relocked the cupboard and pocketed the key. "Let's hope you can wing an undesirable likewise. Now then, where's Frost?"

"I don't know, my lord." Dobson sounded worried. "We went in different directions, acos he can run faster than I can. He's maybe back in the hall by now."

However, when they entered the hall, although it seemed full of people, none of them were Frost. Dobson cast a worried glance in Jamie's direction. It was obvious the man shared Jamie's own disquiet.

"Right," Jamie shouted over the clamor of everyone trying to voice an opinion at once. He caught Theresa's attention and raised one eyebrow in query. She nodded infinitesimally. It was a relief. "Roberts?" He sought out the major-domo, who appeared from behind Mrs. Penicuik, who, now dressed, stood arms akimbo near the front door.

Roberts moved forward. "My lord?"

"Roberts, is Frost back yet?"

The man shook his head worriedly. "Not yet, my lord. I've popped my head out for a look several times and the square seems empty."

That was what Jamie had been afraid of. "Then you check that the house is secure. Miss Theresa will be in charge in here, of course. Do you have someone who can patrol the garden and the rear of the house?"

Roberts looked toward Theresa. She smiled. "His lordship knows more than I about how to conduct these things. Do as he decrees."

He smiled the smile of a man relived to have someone else take charge. "Whatever you say, miss, my lord, I'll do whatever you think fit."

"Then maybe a couple of the sturdier footmen in the gardens and Bill the boots could go and ask the grooms to keep an eye on the mews?" Jamie suggested.

"Ah, I'd do that and nobudy'd see me," Bill said. "Anything for you, miss."

"I'll leave it up to you both then and take Dobson to do a scout around the square," Jamie said. There was no need to waste words or time explaining each little thing to be done. The men understood. "If we are not back in thirty minutes, send someone who can move in a hurry to my house and tell them we need reinforcements. Damn, I need paper. Whoever answers the door will know who to send and what to do."

"Here." Somehow Theresa had found some strips of paper in a small book and a pencil. Jamie looked at the tiny tablet and his dark mood lightened a little. "A dance card?"

She grinned. "For, ahem, work."

Now he understood. So many young men were ignorant in the etiquette of dancing at a ball. "Not any longer," he muttered as he scribbled a few lines and handed it to Roberts. "Let's hope we don't need it in any manner or form."

Roberts took the note and tucked it in his pocket. "My lord, if I might suggest a less…er, pristine jacket?"

"What?" Jamie looked at his attire. Probably not the best to go chasing a villain in. It shrieked 'ton'. However, what other choice did he have? "It will have to do."

"Put this one on." Theresa handed him a homespun. He hadn't even noticed her leave the hall and return. "It's the gardener's but it's warm, thick and is a better shield against knives. Not only that, you look less like a toff."

To be honest, he wasn't sure a threadbare homespun jacket would be any more protection than his own, but he appreciated the 'less like a toff' argument. Jamie struggled out of one garment and into the other. "Right, let's go."

* * * *

"How long is that now, Roberts?" Theresa appealed to her major-domo, who glanced at the clock with an expression of doom. It took all of her patience not to snap at him to look less worried. She had enough fear already without any encouragement. But she knew Roberts was concerned, and in a perverse way that helped her cope with the waiting. For the first ten minutes or so it had been all hustle and bustle but now everything was in place she had time to fret. The rest of the staff had dispersed to go about the various duties they had been directed to do. Mrs. Penicuik and two of the kitchen maids were preparing a simple, but in her words, filling supper. For as that redoubtable lady had said fiercely, they would all need sustenance after the bastards had been caught and handed over to the authorities.

Roberts coughed and brought her out of her musings. "Only fifteen minutes, miss. Hardly time to do once around the square if they are checking things. And — What's that?"

Theresa cocked her head and thought she could discern a faint shout. "Is it — ?" She didn't get to finish her sentence.

"Hold on, miss." He darted for the front door and flung

it open. "Oh my goodness." Roberts disappeared down the steps at a fast pace.

Theresa took three steps forward and grabbed onto the back of the nearest chair for support. Two men appeared, carrying a third. For one awful moment she thought it was Jamie who was carefully deposited on the hall settle. Her pulse accelerated, a large lump of dread lodged in her throat and the world went dark.

It is not, it cannot be. Breathe and look. Theresa opened her eyes and common sense reasserted itself. She saw it was Frost who held one hand to his head and moaned and Jamie was the person who straightened up and smiled at her reassuringly.

"Hit on the head. Northing much to worry about, he's got a hard skull. Plus, there's a nugget the size of a duck's egg on there and he'll have an almighty headache, but apart from that, all is well. No broken bones, but sadly no sight of his assailant."

"Talked like Kimmie, miss." Frost's voice was low and uneven. "I swear it could've been her brother, 'cepting she ain't got none."

"Kimmie?" Jamie queried. "Which one was Kimmie?"

"A maid," Theresa explained. "She hails from Devon. Are you sure, Frost?"

"Aye, miss. Caught me from behind, he did, but I heard him say that was '*un of us varmints gone*'. The bu...blister. I didn't have a chance. I were following another un and this un crept up ahind me. Never heard him." He sounded disgusted with himself. "Played for a right one I was. Never heard a blooming thing."

"You wouldn't have," Jamie said reassuringly. "They enacted a clever game. Experts, both of them. Now, before Mrs. Penicuik tends to you, do you remember anything else? Did they say why you, why here or who sent them? Any clues as to what was supposed to happen next?"

Frost scrunched up his face in concentration and went pale. Theresa felt sorry for the lad. He had been battered, bruised and interrogated all in a few moments, and she bit back the demand that Jamie leave him be. She knew Jamie had to ask the questions, and Frost wouldn't be very happy if she intervened. To her it was obvious that in Frost's eyes, Jamie understood the servant would feel less a man and unfit to work for Theresa if she did so and Jamie knew that was not at all what she intended. She was sure he would set her mind at rest later, when they were on their own, that she had done the correct thing. However at that moment it was not up to her to comment further.

"I think," Frost said in a slow and ponderous manner, as if he was choosing his words with care. "but I can't be sure, mind, that I heard sommat about how the dishonourable pisser, Percy was up to his tricks again, but I wouldn't swear on the Bible."

"You wouldn't need to," Jamie said. "That is enough for me. Right, if Miss Theresa has nothing to add, off you go and get sorted out."

Theresa shook her head. "I've nothing to say except thank you, and you are not to report for duty until the doctor has been tomorrow, Frost. Unless you think we need him now?" she asked Jamie. She appeared worried and he hurried to reassure her.

"No, not unless you get double vision, Frost, and then you come and get me. Do you understand?"

Frost nodded gingerly. "Ah, but I reckon I'll be fine."

"I'll keep a glad eye on him," Dobson said as he helped his friend to his feet. "I'll take him up now and then get us a bite, shall I?"

Theresa inclined her head. What was the world coming to? She gave thanks that Jamie was about. She could have and would have managed but, she allowed, it was so good to have someone else to aid her. It had been a long while since she could say that.

Jamie stood beside her silently, obviously deep in thought, while Roberts locked up. The major-domo swung the large key between his thumb and forefinger then put it on a high shelf to one side of the door before he shot the bolt with a loud scraping noise and turned to Jamie.

"What shall I do about the men outside, my lord?" he inquired with an apologetic glance toward Theresa. "Bill the boots says the grooms are going to take turns to patrol the stables and the mews. I've two men in the gardens and two to give them a spell later. Is there anything else I should do?"

"Go to bed and sleep," Jamie said with a smile. "Tomorrow we're all going to be busy."

Jamie waited until the hall was empty except for him and Theresa and held out his arms to her. She sighed long and deeply, entered inside their circle and grabbed him tightly. He held her close to him and kissed the top of her head. "All right, love?"

"Why do you always do that?" she asked in a curious tone. "Kiss my head?"

"Because it's often the only place I can reach with ease when I don't want to move you," Jamie replied and grinned. "And I needed to hug you and kiss you, and remind myself you are safe and well." *And that this is not a game, or just to thwart certain people, it is our lives, and hopefully our future.*

"Fair enough." She tilted her head up, stood on her toes and kissed his chin. "There, that's almost where I want it to be." Theresa sniggered. "Or I could get on my knees and reach the other place I want to take into my mouth."

That place went from soft to hard in a second.

"But perhaps not in the hall," she added with a laugh.

He winked. "Maybe not, and as much as I'd like to say to be continued upstairs, I think, judging by the hour, we'd better sleep, not play."

Theresa's face fell. "Damn it, really?"

Jamie stroked her cheek and pinched it gently. "Yes, really. I worry what tomorrow may bring, and we both need to have all our wits about us."

"I suspect you are right. Come on then." She slipped under his arms and took his hand. "Last one ready for bed blows the lamp out."

* * * *

It was not the same, going to the theater without Jamie by her side. *I'm getting soft.* Theresa glanced at Maria and sighed. "Why, when after years of plowing my own furrow, does it now seem strange to do so? As much as I am glad to have the chance to enjoy an evening with you, I wish Jamie were around to meet us as we leave. But he is busy showing face at a card game and trying to hunt out news. He offered to meet us, I said no and will meet him later. Now I wonder if I am a fool."

Maria patted her arm. "Propinquity doesn't come into it at all, does it? Perhaps this is all part of you moving on, and moving on alone no longer holds any appeal."

"Perhaps," Theresa said doubtfully. "Or is it just that the play is boring? After all, you didn't seem enamoured either." She looked at the now empty stage and the chattering hoards who streamed toward the exits of the theater. "Nor did they, judging by the sounds of disinterest and the boos. I must admit I agree with them, although it was getting embarrassing."

Maria laughed. "Oh I know. And as for the snores of the gentleman in the next box? I thought his companion would have an apoplexy. How loud were they?"

"Lord Stowe," Theresa said with a snort. "He always does that, but not usually quite so early in the proceedings."

"I think tonight it was acceptable. To be honest, I would normally say any visit to the theater is a treat," Maria confessed. "But the greatest treat tonight was the champagne. That was of the finest quality, but sadly I agree the acting was not."

They made their way out of the box and along the corridor to join the now thinning crowd in the foyer. "I have the itch," Theresa said under her breath. "The nasty something-is-about-to-happen itch."

"The one where poisonous Percy appears?" Maria asked as she put her hand on Theresa's waist and turned her to look slightly to their right. "Because he is near the far door."

"Damn." She should have agreed to let Jamie meet them. It served her right for trying to show she was independent. Now she accepted she was not.

"Exactly my thought," Maria said in an undertone. "What do you want to do?"

Theresa thought fast. "My carriage will be there and so will the coachmen. We'll head past him. Surely he won't cause a scene or try anything with so many people about?" Or so she hoped. However with Percy, Theresa was rapidly coming to accept nothing was certain. "If he does, I'll create a scene of my own. It will embarrass him much more than it will me. You might want to take a step or two back just in case. I would not want to hurt your business."

"I will not move back one inch," Maria said and let her indignance show. "I am a better friend than that."

"Then come on, better friend than that, let us go." Theresa linked her arm with Maria's and strode forward. Out of the corner of her eye she watched Percy take a step forward and block their passage. "Leave him to me," she said in an undertone to Maria, who hesitated and finally nodded.

"Excuse me." She glared at Percy. "You are in my way."

"I need to talk to you," Percy said and put his hand on her arm. "Now."

Theresa stared at him and hoped all the contempt she felt for him and his actions was reflected in her expression. "Remove your hand before I call someone in authority. You, sir, are blocking my path." Theresa spoke clearly and watched several people turn to see what the commotion was all about.

Percy hesitated and dropped his arm. "Please let me explain. You must listen. My godfather—"

"Is not you." Theresa had had enough. She sidestepped him and, followed by Maria, found her carriage.

By the time they had dropped Maria at her home, Theresa

had reiterated for the fourth time that she was fine alone for the last ten minutes of the journey because her footmen were armed. Plus once she reached home, Roberts and the house staff would be on high alert, and if Jamie was not waiting he shouldn't be long. Theresa was tired.

Even so, as the coach drew up and a footman descended the steps to open the door the itch was back.

Sure enough, as she reached the bottom stair, Percy exploded up the area steps and grabbed her hand. "You must let me speak to you, my...er, Miss Kyle. Please, you must. I will not do anything untoward, I promise. Hell, you can have a maid with you but please, give me a mere fifteen minutes of your time."

Theresa regarded him stonily in the light of the doorside sconces. He didn't appear penitent, more bombastic. The manic gleam in his eyes sent goosebumps skittering over her skin and she wanted nothing more than to rub her arms to dispel them.

"Tomorrow," she said at last. "Around five. You may have ten minutes, that is all."

He scowled. "But..."

Theresa tapped her foot. Next to her the footman hovered, ready to intervene if necessary. "That is it, take it or leave it."

"Oh I'll take it and so will you. You best make sure you're ready for me, for it will be you who comes off worse if you do not take heed of what I have to say," Percy said menacingly.

"Miss, may I sling him away?" the footman asked. "'Twould be easy."

She laughed. "Not this time, James. He is going, aren't you, Percy?" Not for anything would she let him see how much he worried her. If only Jamie would appear. Of course, wishing didn't work. However, Theresa very deliberately let the butt of her pistol show out of the side of her muff. Percy stared at it and took one step backward, then another.

"Tomorrow." He spun on his heel and walked rapidly

along the side of the square and into the adjoining street.

"Good riddance," Theresa said, in a much more cheerful way than she felt as she watched him disappear around the corner. "Now supper, I think. I'm ready for it." She wasn't sure she could swallow food, but she was not going to share *that* tidbit with her staff. They were worried enough as it was.

She hoped Jamie wasn't going to be too long. She wanted him with his arms around her. Preferably in bed together.

Chapter Eleven

"And that is the story so far." Theresa stood still as Maria nipped, pinned and tucked the pretty unusual material around her and talked under her breath as she did so. "Jamie arrived after midnight, heard me out and muttered things along the line of enough is enough. Told me he hoped to be back before bloody Percy arrived and set off before it was full light.

"As far as I can gather, he's gone out of town to speak to someone in St. Albans who might be able to shed some light on why Percy is so adamant he needs me or whatever. A friend of a crony's cousin or some such thing. Jamie was a bit vague there and refused to name names."

"He can be as tight as a duck's arse when need be," Maria said with a twinkle in her eye. "More than either of his brothers, and they are both bad enough. Once a Weston has shut his lips on a secret, you'll not prise them open in a hurry. Not unless they want you to."

"Well, he told me that this is, sadly, not something to share. That it was only something he could do but if he discovered it was fit for my ears he would share when he had whatever it was confirmed. He insisted that if it proved true it would show someone in a very bad light. I presume he meant Percy, but I can't imagine anything that would show him as worse than he is already. I didn't like to say that there is very little not fit for my ears." She looked at her reflection in the mirror with critical eyes. "Hmm. I'm pale but I do like this color. Now where was I? Oh yes. Frost has a black eye none of us noticed before, and a headache to end all headaches. Dobson woke him every hour to check he was fine so neither of them are fit for work today. Mrs. Penicuik has hunted out the biggest, heaviest rolling pin I have ever seen, and is hefting it about with her wherever she goes. She says her pistols need to be elsewhere. Roberts has men all over the place who pop up just where you do not expect them and almost give you a heart attack. Heavens, I double-checked every nook and cranny in my bathing chamber and made sure the shutters and doors were locked before I dared use the commode. Even then I tried to 'go' quietly." She laughed. "That apart, the staff are jumping at the slightest sound. I was glad to come here for sense, silence and sanity. At the moment everyone is falling over themselves to be the person with me when Percy appears, so even if Jamie is not back I will be protected at all times. The last thing I heard was one intended to be in the room with me and two more would be hidden in closets and the servants' corridor. So sanity please, and I wish to ask your opinion."

"Mmm?" Maria added one last pin to the hem of the garment she was fussing with and removed the other three pins from between her lips. "Opinion on what?"

"Oh, this and that." Theresa turned from one direction to another to look at herself in the mirror. "You are so clever, this is perfect." The teasing hints of body that showed as the material swirled over her, she hoped, would arouse and please Jamie. "Do you think Jamie really is interested in me, or just in foiling his mother?" She waited anxiously for Maria's reply. She could think of no one more able to give her an honest answer.

Maria stood and stretched. "Are you really interested in him, or is it just to foil Percy?"

Touché.

"Oh I'm interested," Theresa said honestly as she let Maria help her out of the half-made night-rail. "Very much so, and I can tell you, it is a surprise to me. I cannot imagine life without him now, which if I am merely a convenience will be a hard thing to overcome."

"You're not," Maria said with a twinkle." I could have told you that, even if not five hours ago Jamie hadn't asked me the same questions with regards to you and given me the same responses on his behalf. I did tell him there was no need to invade my breakfast over it. Or drink my coffee and eat my pastries. Which I must point out he did all three of. He didn't even blink at my attire."

"Roses and voile?" Theresa knew what Maria chose to sleep in. A bit like herself. Why be frumpish just because you slept alone?

"Of course."

"He'd already had his breakfast before he left," Theresa said. "Typical man."

"Well, maybe he doesn't want to break off from whatever he is doing to eat lunch."

"Maybe. And maybe he just decided to eat because it was there."

Maria laughed. "You could be correct. Men do tend to think with their stomachs, don't they, unless it is with their cock. Or so I'm told."

Theresa raised her eyebrows skeptically. "Sparkly shoes?"

Maria colored. "Yes, well." She bent her head to fold up the half-made garment and her hair fell forward to hide her face.

"This material?" Theresa gave her friend a break. "It is amazing."

"I intend for the dress to shock, entice and draw in Jamie. If it does that, it is all worth it. After all, backless, long sleeves and contours such as it has? If he is not enthralled he is less a man than I had thought."

"Perfect. I can ask for nothing else. It is beautiful and I thank you." Theresa decided not to tease her anymore. It wasn't fair, and Maria had been very careful not to do that very thing to her. "That apart, we need to discuss Percy. I've been thinking about the way he performs — or doesn't."

"And now you wonder if he prefers men?"

"Why yes," Theresa said in amazement as she sat with

a thump in a nearby chair. "But why do you say that?" It had been an idea that had been growing over the last few months. If he did she had no problems with it. As long as he left her alone. "I mean, he was never enthused, but at first I put that down to the fact he felt belittled at being coerced to come to me. Then I got thinking. So you?"

"Gossip," Maria replied matter-of-factly. "All very nebulous but even so, enough to make me wonder."

"I also have wondered more just lately," Theresa said. "The more I pondered, the more so many things added up. His lack of interest, lack of real effort. The way he was so secretive and… Oh well, lots of little things. He always seemed to be going through the motions, no more. Poor man, if it is so that he prefers his own sex, his life will not be easy. I then wondered if he were being blackmailed and that was why he was targeting me."

"To be fair, he did his best to make yours not easy as well," Maria pointed out with a snap to her words. "But marriage?"

"An even better façade I suspect," Theresa said. "Percy's family is very straight-laced and he, well, he as far as I believe, hates confrontation. It is unfair, and all too common. None of us can help what we are. However, if he is that way inclined, I haven't heard any rumors, and I would have. Well, I would have back then. It could well be something else that his family would not approve of. Don't ask me what, I do not have a clue."

"Nor I."

"But, let's be honest, I know, and I suspect you do too, of several gentlemen who only married to look as if they conform to what is acceptable in their world — for whatever reasons."

"Ohh. Who? Do tell?" Maria fluttered her eyelashes in a parody of one forward young lady who was fast making herself very unwelcome in many circles. "And what those reasons might be. I am sooo interested. Damn, I forgot the lisp."

Theresa burst out laughing. She was so glad she had Maria to confide in. "Maria, you are a minx, however not even for that oh so clever mimicry, lisp-less as it was, will I tell you that a younger son of a very noble family has used his elder brother's income to foster his own lifestyle and is about to be found out. Plus a certain gentlemen who your mimicked one has her eyes on has *his* eyes on that young lady's brother. If you understand me."

"Oh lord, what a mess," Maria said. "I wish people would just let live and do as they know is right for them. As long as it's not maiming or murder. So what do you think Percy is up to?"

Theresa shrugged. "To that I have no clue, more is the pity. All we can do is keep our ears open."

"And your wits about you," Maria said. "I admit, I'm not easy about him. Not at all. If rumors are abounding, he might do something stupid. I overheard something today which makes me very apprehensive. It seems he dipped deeply at La Gresham's gaming hell last week. Very deeply. And, well, he isn't overplump in the pocket, is he? Doesn't he rely on his godfather to sport the blunt for him?"

That was something Theresa was also very aware about. Percy was weak where cards were concerned. And also horse racing, cock fighting and anything else men would wager on. Was that partly behind all his demands?

When she left Maria, with Frost a mere two steps behind her, to her annoyance, Theresa couldn't help but check every passerby. Did this one look shady? Was that one following her? Had Frost stopped for a second to check someone out? It was ridiculous but Theresa accepted she could not help herself. Ah well, it would make a few pages of hopefully read-worthy interest in the book she intended to write one day.

An urchin with a pale and pinched face, bare feet and raggedy clothed dashed out from behind a market stall, almost tripped Theresa up and glared.

"Oi, missus, watch yerself." He stuck his tongue out at her

and made his way across the street and into the lane beyond. She jumped, took a step back and stumbled over an uneven cobble. The sensation of falling was most unpleasant, until Frost took those two steps forward to catch her.

"Careful, miss. His lordship wouldn't be best pleased if I let you take a tumble."

"I wouldn't be best pleased if I let myself," Theresa said with a laugh. "I was taken unawares by a tow-headed, mucky-faced bullet."

A stallholder puffed by, cussing as he ran, and Theresa bit back a grin. She might have nearly been run down by a barefoot, filthy opportunist thief, but as the stallholder slowed and retraced his steps, it seemed the child would eat well for one meal at least. It had looked like he'd held a pastry in one hand and an apple in the other.

"My, miss, I thought you were about to come a cropper then," Frost said as Theresa straightened and shook out her skirts. "Little blighter."

"Boys who are hungry will do what is necessary to assuage that hunger," Theresa said quietly as they continued on their way. "Some can do it with ease, others not so." Her mind flitted back to Jamie and his two breakfasts. Had he ever known what it was like to have that gnawing in his belly that some unfortunates did? Perhaps when he had been in the army? A lot of the stories that had filtered back from the various campaigns told of unbearable hardships at times. "Some end up across the world, some lose their lives. It all seems very unfair, but there is little I as a woman can do." Except employ as many people as possible.

"I guess I'm lucky," Frost said as they turned into Berkeley Square. "My ma, she had ten of us little uns, and we never went hungry. Not the best of foods, necessary, but allus filling. She were a dab hand at stretching a meal. Mind you, we were in the country, kept chickens and grew veg. Lord I hated some of it, but there you are, it filled a hole, as me ma said. We picked nettles for soup, blackberries for pies and everyone knew how to set a snare or hide from the gamekeeper."

Theresa chuckled. "I also had the sort of childhood you describe. Scrumping for apples?"

Frost nodded. "Me dad gave us a hiding for that, mind you. Said it were taking food from people as no better off than we were."

"We were both lucky, I think," Theresa said soberly. "And had proper behavior instilled—or thrashed into us." On cue her scars throbbed. *And, scars apart, I still am lucky.* She remembered the day Jamie had seen them and traced them gently. He hadn't said much. Just kissed them tenderly and, later, spoken pensively. *'Parents sometimes have a lot to answer for.'* That had been all, but she knew he cared deeply. He would never do such a thing, that she was certain of.

"Er, miss?" Frost's hesitant voice broke into her reverie. "There's that honorable bloke you told us to keep our eyes open for. Percy Whatsit."

"What? Where?" Theresa did her best to scan the area without moving her head. "Oh tarnation, I cannot see him."

"Over t'other side of the square, miss. Skulking by the hedge. Now he's coming over. What do you want me to do?"

Theresa spotted Percy. Damn him to hell and back. "Stay close and listen first, rather than speak or intervene. Then do the whistle if need be."

Frost looked startled. "You know about that?"

His astonishment lightened the tension, just for a second. "Oh, Frost, when will you men learn? We women know about everything. We just don't always choose to let on. Come on, time for us to accost him. We will take the initiative now, not him."

* * * *

The last thing Jamie wanted when he arrived home, saddle sore and weary after a long and less than fruitful trip, was to be met with the news that his brother was waiting to see him.

"Been here over two hours he has, my lord," his general factotum said as he helped Jamie off with his driving coat. "His grace said he would wait all night if necessary. Refused food but accepted a brandy. He's in the library."

Jamie sighed and nodded. "If he's been here that long he can wait another five minutes so I can wash some of the road grime away. I refuse to meet my no doubt sartorially elegant brother looking like I've been pulled through a hedge backward. Inform him I will join him within a few moments." He nodded at the footman who hovered nearby. "That is all."

He took the stairs two at a time and entered his bedchamber in less than a good mood. Trust Martin to waylay him like this. Jamie was in no doubt what he was there about. He'd meant to visit Martin and explain about the necklace, and why Theresa was now wearing it. Also he had intended to make it clear that he had no intention of asking for it back. What with all the to-ings and fro-ings with regards to Percy it had slipped his mind. Now he had a lot of explaining to do. To someone he suspected would not be easily placated. Martin took his position as head of the duchy very seriously. As he should, but sometimes...

Oh well, wishing wouldn't change anything. Jamie undressed quickly, for once welcoming the help of his valet, and redressed in a clean shirt and breeches. There was no time for more and he decided as he put house shoes on, why should he? It was his house and the only place he had to be was Theresa's. That appointment had no set time. Indeed, she had given him a door key in case he was late. The trust that showed meant more to him than she would ever know.

He descended the staircase as fast as he deemed safe. As he opened the library door and shut it behind him, Martin glanced up from the book he was studying and smiled. "Excellent brandy. I must ask for your source. However, a less than excellent book."

Jamie shrugged and peered at the title. "A friend of Thaw. I do not inquire too much. As for the book? It is no wonder, for it is a century out of date and full of irrelevances. I keep it for amusement, no more. Those on the lower shelf are more up to date."

Martin closed the book and put it down on a side table. "It was to pass the time until you turned up. I'm here to talk to you, not devour your library." He held his glass out. "But I'll happily help to lower the level in your decanter."

"I thought you might." Jamie took the proffered balloon and refilled it before attending to his own drink. When he finally sat at a right angle to his elder brother he was primed and ready to get his explanation in first.

"I have to apologize," Jamie began as he stretched his legs out to the fire. "I meant to call on you once I knew you were back in town, but circumstances overtook me."

"Such as the loss of Mama's necklace?"

Jamie grinned. So it seemed his brother didn't intend to tread softly. "The necklace Mama gave to me," he said matter-of-factly. "Last year. Which if you did not know she had done so, I am sorry. It is not entailed, or so she said. She intimated it was given to her by an admirer, before Papa — or is it since? I own, I am a bit hazy over those specifics. However, she told me to give it to the woman I intend to wed. I am sure she intended it to go to Marion Strawbridge."

Martin nodded. "And did you?"

Jamie raised one eyebrow as Martin's lips quirked.

"You know I did," he said equably. "You also know to whom I gave it. Theresa Kyle. You asked her about it."

"And she refused to say where she got it or from whom," Martin said. "For a while I was somewhat worried. Then I suppose you could say I came to my senses. I was damned sure Mama would not have given it to her, and equally sure if it had been stolen I would have known about it in no uncertain terms. Our parent is not one to lose any of her possessions. A little bit of research told me who Miss Kyle was. Freddie, I decided, wasn't old enough to know what to do with a courtesan, let alone give her a gift. Then I was told by no few than five people that you had either lost your senses or struck lucky — with the very same courtesan."

"Ex-courtesan."

Martin inclined his head. "I stand corrected. Ex-courtesan. Even so, I am sure you will agree I was entitled to be somewhat concerned. Now are you willing to explain?"

"Of course. It all started at a ball."

"When does it ever not?' Marin said as he sat back in his chair. "Go on, I'm ready to be entertained."

"One I attended to play cards, not dance attendance on any woman. I knew there would be a good card room set up, and if nothing else it would pass the evening pleasurably, and I assumed profitably, until my other skills could be used elsewhere."

"Well, naturally. What is unusual about that?" Martin retorted. "I would be both astonished and ask what ails you if it were otherwise." He smiled and his severe expression and the angular planes of his face softened and he became the brother Jamie remembered from their younger days. "Your skills in both areas are legendary."

"Are you telling this tale or am I?" Jamie scowled and asked mock-severely. "For if you want to, feel free. I will sit back and contemplate my navel."

"Oh, carry on with either," Martin said, affable as he could be when he chose. "I've had the day from hell so anything will be better than what I suffered. Mama, Persephone Bolsover who I almost called Bolster because she looks like one, and a leak in the roof of the townhouse. To say nothing of the new enclosed stove not heating to the chef's satisfaction, and over this past week several of the grand dames suggesting subtly and not so subtly that it was time I remarried and they knew just the person. If that was not enough, Leonard Fitchet has been a perfect pest and begged me to buy his chestnut."

"Not that bloody horse again?" Jamie said. "He's asked

everyone in the ton with no luck. It's a bolter and a biter."

"So I heard. Well, he got no luck from me either. Anyway, that's my life story up to date, how was your week?"

He couldn't help it. Jamie guffawed. "And I thought I had problems. At least it is only Mama and Lady Strawbridge doing their best to alter my marital status. Poor you and the bolster. How did you get round that?"

Martin snorted and reminded Jamie of the brother he had been before his loss. "Told Grosvenor to say that I was out and hid in my room. Unfortunately she found me with Mama in the park later and simpered. Simpered, for goodness' sake. I told Mama in no uncertain terms that if she dared meddle again my house would not be open to her."

"Well, she is not coming to mine," Jamie said with horror. "Can we purchase her one? Not too close to either of us."

"Oh do not worry. It's set in motion. Anyway, I interrupted. What else happened with you and Marion?"

"You would never believe it," Jamie said in a mocking way. "Or maybe you would. I decided our mothers went over the top at that bloody ball." He explained the locked-in-a-room scenario to Martin, and how Maria had come up with a solution. "And to my amazement, both I and Theresa said yes to it, and became the ton's latest on-dit."

"Is that all?"

Jamie shrugged. "No, but I have no idea how we progress from here. I couldn't give a tinker's damn about the ton or its archaic customs, but neither am I prepared to let Theresa be at the mercy of them or their proponents. It's a bugger, that's for sure. If I can't be with Theresa I won't be with anyone, leg shackled or not. However that's not all. Bloody Percy Prendergast has decided she should marry him and will not bow out gracefully. He's used most of the tricks in the book and I'm under no illusion that he won't try the rest before long."

"Prendergast? Old Luscott's heir? I thought he preferred men?"

Does everyone know that fact?

"He does. He's been with Peter Fitchet for years," Jamie replied. "And I suspect that is nothing to do with why he is annoying me and making Theresa's life hell. Hell is the word. To whit a gaming hell. He is badly, deeply in debt and has no way to pay, unless his godfather coughs up."

"What will that do? If he marries Old Luscott will help out?"

"Luscott is old school." Jamie nodded. "I have heard, and not from Theresa but from Luscott himself, that he asked Theresa to do her best with Percy. In Luscott's words, help the boy at least have a taste of a woman. It would, he told me, be good for him to be able to discourse knowledgeably about how it was to be between a woman's thighs. I imagine it wasn't an easy task for Theresa. Percy had always thought his ideas were the only ones that mattered."

"Poor woman." Obviously now Theresa's ex-employment was known to Martin, it didn't faze him. "I remember well how Florence said one of her friends told her in strict confidence that the Prendergast males were not renowned for size or staying power in the cock department," Martin went on. "They did their duty and no more, not even with the demi-monde."

"So now we probably know why." Jamie had a pang of pity for Percy. To be different wasn't easy and to prefer a man was a hard path to follow, even in these so-called 'more enlightened times'.

"Before our era, perhaps even before Papa's, but I have a feeling one of his ancestors fled to the continent with his male lover," Martin said. "Poor saps, life was no easier then than it is now for those who prefer a partner of their own sex. I thank god it is not for me."

Jamie looked at him speculatively and Martin shook his head with a laugh. "No, not even at Eton. I preferred the petticoats." He was silent for a moment. "Then I met Florence, and wanted only one petticoat."

"And now?" Jamie asked. The lost and forlorn expression

on his brother's face hit him hard. "What do you want now?"

Martin shrugged. "It is three years and I still mourn her— she was my love, the other part of me—but I accept life must go on. However, at my speed and in my direction, not anyone else's. Just, I suspect, like you."

"So what now?"

"Now," said a light, feminine voice, "I apologize for intruding, but your manservant told me you were both here, and well you are the two people I need to speak to the most. Or rather, my companion does. I have brought someone who wishes to address the pair of you."

Theresa stood in the doorway and moved to one side. "I think you will be interested in what he has to say." She turned and thrust a petulant-looking Percy into the room. "He, however, is not being very cooperative."

Percy scowled, narrowed-eyed and peevish, and glared at Jamie. "Why any of this had anything to do with you or your brother I have no idea. She made me come."

"She has a name," Jamie said. "I suggest you use it."

"Oh, Miss Kyle, then."

"Only partially true," Theresa said. "I suggest you repeat to his grace and his lordship what you said to me."

Percy firmed his lips.

"Or," Theresa added in a voice that sent chills down Jamie's spine. It obviously also affected Percy, who went as gray as the leaded sky outside. "Or, I might just take my gun out again and try and find your bollocks by blasting in the general direction of where they and your piteous prick should be."

Percy swayed and Theresa bit back a grin. Really, he was too pathetic to spend more than the minimum amount of time on. But, and there was the rub, he was becoming more than a pest to be brushed off with ease. He was an impediment to her future.

"Tell them what you said to me."

"It was in jest," he said. His desperate and wild glances around the room, along with the way his fingers twitched, showed how agitated he was. "A jape to annoy her. She is so sure of herself I wanted to take her down a peg or two." He gulped. "It seemed an excellent idea at the time."

It was a good thing the windows were fastened shut, Theresa thought, or he might decide to dive out of them. What a furor that would cause.

"Rubbish," she said. "If you are too pathetic to say to men what you say to me, I will tell them. And believe me, you'd prefer to own up to your own misdemeanors."

He gulped. "Oh very well. I said you had to marry me."

"Because," Theresa prompted in an icy voice. "Do tell the others in this room what your idea to disgrace his lordship and myself is."

Percy gulped.

"Or are you too much of a coward even to stand by your statement now you are confronted with men, not me?"

"I said that if you don't marry me, I will tell everyone you have the clap and passed it on to him. He's the reason you turned me down. He shan't have you," Percy said, truculent now he had found a little courage from somewhere. "If he wasn't around you would have married me. I would have seen to it. It isn't fair."

"It isn't fair," Jamie parroted with contempt. "Lord, what next, his cock is bigger than my cock, it isn't fair? You worm. Be careful. Be *very* careful, because if you put it about that either my lady or I are infected, I will be the one to say who infected us. Oh my, isn't it amazing what pus can come out of a tiny pencil."

Percy gasped and appeared deflated. It was evident he'd lost whatever bravery he'd discovered. Theresa did her best not to smirk at the crudity. Was she a bad person to admit how much she appreciated it?

"You wouldn't," Percy said. His voice rose. "You couldn't."

Jamie essayed a most unpleasant smile. "Why not? You

intended to."

"I didn't, really I didn't. It was to frighten her," Percy said his words tumbled over each other in his haste to explain himself. He darted a glance toward each of them in turn, with a wild-eyed, scared expression. "I have to marry someone and get an heir and… Oh hell." He bit his lip and shook his head, before he ran his hands through his hair, a picture of abject misery and despair. "To be perfectly honest she is the only one I can get it up with."

"Just," Theresa added sotto voce and watched both Jamie and Martin hide their grins.

"Apart from your lover?" Martin said.

Percy swayed and Martin pushed him into a chair. "Sit down before you fall down."

"How do you know that?" Percy asked, hoarse with emotion. "Please don't tell me it is common knowledge."

Martin shook his head and Percy let out a long, relived sigh. "Thank God."

"That brother of yours is omnipotent," Theresa whispered to Jamie, who grinned.

"Omnipotent? Not always, and definitely not when it is family."

"Not common knowledge," Martin continued. "But Terrence is an old friend and I know he suffers as much as you do. However this is not about him and your preferences so tell the truth. Before you have no cock to do anything with. Fess up to your inadequacies as a gambler."

Percy gaped. "You know that?"

"*How* does he know that?" Theresa asked in an undertone.

"I told him," Jamie replied just as quietly as she. "I just found out today. Lord Luscott was very forthcoming. Insisted he didn't know we were a couple and thought you would be the steadying influence. Percy is incompetent at gaming. Owes thousands."

"I imagine he was able to disguise his activities more easily in the country and at various house parties. The male only, hunting, shooting and fishing sort. Does your godfather know how incompetent you are?"

"Yes, well, why else did he say I should marry you?" Percy trembled. "I have an inheritance due to me, one that will more than pay my debts, and as he insists, take me to the Indies away from temptation. But I have to be married by the turn of the year or it all goes elsewhere and the estates in the Indies split up."

Theresa scowled. "And I was to be the sacrificial lamb, eh? God, you make me sick. *Argh*. Throw him in the gutter, someone."

Both Martin and Jamie took a step forward and she hid her grin. Percy was whiter than a sheet.

"No, really no, I was at my wit's end." Percy's bleat was so plaintive and pathetic that Theresa once more lost any sympathy she'd had for him. "I didn't mean to threaten her."

Theresa changed an incredulous snort into a cough. "If you believe that I believe Bill the boots really did see a unicorn in the bushes," she said with scorn. "Lord, Percy, I know men's brains are in their pricks so therefore you must have very few, but use them wisely. The whole idea was to intimidate me into marrying you, save your bacon and let you escape unscathed. You are no man."

"I did what I thought was best."

"For you maybe," Theresa said in a flat monotone. She dared not let her temper out or Percy would be singing soprano forevermore. "Not for me. If you think *I* think that, you are even more naïve than I thought possible."

He shrugged. "You would have status."

Theresa shook her head in amazement. Although really, nothing he said or did should surprise her, this did. "That of being married to an idiot? I would prefer to be known as a courtesan, thank you."

"When in reality you will be neither," Jamie said with a look on his face that dared her to contradict him. "You will be my lady."

Theresa went hot and cold and hot again. What on earth

was he talking about? She opened her mouth to ask, but Percy blinked and forestalled her.

"Your...?" His voice trailed off and he took a deep shuddering breath. "Oh hell."

"That is a mild way of putting it," Martin said. "Perhaps you should have said how sorry you are and offer your congratulations."

"Oh yes indeed," Percy stammered. "I do."

Gone were the swagger and the arrogance, Theresa decided. Instead was a broken man. One worried about his future. "What will he do?" she whispered. "He can't be left to flounder."

Jamie sighed. "You, my dearheart, have a soft center," he said under his breath. "Much too soft."

"Well, of course, or why else would I have stayed with you?" Theresa said, indignant he might have thought otherwise. "You have given me less to no encouragement."

It was true. She nodded and looked at Jamie, who sighed and turned to face Percy.

"So, how much are you in debt?"

Percy told him and Jamie whistled. "Not to be sneezed at. No wonder you were scared. Your godfather and I have come to a deal. I am to buy the estates. He will pay your debts. And you and your lover—if he chooses to retire to that estate—work for me and stay. If after ten years you are debt free and show you have tried to make something of your life, the estate will be made over to you. If not?" Jamie shrugged. "You go it all alone without me, my money or the estate, which I will keep."

Percy's eyes lit up. "You mean you will send me on my way? That will be it?"

"With the provisos I have just mentioned. Do you not wish that?" Jamie asked. "For if so, something else will be arranged."

"Oh yes, I do, but..." He turned to Theresa and smiled wanly. "Miss Kyle, I truly am sorry for any hurt I may have caused. My only reason is one of fear."

"Well, fear no more," she said, unable in the light of his despair to extract any more vengeance, even if he had forgotten to add 'and greed'. "But for goodness' sake, get out of my sight. Forever."

Wild-eyed and with a high color, Percy gulped. "Yes, yes," he gabbled. "Tomorrow."

"Tonight," Jamie said flatly. "Even if just to St. Albans. The Boot will do you well."

Percy didn't even begin to argue. "Yes, right, right."

"Attend Danvers, the solicitor, at noon tomorrow and he will tell you all the arrangements that have been made. The monies will be there for you, and just to show I am not that trusting, a contract setting out your new life. Now go."

Percy bowed and dashed out of the room. Seconds later they heard the front door bang.

"So now he is gone," Martin said with satisfaction. "Will it work, do you think?"

"Oh yes." Jamie was definite. "He knows I mean what I say. I'd press him if need be."

"Then all we need to do now is sort you two out. Or rather, your future together?"

"Definitely," they both said at once.

Martin laughed. "All I can say is that is a good start." He sobered and looked from one to the other. Theresa wriggled uneasily.

"Why are you championing me?" she asked in a blunt way. She needed to know, there and then. Not to wait and wonder. "I'm a commoner, a courtesan. My papa was a carpenter and before they had me my mama was an assistant to the local seamstress."

"Ex-courtesan," both men said together. "Do not forget the 'ex'."

"Oh very well, ex, but even so."

"And your mama was the fourth daughter of a third son of a lord," Jamie said and rolled his eyes. "You antecedents are fine. Next excuse?"

"They have cut me and my family out of their life."

191

"More fool them. Anything else."

"My own past, and well, Mama and Papa," Theresa said, choosing her words with care. "My papa was not a nice man." On cue her back ached. *Damn it. Damn him.*

"Your point is?" Martin said as Jamie rolled his eyes. "Our mother was and is a snob who wouldn't know one end of a needle from the other. She is the lesser of the two of them. Her grandmother was a mere commoner as well and *her* papa was a curate. We never dare remind her of that fact. Our papa was a waste of space."

"If she could erase Great Grandmama Hobson I think she would. But Grandmama will not let her," Jamie added. "And nor will we. But I do wonder, brother mine, how we can sort things to Mama's satisfaction."

"Would it bother you if we didn't, but you two were still together?" Martin asked.

"Not at all," Jamie said. "As long as we are together."

"Yes," Theresa replied. "I will not be the cause of turmoil in your family."

"Well, I'm on James' side, so the nos have it," Martin said. "I'm afraid, my dear, you are overruled."

"But how?" Theresa said. Dare she hope there *was* a way?

"First, let me ask you both. Do you mind where you live and would you be prepared to marry over the anvil?"

"Gretna?" Jamie said and laughed. "Oh I'm agreeable. And then take over the Scottish estate?"

Martin inclined his head. "Exactly. For now, until the ton are on to the next scandal."

"Well?" Jamie turned to Theresa. "My love, what say you? It is a beautiful place, lochs and glens and mountains." He grinned. "And me."

"And midges?"

"Not where we will be. The estate is on the east coast not too far from Perth."

"Well…" She tilted her head and stared at him. "It sounds perfect, but there is one important thing missing."

"There is?" he asked and raised one eyebrow in question.

"What is that?"

"You haven't asked me yet." She looked at Jamie and pouted with what she hoped was teasing provocation. He folded his arms and stared back.

"Do you have faulty hearing, my love?"

"Well, not recently anyway." She amended her statement. "And not one I have yet to answer."

Jamie laughed and turned to his brother. "Martin, please leave. Go and smell the horses or something."

Martin grinned. "I will go and find some champagne. Don't take too long, I want to drink to your health and get home at a sensible time." He bowed and left the room.

A coal slipped in the grate and sparked to life. Jamie looked at it, picked up the coal shovel and thrust the blazing lump farther into the grate before he turned to Theresa and held her hands in his.

Good god, he is trembling. That tiny sign of nerves steadied her own jumping pulse. She gripped his fingers and smiled up at him. "You don't need to ask, you know. All I want is to be yours anyhow and any way."

"But I do need to ask you," Jamie argued. "I need to ask you, my love, if you will do me the honor of being my wife? To live with me and be my love. Even if we are only wed by word in front of witnesses not a cleric."

She bit her lip as tears of happiness welled at the corners of her eyes. Did he know just what he was giving up? One look at his face told her the answer. Of course he did. His love shone out of him like a beacon to guide her home.

"Oh yes. It will be my pleasure."

"And mine." She grinned. "I do believe I owe you one hundred guineas?"

"Save it for something special."

Her mind flashed to those who perhaps could be in the Daring Ladies Club. "Oh I will. But now may I share *my* pleasure?"

"*Our* pleasure, my love, eh? Our pleasure. Our life."

Fairground Attraction

Excerpt

Chapter One

Tinny music blared from all directions, multicolored lights flickered, teenagers shrieked, pushing past families and older couples arm in arm. Generators — their cables snaking across the ground, ready to trip up the unwary — added noise, plus their particularly oily smell, to the other odors of grease and popcorn. All the fun of the fair. He loved it. Every last screaming child or puking teen. Each was a part of the whole.

His world. Even if he had to leave it and go back to his other life soon, for now this was all he wanted.

Raig stood and watched the crowds, always on the alert for anything untoward. Kids on their dad's shoulders, mums pushing prams, couples holding hands as they decided where to go and what to do. A group of teenage boys, all swagger and bravado, stalked by and similar groups of giggling girls nudged and shoved one another. A normal evening at the fair.

He got the odd admiring glance, and ignored it. Something he found easy to do. One couple in particular caught his eyes. They were resolutely dragging an older woman in his direction. She looked as if she'd prefer root canal treatment. Ah, show time. Suck it up, Raig. Whether he liked it or not, a promise was just that — a promise. He didn't make many, but those he did, he honored.

"Come on." He heard Lorna, the younger woman, urging the older lady. He looked down at the other lady's feet to see them encased in sensible ballet flats, albeit with something sparkly across the toes. Go figure. Semi-sensible then.

He glanced up at her face and his heart missed a beat. More than just a beautiful woman, she reached out to his soul, making him ache to know her in every way. What the fuck? That jolt of recognition, the electricity in his body, scared him. Was this what his da had meant? Recognizing a woman as his? Shit, if it were a film, the violins would be playing.

He'd always thought that his da had just been fanciful, making up the love-at-first-sight thing because it sounded so romantic and made his mum laugh, blush and poke Da in the ribs. Now? Well, now he wondered if maybe all those romance writers had hit the nail on the head. Shit, never mind the nail, he felt as if he had been hit on the head. With a sledgehammer. Him, a normally straightforward, hard-talking, no-nonsense businessman, thinking of roses and champagne, soft music and…yeah, and sex. Okay, so the sex bit was normal, the rest wasn't.

"Mum, stop lagging."

Mum? Oh fucking shit. This vibrant, sexy woman was Vairi, Lorna's mum? The woman he was going to give a good time? Whew, 'give a good time' just took on a whole new meaning. It was unfortunate, but he suspected it was not the one Lorna and Denny wanted him to give her. The woman sighed deeply.

"I need to lag. You go on without me. I'll sit and…smell the daisies."

Raig chuckled. The stare she gave him should have withered his balls. He winked. She scowled, leaned on one of the security fences around the galloping horses and looked in the other direction.

"What shall we go on first?" Lorna shouted, her voice pitched above the noise. She sounded eager as she looked toward the chair-o-planes, the longing expression on her face there for everyone to see. The older woman rolled her eyes, raised her eyebrows and took a deep breath before exhaling heavily.

"You two can go on that torture ride. I'll be here watching you and not losing my tea."

Time to make his presence felt. He moved closer to her. "Ah, pretty lady. Sure, you'll not lose your tea, but you can't be at the fair and not have a ride."

She whirled around, her long curls—the color of a raven's wing—flipping across his face. He saw chagrin in her eyes and something else. Attraction? He and his ever-tightening body hoped so. His mind went to those classic novels his sisters had force-fed him. Lady Chatterley's Lover, Wuthering Heights, The Story of O. Okay, that wasn't a classic per se, but he could imagine them both in it. He wondered what she saw when she looked at him. Six foot three tall. Inky, almost black eyes, overlong, dark, curly hair, one earring. Tattoos almost hidden with just one tantalizing bird's wing showing. Tanned and toned.

He chuckled as she put her nose in the air, but not before she stared at him as if to reach into his soul. The sort of stare he would bet had nailed lesser men than him to the floor and kept them there and reduced them to babbling wrecks before they slunk away defeated. Not him.

His tone teased, low and husky as he leaned in a little closer. "So, what will your pleasure be?"

Did he really hear her say, 'You naked'?

"Pardon?" Say that again.

"I'm sorry I need to go." Pure frost. "My son-in-law is waiting for me."

His smile was, with a bit of luck, wickedness personified. "I see him." He raised his voice to be heard over a distorted rendition of Greased Lightnin'. Even John Travolta had trouble beating a fairground's volume. "Are you well then, Denny?" He waved. "I have her. You and your lovely lady have a good evening now. As we will." A laugh, a wave, a swift hug of her shoulders. "Now then, Lorna's mum. What will be your pleasure?"

Vairi rolled her eyes. "For you to cut the crap and that phony Irish accent, to be sure." She mimicked him. "'Tis as fake as that Rolex you're wearing. Own up to whatever shit you and your co-conspirators have thought up, find me a taxi and pay for the bloody thing." There was the stare again. "Give me a break and don't follow their well-meaning but unwelcome footsteps and try to" — she mimed quote marks — "make sure I have a good time, and show me what I'm missing. Seriously, I'm happy with my life and would be a lot happier without well-intentioned people trying to change it," she finished with a snap. "So thanks but no thanks whatever you're about to suggest. Unless it's to escort me to the taxi rank."

Oh ho, feisty. "Ouch. Oh, a chuisle, you pain me, indeed you do." Did he sound as wounded as he felt? "Not shit at all. The Rolex is as real as those deep blue eyes of yours."

"Bugger."

Her stern expression relaxed and he swore he could see how she fought with herself not to give in to humor. Hopefully she wasn't so annoyed as she'd tried to project.

"Now if only I could say I wore colored lenses. However, like George Washington, I cannot tell a lie. So Mister…"

"O'Shea. Padraig O'Shea. And you?" He bent over her hand and kissed it. A soft kiss, full of promise. Theatrical, but what the hell, he meant it. He, who had always steered clear of commitment, of ladies who clung, demanded attachment and wanted more than this. He had no idea why, how or when. Just that he did. Her laughter surprised and delighted him.

"Vairi McQueen." Her voice held an absent tone. "Oh my God. Never. Paddy O'Shea. Next you'll be telling me 'indeed and there's a leprechaun on my shoulder'."

He contrived to look wounded. "Never, ever would I be joking about leprechauns, lovely lady. Also, no, I'm not Paddy O'Shea."

"Told you." She huffed, her eyes glittering in triumph. "I knew it. Lies, all lies. So who are you?"

"Paddy O'Shea is my da," he continued as if she hadn't spoken. "I'm Raig."

"Rake? That sounds about right." She shook her head. "I don't half get them. Any oddball or weirdo and they come my way. And there's something else. How do you know Denny?"

He chose to ignore her. "Now, I cannot be escorting a lovely lady and be calling her 'Lorna's mum'. I'll be calling you Vairi My Queen."

She glared. "You're not escorting me anywhere long enough for that."

"Now that's where you're wrong, love. God knows what's in the water around here, but I can't help it." He bent his head and kissed her cheek, hoping to hell he wouldn't end up with a black eye for his trouble. "You've bewitched me."

Vairi shook her head. "You're well-named, Rake O'Shea."

In reply, he put his arms under hers and swung her around until the lights swirled. As he slowed she staggered and he held her close for a second, liking the way she felt as she rested against him. "How's your dinner?"

"Bastard. My stomach wishes it had never met you. I can't say it's a pleasure to have done so."

He could. His stomach was so churned up, a brass band could had taken up residence and was fighting the fairy folk for space. She was all woman, and his gut told him she should be all his woman. There was no rhyme or reason, just a certain 'this is it, I've found her' feeling. Something he accepted did happen to people, but never to him—until that moment. "Well then, Vairi My Queen. Tonight is yours. Requested, arranged and plotted by Lorna, who says you don't get out enough. Denny and I were at school together, almost six months of every year when the fair overwintered. He knew I'd be more than happy to escort a lovely lady and show her the...sights." It might have started as a favor to someone who'd helped him out of more scrapes than anyone could imagine, but now? Oh now, thank you, Denny!

She waited, and watched him with close attention. He had no idea why. Her reaction was most perplexing. If he wasn't mistaken though, Lorna and Denny would get a piece of her mind when she saw them next, which left him wondering what would be her follow-up move.

"All mine? To choose or discard things?" she asked and licked her lips.

Oh fuckety fuck. His dick tried to thrust through denim. Sweet lord, did she know what that did to him?

"Use or loose as I please? And you'll not argue?"

Shit. "I'll try not to," he said honestly. "I'm not saying I'll succeed."

"Honesty. I like that."

She did that bloody arousing lick over her lips again.

"Okay then. The galloping horses. Then the big wheel." She laughed up at him. "A hot dog and onions and some candy floss. So, Rake, you game?"

"Oh, Vairi My Queen, more than game. A woman after my own heart."

She giggled. "That's one thing I'm not. After your heart," she elaborated as he stared at her blankly. "I have enough trouble with mine, let alone anyone else's. I'm just after your fairground rides for a wee while."

Raig tucked his arm inside hers and executed a mock bow as he led her across the grass toward the ride she'd requested. "That can be arranged. Let's go." He interspersed the short walk with a few words of caution—'mind the cable now' and 'sure, and don't be falling over the bin'.

As he was at least seven or eight inches taller than her, Raig found it easy to maneuver Vairi tight up against him, as he enjoyed her subtle scent and feeling her soft body next to his. If he had his way, there'd be a lot more feeling and soon. It was a strange sensation. Usually he kept his distance with any woman. With his other employment it paid not to have anyone around who the alleged opposition could use as leverage. Raig was invisible and intended he and his stayed that way.

So, no long term lovers.

Oh, he'd enjoyed his share of affairs, but no one had managed to get through his social mask and into his mind. Until now.

When they reached the side of the first ride, he turned her into his arms and lifted her effortlessly onto one of the painted horses before he stepped up after her.

"Now then, that's you seated on Sword." Oh, so aptly named. With luck, he'd have her seated on his sword before long. "Scoot forward so there's room for me tucked in behind you."

He imagined his eyes twinkled and dared her to disagree, as she scowled and rose to the challenge.

"Oh, Mr. Rake, I'll show you. I may be way into my forties, but hey, I can flirt and enjoy, if I can remember how to do it."

Interesting. She looked about thirty. Impossible, he knew, if she was truly Lorna's mum. "So, how old are you?"

Vairi narrowed her eyes, very wary and on the defensive. "Why does it matter?" Her tone was full of suspicion. "Is there an upper age limit to riding these things?"

"It doesn't matter as far as I'm concerned. I'm just a nosy bugger. I go by the adage, you're as old as the person you feel." He smirked and hoped she would get the allusion to his age and the possibility she would be touching him. To make sure, he took her hand and placed it on his chest. The warmth of her touch hit him even through his shirt. If the material had scorched, he wouldn't have been surprised. "Now think on, I'm thirty-one. Therefore, by that rule, QED, so are you."

"Fuck." She snatched her hand back as if she'd been stung, and shook her head. "Sod it. If you're that age, that makes me almost old enough to be your mother. And if it works both ways, you'll be feeling geriatric."

Raig roared with laughter and gave in to the impulse to peck her on the cheek again. "Nah. It matters not. You are what you are. Which is perfect for me. So, Vairi My Queen, ready to roll?" He swung onto the horse behind her, moving her forward until she was stopped by the pole, which he imagined was tight between her legs and rubbed up against her pussy. When they began to move it should be more than arousing for her. And agony to watch and not participate for him. Raig's cock strengthened, lengthened and hardened against her. Would she complain? Or comply and lean back into him? He had no idea. She wriggled and moaned softly under her breath as his dick did its best to chisel into her ass.

Steady. At least she didn't turn around and thump him.

All he could do was to try to arrange things in his favor. Raig bent into her and whispered, "Ah, Vairi My Queen, this is what you do to me. Giving me such a hard-on, I'm wanting to bury myself far inside you, so deep, until you cry out my name in passion. But until you're happy with the idea, we'll be riding the horses." Oh, how he wished he were a mind reader. Judging by the look he saw on her face as the mirrors on the ride flashed by, maybe it was a good idea he wasn't. Had he gone too far too fast? Ah well, he'd rather be open and honest than coy and calculating.

Nodding at Jonny, a tall, skinny, blond-headed man who was in charge of the roundabout, Raig held Vairi firm as the ride quickened, each horse going up and down to its own pattern. As the roundabout began to speed up even further, he felt Vairi stiffen and hold on to the pole so tight her knuckles were white. Why the hell did she choose the ride if it upset her so? Unless the hardness of the pole on her pussy was worth it. So he would make sure the sensation of his cock crowding her ass surpassed anything else she may feel. From the subtle shift of her hips, he could tell how turned on she was. Well, fuck, if the pole did the job, who was he to complain? He could replace those emotions later.

He said softly, "Sway with the motion, move with it. That's good." He encouraged her as they spun around, lights blurring together, music flowing from one ride to another. A good thing about being the boss—they could stay where they were for as long as they liked. Raig could sense her becoming aroused. Her breathing changed pace and her body shook as the friction between him and the ride increased and intensified.

"Fuck you, Raig. This is so not me," she said shakily as her skin flushed and the silken sheen of arousal slicked over it.

"Why not, love? Just let go."

"I can… I can't not… Oh shit…" Vairi leaned back into him before she shuddered and shivered her climax. Fuck it, how he wished he could have seen her face as she came.

The roundabout began to slow for the third—or was it fourth—time. Raig pressed gentle kisses along her neck. "I need to be an active worker for this go around. I'll be back before you know it, well before your ride has finished. I need to help Jonny there to collect the fares." He moved away, with reluctance, and off the horse. "I need to be with you. Hell, I'm needy."

"Ditch the accent," she said huskily. "Be natural." 'Or else' was the inference.

"Ah, Vairi My Queen. It's mine," he said easily. "God's truth. My voice. The voice I'll use as I make love with you."

Nimbly, he moved away before she could reply, swaying easily as the motion of the ride picked up once more. Raig glanced over at Vairi and frowned. Was it a case of once around too often? My, she does look pale. He could only hope she didn't toss her cookies until he was able to get her off. He motioned to Jonny to go to her and check on how she was coping.

Raig took up the fare from three squealing teenagers and sensed Vairi's eyes on him. He noticed her wan smile in response to Jonny, as he spoke to her. As soon as all the fares were in, the ride would stop. Why on earth did she ask to go on something she couldn't handle? Women. Would any man ever understand them? One minute he was watching her come, the next about to throw up. Mind you, four rides on the trot probably was a tad excessive.

As the ride slowed, he made his way back to her. "Now then, Vairi My Queen. You're looking green. Ah, you've made me a poet, sure I didn't know it."

"You oaf," she said thickly. "Think yourself lucky I didn't thump you. Please, please, get me off this ride. Sheesh, what planet am I on? Wherever, I've left my common sense behind, that's for sure. I hate bloody things that go round. Oh hell, help me off now, pretty damn quick, or I'll be sick. Oh fuck, you've got me doing it now."

Watching her face, it was easy to worry. "Ah, love. It's stopping. There now, I'll get you down. Whoa, let me do the work." She slumped against him. "That's my girl." Gently he lifted her off the ride. He was sure if she hadn't felt so ill, she would have been embarrassed.

Worry churned Raig's gut. He had entered into the spirit of the evening reasonably uninvolved. He had agreed to help Denny and Lorna out when they had requested he entertain Vairi for a while, as he knew he would be at a loose end during the early hours of the fair's opening. He was the boss man. The one to wander around and keep an eye out for anything and everything, but he wouldn't be the only one doing that.

I'm the spare part, really. Some saw him as a part-timer who played at the fair. Raig knew he didn't and spent as much time there as humanly possible. What some people didn't understand, was if he didn't do other work—even though they weren't told exactly what—the fair wouldn't be as it was. Takings never covered the running costs. His alter ego was needed, even if it was a yoke around his neck at times.

Raig understood Lorna's worries, had heard how she felt all her mum did was work and garden. How she never went out and enjoyed herself. He knew if it had been his mum, he'd want her to have a life as fulfilled and interesting as possible as well. And, he'd reasoned, all they wanted from him was a few hours of his time. Not much to ask of a good friend. However, it seemed, after he'd looked into a pair of dark blue eyes and watched the bravado there, he'd gone from fancy-free to entwined in thirty seconds flat.

It didn't scare him. That was a first. Raig had always thought of commitment as akin to the plague. To be feared and avoided like, well, the plague.

Now this gorgeous woman with a slim body, legs encased in deep navy denim that seemed to go up to her ears, breasts that would be—he was sure—the perfect handful and a smile to launch ships, had him aroused in seconds. Her eyes were, he decided stupidly, liquid pools to drown in, and her loose gray blouse hinted at mysteries to be found. Although the sallowness of her skin and the misery in those eyes had him worried, he was still hot, horny and hard. Signaling to Jonny he was going, he lifted Vairi tight into his arms and carried her through the crowds to his trailer.

He could no more ignore the elegant line of her neck than stop breathing. It invited soft, nipping kisses. Fuck, he knew she was suffering, but he was suffering, too, though not with motion sickness, more like with lack of motion. Of the in-out variety.

She moaned softly in his arms. Ah, shit, Denny would kill him. After Lorna had. In his defense, no one had thought to tell him she got motion sick. What exactly had they imagined they would be doing all evening? Playing bingo, for fuck's sake? He had more than an idea what he would like to be doing with Vairi. Somehow he didn't think Lorna would have the same idea.

In his arms, Vairi struggled to sit up. "What the hell?" she asked huskily and coughed. "What was that?"

Well, that was spoken loud and clear, at any rate. "Hush now. You were feeling not so well on the ride. I'm taking you somewhere private and quiet to rest a while."

"White slaving?" The chuckle, although weak, was definitely there. "Toss your cookies to be taken?"

Ah, that deserved a kiss—this one on her forehead. Christ, when was he going to bite the bullet and kiss her, firm and possessive, on the mouth? When she didn't look as if she was going to pass out. Or throw up on him.

"If that's what you're wanting. If not, just to my trailer until you don't look the same color as that lovely blouse you are wearing." He smiled at her nod. "Seriously, I was worried."

"And me. I've not been that bad before. I wanted to die."

"You and me both, love, you and me both," he said fervently. Raig skirted the big wheel and took care not to trip over the trailing cables before he walked quickly toward a large olive-green caravan. "Hold on a sec." He mounted the steps and held her steady while he fumbled in his pocket to find the key. "Can you stand a moment as I unlock the door?" Damn, he was losing the brogue. Even though it might not be needed, as camouflage it was good enough. Did he still need to hide who he was? He had no idea. Think, Raig. "Yeah?"

She nodded again. "Think so."

"There's a girl. Be holding on to me now." With care, he set her down on the top step and unlocked the door, propelled her in and helped her to sit on a long, comfy bench settee. "Now then, my brave one, I'm thinking a cup of tea might just help."

"No, honestly, I'm fine now. A glass of water, then I'll get something to eat." She blushed, and nibbled her bottom lip. "Like I said, I'm not usually anywhere near that bad. No dinner combined with the trauma of being abandoned by my family might have a lot to do with it."

"Ah, well, I'll be thinking most people would be affected

that way." He poured a glass of water as he spoke. Vairi took it with a murmur of thanks and sipped slowly. Then she nodded, put the half-full glass down on a side table and cleared her throat. Unease traveled through him at the look of determination on her face.

Uh-oh. It was the universal 'cut the crap, ditch the shit and open up and be honest' look so many women had down to perfection. Usually it annoyed him, this time it worried him. *Fuck, I have it bad.*

"Right then, Rake O'Shea. Gloves-off time. Who are you, why do you keep using that phony accent, and what the hell is going on?" Vairi demanded in a tone sharp enough to split logs. "No bullshitting me, or this water might find its way to your face."

Hell on wheels. He winced as he realized he had to think on his feet. Fast. *Jeez, that sexy shoe was tapping on the floor and those glittery things that decorated it caught the light as she moved. Cool it, Raig. Concentrate. Use your brains not your balls.* Not easy when said balls vied with his cock over which was the hardest. It was a close-run thing and walking would soon be difficult without emulating John Wayne.

"My name is Padraig O'Shea," Raig said carefully. "I have known Denny since we were young. He and the lovely Lorna asked for my help. I wasn't going to say no. I'm bloody glad I didn't."

"How young?" Vairi ignored the latter part of his statement and picked up her glass again. He eyed it warily. "Define young," she added.

Hell, that voice could break eggs. Bite the bullet, Raig, you're not going to wriggle out of this. "He was five, I was seven. So I'll do the maths for you in case you've forgotten how. I'm thirty-one. Born in Dublin. Single, solvent and clean. My da always was working with the fair. He met my ma when it was set up there. He said it was love at first sight for him, but it took her a while to believe him. Married thirty-five years and as daft for each other now as they ever were."

"'Was' as in not now?" Of course she'd pick up on the 'was', being as she was no slouch in the brains department. Her erotic, foot-tapping rhythm said 'take me, fuck me' and was making him hot as it sent messages from his brain to his cock and back again. Those sodding, fecking arousing scenarios were playing havoc with his concentration. What was he supposed to be answering? Oh fuck, Da and the fair.

"Ah well, Vairi My Queen, that's the rub. Sometimes, although now more for the craic than the necessity." Why did the look she was giving him have him wanting to cover all the strategic parts of his body? "Otherwise he's at home with my ma and playing lord of the manor, so he is."

"For fuck's sake, cut the crap." The water in her glass rippled violently as she slammed it down. She stood and paced across the trailer before swinging to face him, her hair following the motion in a forceful sweep across her face. Ah, that was why his hands, hovering over his cock and balls, were ready to take evasive action—her frustration was palpable.

"I, ah... Okay, tell me what you want," he said slowly, his mind racing. "And I'll do my best."

"Please, Padraig. Okay, I'll accept I've been set up," she said in an exasperated voice. "Now I know why Lorna was so insistent I came to the fair with her and Denny. She knows I don't do rides well. But what exactly was I set up for? Surely my daughter wasn't pushing me toward an evening of sex and satisfaction?"

Laughing at the look of horror on her face as she realized what she had said, he made to reassure her. "No, no, Vairi My Queen, that was not in her mind." It is in my mind though. Oh, by God, is it in my mind. "I was out with the two of them on Tuesday, and Lorna was saying that you'd been commenting you were in a rut and needed get out or drown in wallowing crappiness. Her words, not mine. She wanted to help you—all work and no play is not good. So I said if they brought you with them tonight, I'd show you a good time. I wasn't thinking you would go a strange shade of gray when I did."

That elicited a reluctant laugh. "Okay, I concede that's my own fault. I decided to jump out of my rut. I forgot the parachute. Hell, I should know better. I even get motion sick in the passenger seat of a car. Should have stuck to hook-a-duck."

He chuckled with her. "Would looking at the water round those cute little ducks not be making you seasick then?"

"Jeez, Rake, drop the accent, why don't you. You keep dipping in and out so much I'm giddy. It's not real, it's phony. You sound like a stereotypical B-movie. Yes?"

He shook his head as he looked at her and replied with not entirely faked sorrow. "That's where you are wrong. I'll admit I've been piling it on. Lorna said you were a romantic, inspired by sexy accents, and as I've been told over the years, the Irish accent is just that, sexy, so I thought, well, why not? To be honest and truthful, the lilt is always there. It's just been weakened over the years. I resurrected it for you." He watched her, as she seemed to mull over his statement. He could imagine her dissecting every word and pulling up to consider the bits she chose to.

"I'll buy into that. Right." She took a deep breath and smiled. A look hot enough to split his jeans if he wasn't careful. A lesser expression than that had started wars, he was certain.

"So, Rake." The way she purred his name sent his libido sky high, and he swore there would be a stain on the cloth. "A good name, by the way. Now, what are you going to show me?"

His cock understood what he wanted. It was hard and tight up against the fly of his denims, straining the zip in its effort to be free of its confines. He was glad Mr. Levi Strauss knew a thing or two about the strength of that particular cloth.

"It depends on how much you want to fly." His accent was now upper-class English. "I have an idea about what

208

I'd like." He saw her considering his statement. "I'll be open and honest. I agreed at first because of a photo in Lorna's purse. The pair of you, somewhere sunny."

"Barbados," Vairi said, her voice faint. "Three years ago, just before she married. It was my birthday present. We ate, drank and sunbathed. No sex." She giggled. "Lord that sounds icky. I mean neither of us went off and had sex with anyone."

"Shame." He laughed. "Does your daughter not understand you are a living, breathing, sexy woman?"

She laughed with him. "Probably not. No girl or woman or, I suspect, male likes to think their mother knows about, you know, sex. Okay, we've had the kids, but then? Zilch. Won't they be in for a surprise when they get to that state?"

He nodded and decided to use the element of surprise to catch her off guard. "So, Vairi My Queen, did you come on the horse? With its rod pressed hard where my cock wanted to be?" He took a gamble and guessed — hoped — she wouldn't be shocked or offended by his frank speech. Vairi blushed, but no angry words accompanied it. So far, so good. Now he intended to make her less self-conscious.

"I could have done," Raig remarked frankly. "Very easily. Hard up against your ass, with you rubbing against me and that bloody pole. Knowing it gave you more of a good time than my cock was gutting. Gutting. What I really wanted was my cock in you, never mind the pole. I would be your pole. Hot, hard, and fuck you into oblivion. Hear you come. Feel you come. That's what I want. To feel you milk me to fruition."

"Ah..." She seemed to struggle for an answer. Vairi stroked her index finger across his cheek and seared a line down to his lips, which she tapped twice. "So? Why are you waiting? Be that pole, Rake. Because all I thought about as I got hot and bothered was you. You inside me, making me come. Now's your chance. If you're not worried how old I am, why should I be? Cougars of the world unite and all that. Show me how you're going to fuck me, Rake. Show me what you want, how you want it. Let me shout and scream for you."

He was nonplussed. Of anything he'd hoped she say, that went over and above it. Boy, she surprised him. Big time.

"Love." He had what he wanted, and now he was hesitating. What the fuck? Get real, Raig. "Are you sure, Vairi? God, I want you, do I ever. I want to hear you moan, see you writhe as I fill you and fuck you hard. Make you come as you scream my name. But I don't want you to be wishing we hadn't, come tomorrow."

She sniggered. "That statement could be taken two ways. I'll not wish I hadn't come, come tomorrow, I promise."

He smiled. Trust her. "Good but, love, listen well. It'll mark you. Make you mine. I'll bite, nip and scar. I'll take you. Brand you. I may have only known you for a few hours, but by God, I know the type of man I am. If I make you mine, it'll be forever. I know my own mind, I have faith in my intuition, and it's letting me know this is 'it'. So think very carefully, my Vairi. Are you up for taking that risk?"

The silence was total. Raig was glad. Glad she was taking his statement seriously. It mattered to him more than he'd ever imagined possible.

"I think so." She spoke clearly, her voice unhurried. "But I'm not sure, Rake, and I need to be. Oh, not about the nipping and biting bit. I'll give as good as I get. But forever? After only knowing you for a few hours?" She shook her head.

Not in negation, he thought, more in bemusement. He understood how she felt. He didn't understand this connection between them himself. He just knew it was there.

"Get real," Vairi continued. "What happened to try before you buy?"

"In this economic climate? Not a snowball in hell's chance. It's all cash on delivery these days. Or rather, no sale and return. That's the price we pay. If you want us, we're here for the taking. If not?" He shrugged. There was nothing else he could say.

With such an expressive face, her thoughts and doubts were easily read. He was ready to bet she'd now come out with a flat 'no', and he'd be driving her home and not driving into her. Wisely, he kept quiet, knowing it had to be her decision. He'd been taken aback by how easily he'd realized she was the one needed to make his life complete. As a kid, Raig had laughed at his da when he had told him that one look at his ma and he'd known she was the one for him – the shoe was now on the other foot. The photograph he had seen had whetted his appetite but not prepared him for meeting Vairi in the flesh. With the first look, he'd been smitten. He could have beaten his chest, Tarzan-style, jumping up and down, shouting 'mine'.

Vairi's shoulders straightened, almost because now her decision was made, it was time to impart it.

His cock shriveled as if it needed to hide – just in case. For fuck's sake, in case of what? Get a grip. Hell, I'm acting like a wuss. Man up and face the music. Or whatever.

Raig held his breath as he waited anxiously for her to speak and decide their fate. How on earth he would handle it if she came out with a flat 'no', he didn't want to imagine. Conversely, if they made love, and she said 'thanks but no thanks', would that not be worse? Bloody hellfire, he admonished himself angrily. Stop second-guessing the woman and let her speak. And expand your vocabulary, why don't you? 'For fuck's sake' and 'bloody hellfire' are well overused.

"Have you done muttering?" Vairi inquired as she sat down next to him. As he nodded with a wry grin, she smiled at him, her face lighting up. "I'm as worried as you are. It's not a one-way street, you know? You looked like a toddler who's been told he can't have a third lollipop. Man up."

He guessed what she was going to tell him would make him feel he wasn't getting a fourth. Even so, his cock reacted predictably to her smile. She noticed, of course. It would be difficult not to when his jeans now seemed two sizes too small.

"Down, boy. You haven't heard what I'm going to say yet."

Ah, did he really want to?

More books from
Totally Bound Publishing

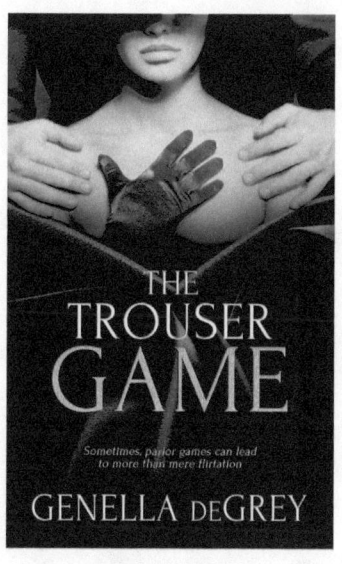

Sometimes, parlor games can lead to more than mere flirtation.

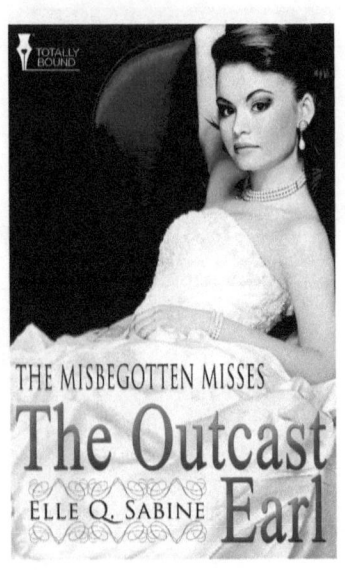

Book one in the Misbegotten Misses series

Charles anticipates a carefree bride who can focus time and attention on him. Abigail is drawn into a dutiful marriage while preoccupied with her family. Can this couple find a way forward that suits them both?

Pearl longs for something more from her staid life. When her friend Frances suggests they become gentlemen's harlots for the evening, Pearl's life changes forever.

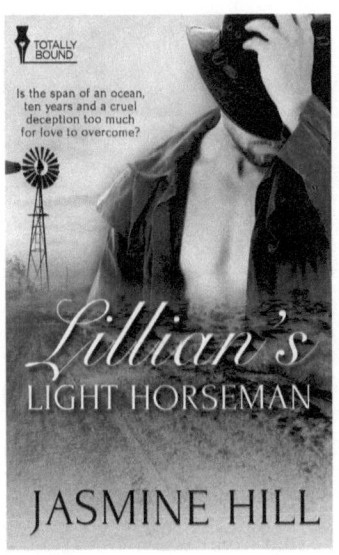

Are the span of an ocean, ten years and a cruel deception
too much for love to overcome?

About the Author

Raven McAllan

A multi-published author of erotic romance, Raven lives in Scotland, along with her husband and their two cats—their children having flown the nest—surrounded by beautiful scenery, which inspires a lot of the settings in her books.

She is used to sharing her life with the occasional deer, red squirrel, and lost tourist, to say nothing of the scourge of Scotland—the midge. As once she is writing she is oblivious to everything else, her lovely long-suffering husband is learning to love the dust bunnies, work the Aga, and be on stand-by with a glass of wine.

Raven McAllan loves to hear from readers. You can find contact information, website details and an author profile page at https://www.totallybound.com/

Home of Erotic Romance

www.ingramcontent.com/pod-product-compliance
Lightning Source LLC
Chambersburg PA
CBHW020415180626
46812CB00003B/995